{The Drifts}
Thom Vernon

Coach House Books
Toronto

Published with the generous assistance of the Canada Council for the Arts
and the Ontario Arts Council. Coach House Books also acknowledges the
support of the Government of Canada through the Book Publishing
Industry Development Program and the Government of Ontario through
the Ontario Book Publishing Tax Credit.

LIBRARY AND ARCHIVES CANADA CATALOGUING IN PUBLICATION

Vernon, Thom, 1963-
    The drifts / Thom Vernon. -- 1st ed.

ISBN 978-1-55245-228-8

    I. Title.

PS8643.E75D75 2010   C813'.6   C2010-901664-5

for Sarah, Doodle, Aunt Ale and Cubby

'Before us the thick dark current runs. It talks up to us in a murmur become ceaseless and myriad, the yellow surface dimpled monstrously into fading swirls travelling along the surface for an instant, silent, impermanent and profoundly significant, as though just beneath the surface something huge and alive waked for a moment of lazy alertness out of and into light slumber again.' — William Faulkner, *As I Lay Dying*

'The angel would like to stay, awaken the dead, and make whole what has been smashed. But a storm is blowing from Paradise and has got caught in his wings; it is so strong that the angel can no longer close them. This storm drives him irresistibly into the future, to which his back is turned, while the pile of debris before him grows toward the sky. What we call progress is this storm.' — Walter Benjamin, *On the Concept of History*

{ *Julie* }
6:26 p.m.

The glass went brittle when the sun set. Sullen night was bearing down and the shadows were inching towards the light. A numbness'd set on everything the way it does when weather's coming. Charlie'd better'd get his raggedy tuckus back in this house and plant hisself down on that sofa was what was on my mind.

Charlie and me can't talk except through our skin. Some people just don't. We're one of them kind of folks. For us, words never come just like that. Ain't much of anything that comes. Words get themselves worked up to wobble on through pores but when they weave on through, out into the air, they're all warbled like one of them numbskulls that ain't good for nothing over in Lake City. Making love is our words.

A few months ago, when Charlie and I couldn't get words to say what we had to say, we made a mean love on the carpet. That afternoon I almost got free. Oh God. Almost – I almost got through free. But the past piled up behind me the way it does, goosing me through into catastrophe.

The girls had just took off. Just them. Took off. I had been scrubbing fingerprints off the kitchen wall where they all lean to get their shoes on and, at the same time, I don't mind saying it, I was peeking about seeing where in the place we hadn't baptized. In the living room, Charlie, seated on the final stair, was groping around for it too. Ol' Charlie's a groper. A groper through and through. Ol' Charlie's like a blind man in the wilderness. Ol' Charlie probably still don't know if he's coming or going. He'd gotten himself into a rut with me and at his work, the Singer sewing machine factory, and he was feeling around for a way out.

A man and a woman don't have to be near each other for that beast kind of thing to lurch up. One look at him and I know what he's thinking. I don't even have to peek at him to know how the wheels of that brain are turning. Goosebumps came up on my arms. He was biding his time, seated right there. I put my cleaning away and angled myself by the door jamb separating the kitchen from the living room. He sat there prying his boots off.

Soon enough, I was holding on to the slick leg of the couch and gritting my teeth. With no consideration at all, Charlie stuck into me with a shove, digging himself up inside, his thumbs cutting into my hips, his mouth ferocious and hungry. He pumped himself all the way up into my belly, and when he got himself all the way up in, my knuckles was burning in the shag. He hadn't thought of anyone but himself for twenty-five years, he wasn't going to start then. Could be there was better leverage up on all fours so I got one leg up. He got me around the gut, hauled me up and flattened me back. I thought Charlie couldn't get it up no more but, boy, that day he was trying.

Since spring, a mouldy stain on the panelling in the living room had blossomed to look like mums. Every. Storm. That thing. Bloomed. I. Studied. It. Getting. Jerked. Back and. Forth. My grunting turned me. On but, then, I just, forced my mind to, think of Wilson, each and every, spike he made.

'Radio says … you know? About the weather.'

'What … is … that?' Charlie's mind was not on the weather.

'Radio said … this winter was.'

'What … about … it?'

'Said this … winter was going … to.' My words wouldn't come the whole way.

'Said was what?'

'Winter was a lot of … oh … was.' He had me around the neck now.

'Winter … was … what?'

'It ain't going to.'

'Come on, Julie, what'd they say, what'd they say, what'd they say?'

'It ain't going to … be a lot of – '

'A lot of what?'

'A lot of, there's going, to be.'

'To be what … there's going to be what … a lot of what … what's there gonna be?'

'A lot of.'

'Yeah … like what … like what … like what … a lot of what … what's there gonna be … what's there gonna be … what's there gonna be?'

Finished, Charlie walloped my rear end with the fat of his hand and come out, squatting. 'To what, hon?'

I lay there, my stomach seizing in on itself so's it was a call, a pining that couldn't collect itself into something to say. I repeated what I said. Them words were close – I could speak them. 'This winter. A doozy.'

'Hoo, baby.' But Charlie was done with me. First, he screwed himself into a fetal curl, then he yawned out into a square of sun heating the carpet. The leaves had fallen off the crabapple by then so it was just branch shadows flickering on his hot-dogging skin and a robin outside yearning in its migration.

I climbed to my feet, threw my bra around my neck, Charlie's jeans over an arm, kicked his boots to the front door and his shorts at his face. Scrutinizing him, you wouldn't think he was the kind to go out on me. I eyed him lounging in the sun on the watermelon shag with his hair the shade of oxidized copper. Crow's feet were sneaking out from his eyes and etching his cheek. I poked his worn and thin-skinned belly with my toe and asked him weren't he weighing me against Wilson?

'Ah, you know, what's the reason to weigh one against the other?'

He could just kick me. He wasn't even going to deny or pretend. 'I been around the block, Charlie, ain't I?'

'I'm yanking your chain.'

'Are you? You wouldn't go and fool an old fooler, would you?'

Charlie rolled on his back and stretched up to the sun. We had an old tom that'd do that, roll onto his back, squeeze his eyes shut and stretch out. Charlie had chalky pillow fur on his chest and a tiny taut belly spreading like melted cheese to the carpet. That afternoon had got nippy. I wrapped them shirts and pants to me and soon as I even thought of it I got myself back around him, fully against his side. I snuggled close, poking him with my tits. I scooched down. The stain above bulged. The whole damn house was leaking.

I leaned up on one elbow, and my right breast fell flat on the floor the way it did now. Years ago, I'd spend hours in the mirror marvelling at the curves out of my chest, down to the nipple. The only time I saw a pink like that was at the 4-H booth. And there was a cow one year, and they were drinking its milk right out of the teat, and the judge had the teat right up to his wide-open mouth and they squirted milk out of that teat, the same pink as my nipple, into his mouth. These days the skin hangs from my breast, where there ain't the kid muscles, and then falls off past the bone at a right angle. And the nipples are not pink now, they're mauve. They got the tinge of kidney beans and that clay along Interstate 40 the more east you go towards Knoxville.

I ought to have made Charlie confess. But no. Not me.

I beaned my breast into his arm near to where it used to hang and peeked over at him. 'You like that? It's … I'm saying … and it's … I'm doing it easy … it's … don't think for a minute it's a mystery, okay?'

Charlie blinked. 'Jesus. You gotta take a nice easy siesta and make it a pain, you need to do that every time, dontcha? Every single time.'

I hiked a leg up on his thigh like back when we used to dream of Puerto Vallarta.

'You can't put it on the table?' I asked.

'You ain't saying what you're saying, are you?' He turned his head getting all concerned with that ceiling bulge.

'Wilson.'

'What, Wilson?' He rolled away from me to his side, sticking out his lip and facing the window, griping how come we got to keep the heat so low.

I scrunched close against his back so he felt my heat.

He got the lip of the last stair in a grip to where his knuckles went white and smelled his fingers.

I drew his hand to me. I kissed it. 'There's still meatloaf smell in the carpet, huh? 'Member that? When Michelle threw her plate at me? Charlie, what do you say this weekend we go to that place in Lake City and see what they're charging for a room?'

'On account that what?'

I angled over him so I could get a good look.

His moss-coloured eyes were open. 'Got no reason, do we?'

I got into his neck while he had his face buried down in the carpet, sniffing.

'You smell that Summer Rain rug powder, don't you?' I chewed his ear and lay my head on his shoulder. 'It's jus' like it, huh? Summer rain.' I stretched out my leg and the squealing red spider veins clustered at the ankle. My thighs had a little left of what they used to. It's a wonder he didn't smother in all of Wilson's fat but God knows she turned him on more. I bobbed my chin on his arm. 'We have a chance here, Charlie. We can just make it up now, our entire lives, we could just ease on and make it all our way, like a fairy tale. Tanya and Michelle're gone now. Can't you see it? Ain't a thing keeping us back from making our days what we want, you know?' I caught my breath. 'We could be like that crabapple. In a few months, it'll be spring. Couldn't we bloom? Like the tree, just the same? Couldn't we bloom?'

'For what?'

The flat side of my hand ran the length of him, the fine hairs on his pale upper thigh doe-soft. I measured the length and breadth of him, armpit to ankle.

'You butterin' me up?' asked Charlie.

'You don't think I can't see when you got that railroad car in your eyes? I mean Wilson. And it ain't just her – it's … you know, don't you? Don't you know, Charlie?'

'Know what?'

I kept my head up. 'Ain't kids anymore to keep us apart, is there?'

Charlie went on about how we couldn't even rest on the shag without it being so itchy, and then he turned over and faced me. He shut his eyes, drumming his fingers on my toes, saying he never thought nothing. Nothing more than he ought to. Of Wilson. 'Why do you got to insinuate things?'

'Am I insinuating? Look at me.'

'Are you?'

'That's what I am saying about – see, we can't talk straight, can we? It's weird. You're way over there. You got Charlie World, I got Julie World, don't I? We wouldn't know the truth if it was a strawberry in the meatloaf. Would we?'

'That's all boob-tube talk, ain't it?'

I bound myself with that old reeking flannel of his and got to my feet. Then, boy, I got him good. I took a step over him, baring my motherlode. I got my yoo-hoo right in his face. I brandished it. 'It's yours, ain't it? Wilson shave down south?'

'Ugh.'

I pranced up on the stairs then. And I was going to go up but then, at the landing, I got brooding over this trip we took. It was one to the Grand Canyon. We were on the North Rim, looking at stones and scrub over on the other side on the South Rim. I supposed Charlie'd noted it too. I pounced back down them stairs and I seized his neck, and told him that he was like one of those teeny little scrubs we could hardly make out, and I meant there he was, lying right there on the floor, but he was so far off, and then I stopped 'cause I didn't want to say what I couldn't take back, and being married I don't say everything that comes into my head, I pick my battles, and I stopped, but then bolted right up the stairs two at a time for show, and he hollered how come I wasn't leaving him nothing to wear why don't I leave him to freeze to death and, right on cue, that packing box trussed up like a trucker with tits rolled into the driveway toting that cow and ringing the doorbell. It was when that damned animal came.

Being upstairs I couldn't see him. But Charlie would've stayed low, sneaking over to the shades on his knees to see who it was. Who it was was Wilson, that side of a house prettied up like a caboose with gazooms. She was tying her boots, lying in wait. He might've taken the drapes drying on the back of the couch and wrapped them around his waist before he went to the door. His own nipples would've squealed when he cracked the door and September, queerly cold, stung him.

'Get your clothes on! It's one o'clock,' said Wilson.

Charlie would've fumbled with his curtain, then the door, saying how he'd just waked up.

'Just waked up, my foot. Let me in! And what're you covering yourself for, ain't no one out there wants to see you.' That swollen six-toed two-by-four would've walked in.

Charlie'd've shut the door, shivering. He ran up the stairs and put some clothes on. Me, face down on the bed. Then Wilson led him out to the driveway. A calf snorted in the bed of her new pickup. Overhead, clouds elbowed on in and what sun there was got clobbered while Charlie hopped foot to foot warming up.

'What's it want?'

'Its mama.' Wilson scratched the animal behind the ears. It yanked back.

'Probably don't like the driving.' The animal flinched when Charlie first touched it, breathing deep.

''S so little I ought to save it, don't you think? Maybe she ain't caught it yet?' asked Wilson, coming so close her ham-hock upper arms melted into Charlie's.

'Keep it out in the shed if that's what you're thinking.'

'Yuh.'

'Okay.'

Charlie bent his paws into the teeny thing. It stood stock-still. Charlie pondered the front door.

Wilson hooked her thumbs in her belt, her eyes lingering on his. 'County's gonna get me. Hobby or no, they're gonna get me. You watch. They're going to make me put 'em all down. I got the sickuns apart from the gooduns, but I don't know.'

Charlie jumped up into the truck, kicked aside a bunch of straw, untied the calf, picked it up in his arms and jumped back down. He set the pitiful thing onto its wobbly legs, waiting for it to steady. He bent forward, carefully stroking its chin, saying hadn't he ought to tie the thing up?

If they'd been watching, Charlie and that sorry excuse for a mid-size Chevy would have caught me fogging the bathroom window. Watching and breathing. In the condensation gathered there, I drew a cauled stickboned gal like myself and let it evaporate off before I pressed my eyebrow into the stinging iced glass, thinking. Thinking and watching as that crabapple tree on the other side of the driveway screeched and knifed at the sky. It lurched, zigzagging back and forth, a hysterical witch staked to the plain.

That was three months ago when Wilson brought that animal, September. Things have developed some since then – me and Charlie ain't talked since Tuesday. He come home for lunch that day about the same time I come in. My lips wouldn't open so I wiped the kitchen counter. I should've just gone on about my business. I'd never've thought twice about it and I wouldn't've ended up where I am now. I should've just left that official paper folded up in my purse. That's just what I needed: a squirming, twisting, screaming child that leeches nothing but me 24/7. Suck it out of me now, was what I said. I was done with babies.

Not Charlie.

'What do you think of the idea of being a daddy again?' I asked.

He said he didn't think much of it but then he had one arm under the coffee table flipping through piles of *National Geographic*, *People*, *Entertainment Weekly* and *Premiere* and griping about how come they couldn't get just one magazine since they all say the same thing and where was that damn remote.

'Ask your daughters. As soon as they get straight I intend to send them to 'em. I don't read 'em, do I?' That wasn't the whole truth but it was good enough for him.

'I am just saying couldn't we fix the roof with the price of these things?' We speak only in questions now.

'What would you say if Burns said I'm pregnant?'

That got him up on his feet. The fucker did a two-step and clapped his hands. 'Oh, jeez, okay, you sure, are you, did he?'

I slung the dishrag over my shoulder and got my purse from behind the back door, and I told him I had the results if he wanted to see.

Charlie slithered into the kitchen. 'Honey, that's real good news, ain't it?' Then he got smart. He folded his arms real judiciously and shut his trap.

'Yeah, we need another kid like we need a hole in the head, don't we?' I fished in the outside pocket where I keep all my receipts. 'Ain't Burns' head up his fanny?' I handed the stinking paper to him with one hand and got the stock pot out of the dish rack with the other. 'Take it. Ain't he?'

He hmmed and hawed, his eyes grew chock full, his shoulders zoomed up to his ears like somebody about ready to get a prize they won but didn't take for fear of seeming greedy. He'd won all right, on my ticket.

'Aren't you going to take it?'

Then, like lightning, he became one of those detectives on the cop shows. He licked one half of his mouth. He squinted as he snatched the paper. He read every last number burned there, twice. When he was done he put on a show. He made a big wind-up pitch and knocked his forehead into the door jamb. I was his prize hen.

I watched him out one eye but kept the other hid in the cupboard. Us having that baby was not an option. 'Canning's done till fall. Now don't say a word.'

'Well, now that's a how-de-do. Here's my second chance of being a – '

'Don't you say it, Charlie. Don't even speak it once. I did my time. I'm done.'

He slumped onto the counter and stared at his reflection in the toaster. 'Charlie? This is our time now. Now you know that.'

'How come it can't be by the grace of God and include one more?'

''Cause God ain't spreading his legs and then spending all His time chasing it. I ain't never been nothing but a mother.' I was tired. I didn't want to start again. Then the pipes burst. 'For crying out loud, I KNOW, CHAR-LIE. I wasn't hatched on Monday, you're such a goddamned – I love you. And I bet Elaine Little's been preaching, hain't she?'

'If this is what the Lord wants –'

'Goddamned snaky proselytizer – that's where you get all this God now.' I shook my fists like in a TV movie. I climbed on a chair to put the pot away.

'Maybe the Lord needs me to be a daddy again.'

'Really, Charlie? The Lord needs you?'

It ain't a secret he's a lousy father. And I nailed him there the day Tanya and Michelle left for Hollywood. Where was he when Cole Little was feeling up the girls? Huh? Both of them? Where was he when Tanya was mowing that perfect lawn – 'peaked and peerless,' the magazine called it, though it was just St. Augustine's weed – and hit that smoke-tree stick that nailed straight into her leg? Where was he when the basement windows got so piled high with snow the glass broke on Michelle's head when she was cleaning the stairs? Huh? Where was he when their bleeding came? The way I see it is I was pleased to see the girls leave. Being hurt at the time, I told him we were not the best lover operators. 'We're a nice roll in the hay, okay? The girls're alive, and they're gone, and God hate me but I'm gladder for it.'

I didn't know that day what I knew later wobbling on that kitchen chair. I squatted on my haunches, teetering for a fall. Charlie and I, eyeball to eyeball. 'You got another think coming, bud.'

'I, for one, could do better this time.'

'Have it yourself then because I am done. D-O-N-E.'

'Naw.'

I cornered the lizard, poking my finger into his chest.

'Don't even start with me. You proposing to raise it up? Three, three, three years ago we chewed that gristle – and we decided, Charlie. Goddammit, we decided! I don't know what I was thinking then but I am for sure certain what I am thinking now.'

He coiled up against the moulding.

I pushed up his stubby, hooked chin so he could see beyond his belly button and over my shoulder. 'What you are not done with and what I am going to give you a second chance at is the grime on that ridge up there which is ready to grow legs and feed an army of cockroaches.'

He matched his attack to mine. 'Ain't no cockroaches in Arkansas!'

'Hah!'

'Okay, there's two in Jonesboro!' He wiped dust off the ridge. 'I can clean this up.'

He made peace.

'You do that.' And I lurched off the chair, curling against the stove and into his fur. 'Can't you just taste our future, baby? Can't you?'

His stomach pressed against mine. The still unfixed gas leak in the stove spread a noxious sulphur perfume.

'We did our time, hon. The girls're grown, it's us now.'

He got me in his arms and let me rest on him. 'Well. It'll work itself out in the wash, won't it?' He surveyed the back forty through the sink window, scheming.

And he ain't slunk hisself back to my gaze since.

{ *Charlie* }
6:28 p.m.

Charlie set his foot on the poplar porch but took his weight off the railing where he was leaning

Dont creak shes there

He listened The din of silence Elm leaves Car crick His breathin Snow spiralled into the drifts like the milk white of that old Impala they used to have the one with the cream vinyl roof that got all worn to shreds on account that the tornado sped through tearin to Fort Smith He twisted his knee till it popped

Devil He stayed too long in one place and his knee got stuck

He blew into the cracked skin around his nail

Numbin night Ol Julied have a recipe for that wouldnt she Shed set me on fire Shed burn me clean alive Shed peel the skin off my bones That girld leave the gristle for the coons He could just hear her

Warm up big boy

Thats his girl Go in and have it out That would be that Go in have it out let her know there was no way in hell She was not doin it Go in Dont even think about it She was not havin one Go in and *Doncha ask me to say it you know what Im talkin about Doncha say it doncha say it doncha dare You know the word what Im thinkin Doncha make me* You say things you make em real He put his other foot down

He was gonna go in But well now maybe shes already went out Maybe shes there now Maybe her legsre spread The deeds done the arms pulled the legs ripped the brain burnt her agony to begin again It was a done deal A fact Shes a big girl aint she She didnt need him to hold her hand Go see the doctor Well now Somebody woulda told him Dont go against Heaven Somebody woulda Who Who woulda told him Who did he know at that office The only person he knew enough to nod to was Dr Burns himself and he wouldnt He couldnt hardly splutter out what he was sayin as it was on account that he lost his saliva glands to the cancer The long and short of it was doctors dont have to tell a husband jack shit Charles Ceame beloved husband to Julie Ceame dont mean shit Not these days thank you Jane Fonda You can do anythin you want if youre a woman you dont have to vouch nothin to nobody as long as you got your insurance card You can get any ol pill you want Nobody hasta know nothin You barely have to know yourself Shoot his girls coulda walked right into Burns office and told him they was knocked up and away a babyd go Boom boom down a chrome-plated drain Like that gone Poof Oh God she coulda done it anytime hed never know huh Oh why hadnt he come back sooner

Hell hell hell Charlie

He shoulda been here Oh boy you blew it Goddammit you blew it Yup What would your mama say Now now who is standin up for that little baby his mother hairbrush in hand beatin him into a corner behind the bathroom door *Ill beat the bejesus out of you You grimy little termite* Her shriek in his brain now on the porch *See What See Whatd I say Aint gonna save that child is she You married her Thats wholly the way no good welfare suckers worms into folks They got so much dependence relyin on the government to feed em and then when it comes time to take care of their own they cant They cant cause they dont know how Aint never done it have they Nope Livin is like lickin honey off a thorn bush All they done is wait around for the government to give em handouts So when it comes time to take care of a child growin in em Forget it All they can think of is to kill it Its the governments fault A woman whod crucify her own Charlie these babies barely got They aint got fists They cant fight Can they Whyd you wanna marry a woman like that She aint like us son Shes from Nebraska*

God maybe he shoulda been home tonight He would never forgive himself He was goin be one of those now One of those folks who kill their babies One of those men who wont stand up for the seed hes spilt Hed be one of those butchers Gods Assemblies in Christ II hunted

You couldnt get into this town without seein the Bawlin Boy and his oily eye Since fall Gods Assemblies in Christ IId built up their numbers with an advertisin draw on account of that brother diddled that boy in Bible Study What the Assemblyd done was to have some powder blue billboards displayin shredded babies transformin into doves and flyin away and then one more with a bawlin boys face Under the boys chin asked *Why* in red The boys face hooked Charlies throat His half shut lips his eyes clouded over his hair spun up in a draught It had been nice sometimes to just stand there and watch the boy cryin with the dogwood branches wigglin behind them workin eyes glancin right then left On fish line a motorized tear climbed up the boys cheek through an oil drip pan then slid down like he was cryin The heart rent to see it

But now Hammer Gould and Stuart Krassen politicoed the billboards runnin for Supervisor so much that Charlie could walk right by the Boy now and not look twice He had become shut off to his heart like a soldiers got to Comin into town and drivin past Charlie never once no more thought of the Boy as gettin abortioned He couldntve He just shut his heart to it And that never once no more thinkin choked his throat up now Whens the time whens the minute what exactly took over his feelin Charlie had no idea what the world was comin to In a *Star Wars* story they dont let nothing upset em Now no one feels nothing neither Even for little killed babies

He had closed a door to his heart as a kid His daddy was always callin him a sissy on account of his desire that Charlie shoulda been a fighter like his brother Wayne was But oh God he prayed every night for his draft chit to not come up On account of he couldntve done what they wouldve told him to in Vietnam Holy Tomoly oh no He couldntve waltzed into them villages and left them arms and legs and tongues and titties and heads even stuck on branches dryin in the sun teachin the Viet Cong He seen the pictures and when Wayne come back when Charlie was still in high school he hardly would talk of it One thing he said was in the Seebees theyd go in after Americad gone through and tear everythin apart and destroyin a village and whatnot and the Seebeesd help em to build it back up

And there was one day its why they had to stop thinkin they was feelin at all or they wouldve went crazy was what Wayne said There was one day Wayne and them was on patrol or carryin a load of lumber and this little kid come runnin up a little vc come runnin up and just handed Waynes buddy a shoebox yellin all *Happy Christmas* And they all thought that little vc had his English mixed up that he was sayin somethin else It bein July His buddy took the box and popped the lid and it blasted and they hit the deck but his buddys arms was gone to the elbow Wayne saw the joint ball same as seein a teacup of milk is how white it was And his face ripped right off His whole face gone His mouth only just this this this hole there in where his head was all dented in the blast till he fell down Charlie couldntve felt nothin after that

But now the whole worlds like that How did we get so bereaved like Julie was scarin him tonight She was scarin him same thing like that woman who drove her boys into the lake The Bawl Boy hardly never left Charlies mind But Charlie couldntve come back home till he figured things out And now there aint a thing in the world you can do about it is there Look if shes gone and done it you are alone in the world He could just hear his mama saying *Whered your hmmin and hawins got you to this time Huh*

He put his foot down again

That was the problem Julie didnt know herself neither She didnt know what she wanted She would have known wouldnt she Specially if she just would listen to im Boy he oughta go right in there Lets see its after six shell be on the couch He could be standin over her when she wakes up hell be the first thing she sees The first thing she thinks about Hell be lookin down and shell be lookin up Thats good

Ah here it is He could Ah here it is He could sneak in the back door in through the kitchen to the livin room go up to her while shes snorin put a hand over her mouth and when her eyes shoot open put a finger over his mouth to shush her He means business Enough is enough Hes callin the shots now And if she didnt and or if she killed his baby already

No no no How would he be if he went and treated Julie like that

He stepped back off the porch onto the steps where the chokeberry got hold of his boot What he oughta do is go get the shovel and scrape off the blanket of ice coatin the stairs and sidewalk somebodyll come along with hard sole shoes and crack their tuckus open thatd wake her up or go in and have it out and leave for the night or he could just stay outside he could not go in at all and stay out at Wilsons until this blew over but if he did that then Julie would be upset and that wasnt good for the baby he could always go in and plant himself in the chair by the door while she let him have it He deserved it He could nod a lot as if he understood He wasnt sure what the best move would be If he stepped up onto the porch Julie would hear he would disturb her She needed her sleep didnt she Put your foot down no pick it up He was goin to put it down and step up onto the porch but snatched his foot back from the shrubs and hurried to behind Julies Cutlass Hed left his Luv out on the road

He leaned on the trunk He had a ring to deliver Wilson wanted him to pick it up She was too excited to drive She was probably tossin them back at Averys by now he oughta get on but maybe Julie and hed have somethin to say to each other on account that he actually did have pressin things to inform her of given Vincent and all

Goddamned Vincent their sneaky foreman at Singer pulled Wilson to the Coke machine today Wilson pulled Charlies belt so hed come too

I only want to talk to Wilson

What you got to say to me you can say to Charlie

I got some bad news I think and I dont wanna get in no trouble He wouldnt look them in the eye *All right then*

He shook two quarters in his dicey hands For all of Vincents faults when he thinks he might get punched he isnt the worst boss

Wilson covered her ears threatenin *Dont you dare*

Charlie shuffled *You could tell me*

I aint supposed to If I do you got to keep it to yourself

But Vincent could not decide between Coke Diet Coke Red Faygo Grape Faygo or Lipton He stuck one leg out to the right so his toes got fancy on the linoleum then he flapped his elbows like a chicken and wiggled He sang when he spoke *Ahee havent havent havent said anything*

Even Liberace had the good sense to pluck his piano more than sing said Wilson

A person couldnt tell his singin from pryin a rusted door off its hinges *Its gonna happen aint it* Charlie said

Wilson sprung off *An you an old pussyfooter*

Charlie got her arm *Patience of you know who patience of you know who Dont stand there like the Queen of England Vincent tell us*

No it isnt bad bad

Old Pussyfoot fiddled with the change in his pockets *Well it might be bad bad for some some* He cocked one of his milk trout eyes at Charlie *You might probably have a good chance of staying Wilson Now how come that vending company hasnt put some RC in here* He rocked back and forth on the balls of his feet hummin

Wilson didnt take shit from shinola *Gotta go*

Charlie kept hold of her arm *He aint gonna tell it if its just me Vincent would you just tell it*

Vincent puffed his upper lip out and shook his head *Layoff* His Grape Faygo crashed down *Yes yes Layoff*

You sonuvabitch you said they werent thinkin that Wilson backed Vincent up against the wall She breathed Bud on him

They werent friend

I aint a friend Your pay aint goin

Isnt Wilson We dont have a final word

The hell it aint

Vincent whispered in Wilsons ear *It aint gonna be you Its just gonna be a skeleton crew and* His breath tickled her ears sweet spot

She shivered *What about Charlie here*

Charlie I am sorry but you aint no more special than another man

I know it

Is the union sendin letters asked Wilson

Union gave them the go You pay your money you take your chances In spite of what you might think Wilson I want the best for my best man

I aint a man Got to get a last dig in all the time doncha

Charlie hunkered down close to the bumper He couldnt see her but he knew she was on the couch A person just knows Okay Fine Theyd settle it tonight She was goin to have that baby no matter what kind of world they lived in Jesus Christ who did she think she was killin one of her own children Killin one of his Over his dead body Lord Maybe theyd be one of those couples that split up after their kids moved out

That morning that Tanya and Michelle drove off Charlie had his shears and was takin out the height of that gamma grass coming through the back steps All three of his women got together the way women do in the kitchen Spyin on em through the back door glass he could see how Michelles cheek still had the fat and clarity of a baby She blocked the Mr Coffee sos Julie had to get around behind her It was a good chance that Julie wouldnt see her girls for a real long time if they found work

They werent going with much Julie set her mug on the sink Gently she pulled the hair tighter through Michelles ponytail band Michelle pulled her head away and leaned against the counter He could hear em through the crack at the bottom of the door The air pushing out went right into his eyes and he had to keep rubbing em

Michelle sighed a little fed up *Im sorry Go on Pull my hair*

Tanya eased down from upstairs creaking the old floorboards anyway and leaned on the door jamb Julie crinkled her brow probably wonderin when did the floor start being so loud She chewed the inside of her cheek Julie didnt have no words She was losing what she knowed Everyone wanted her to be happy Charlie wanted her to be happy How come she wouldnt be happy All the words people used when them they love are disappearing didnt give her no comfort *Take care Good luck Drive safe Be careful Oh youre going to have a wonderful time* Words dont salve Her throat clutched around something wrenching a valley to her heart She couldnt hide it from her girls or Charlie The clenched jaw and short breaths Her whole life had been them Now what Holy Hell Julie

Julie struggled to speak *Lonely You dont know nobody Got no quarter nowhere to be Even after I took up with your daddy Twice a week is what I told your daddy Id only see him twice a week till we figured it out Wilson was a girl that was a pop to the head Make men yearn for you Dont make it easy*

Michelle rocked back and forth on the balls of her feet impatient *Mom we dont make it easy Tanya and I*

I can talk for myself said Tanya.

We dont have any ideas about boys

But youre not saying that are you Mom You got to know we aint going to know nobody close Tanya was smart and could sniff through words to more of the truth Her aunt Tammy Julies sister had that

Julie folded her arms to press her hurt back in She chewed the inside of her cheek and screwed her lips out the way she does

Be happy for us Mom Tanya said

Your goddamned daddy put this into your head Dont think I dont know it

It was ours Our idea said Michelle now rocking back onto her heels

Julie knew better and shook her head in short sharp jerks *He and that refrigerator Wilson egged you on*

Mom

They didnt make us feel bad about it

Julie twisted her lips out like she was sucking on a Sucrets She stared at the fingerprints on the cupboard door That was Charlies chore

You ought to do your chores before you go Your father aint gonna help
Michelles mouth came open slightly in disbelief *Mom were leaving today And thats Daddys job We want to get over to at least Little Rock before dark Dont make us feel bad about it*

Im going to tell you something Julie said to Michelle *When I first found out I was pregnant with you there was a big thing with Russia It was the same with my mama Every time a womans having a baby now shes got to think about nuclear war I thought some about not having you I didnt have no right to bring you into a world like this To put you through that Then I come around to the fact that God put us here He has a plan or is running things I dont know Having you girls is what Im here for*

Now that sounded more like his little lady

It aint a choice Animals dont choose nothing except not hurting We are animals Like dogs

God Mom Do you have to be so dramatic asked Michelle *Tanya we got to get these boxes in the truck* As she passed Michelle patted her mothers head *Like a dog Itll be all right Mom*

But Julie wouldnt have it She covered her heart again Then rubbed the cleave in her chest up and down She looked away and started diggin in the grime worked into the edge of the sink Her nose turning red and her eyes waterin A little chirp come out of her She had a big bug in her She couldnt shake it Goddamned Julie

But things had gone on since then Now there was business to get to Tonight Charlie had to duck out to the ring store in Lake City He ought to be excited for Wilson When she slipped the ring onto Dols finger Lord he was gonna cry all over everyone And he ought to want to get his tuckus over to Averys He ought to have wanted to go past from their downfall inside and see Julie He ought to have known how to make things right

{ *Wilson* }
6:34 p.m.

In the purple glow of the early evening, Wilson had sat on the fence watching the sun fade and night swallows swoop down. At first, the sunset had them clouds pressing back the night as a peach parade of sunset shot out over her head.

Most of them cattle weighed over a thousand pounds. The barn door had been heavy on wheels. To let some air in the barn Monday to Friday, she had pulled it back and forth, back and forth. All of them brown eyes blinked at her in her mind's eye.

Now, on the edge of the bar, she dug into the soreness between her bicep and forearm. She pressed hard enough that she could have drawn blood if she scraped it too. She could see it in her reflection in the microwave door's glass. And she meant to draw blood. She had tossed it back and forth in her mind before heading over to Avery's tonight, what she was going to do. Possibly to draw blood from a stone.

She was hungry. Maybe she ought to dig around in that deep-freeze and get her some of 'em pre-fried frozen shrimps and do 'em up in the nuker. Folks didn't eat enough at this place. Warn't no peanuts or nothin'.

She took the lone stool at the bar and scratched her nose. It had been a hard day, what with Vincent's news and then dealing with them cows.

She didn't know what'd come over her years ago when she took up cattle-raising. Partly it was keepin' busy when she wasn't at the shop. Kept her head straight. Probably she felt sorry for her father. When she first got her three head, her father would come out and sit on the fence and watch them. He'd always wanted his own but never got around to having them. And it showed in his thin lips and dull eyes. Wilson's great-aunt always said her father was the saddest boy she ever met. Now that she had had her own herd, she understood her father's grief and why he hadn't gotten into cattle-raising. Couldn't bear it when it come time to slaughter.

She never wanted to look another cow in the eye as long as she lived. The sadness there soaked in same as what it smelt like once they was burning. Jesus, they're the lonesomest animal God ever put on this earth. Wilson's fingers smelt like the sugar char of burnt cowhide and it'd stick on her straight through to April. She ought to have gone in the restroom and tried that powdered soap Avery keeps in there. But it'd take off the top layer of skin and it was too cold for that.

Nobody was looking. She stuck her fingers in her beer and sucked 'em dry. All 'em enzymes eat off the smell.

She and Charlie'd been doing with carcasses all week. She had to put down every last one of 'em save that one at Charlie's for quarantine. If she didn't, the County would tan her hide and she'd never get to have her own heads again. What a rotten business, what a hobby, pressing down the way them winds do twixt her shoulder blades.

Went like this: get the seventeen head in. Line 'em up. Get one through the post. Leave the others by the fence. Their eyes steaming like a pond in August. Lead the animal in, the shadow of the door'd crawl to the rump. Wilson'd roll it closed. Them barn swallows seething at the beams way high up there. Charlie pet the animal, soothing it. Horn flies was all dried up by this time of year but 'em tails would swish-swish coming from habit. Old lonesome heads would come in, their cartoon brown watery eyes taking in a person like they didn't judge her for what she was doing. Every side of the business understood they all had it coming. It was the way things were. The shadow would creep, the door would clunk shut.

Wilson would grip the hammer handle, raise it high above and aim. She'd seat the blow at the base of the skull, right up over the shoulder blades, lifting her up, 'em necks're so strong and the animal didn't right away buckle. Charlie would sink a bullet. The knees'd cave. Every couple head or so, the skull would be weak enough to shoot the innards to the wall. The animal'd loll there like a mixed-up retard. Charlie would tuck his gun in his belt, at which point the animal'd weaken, teeter and then founder. Then they'd hook the shoulders through, yank the pulley and haul her up. The bowels'd loose, and, they not being a professional operation, brains and crap'd make a foot hazard. It never happened yet but oh she was just waitin' for one to wake up, accusing, on the hook. What got Wilson was those blank eyes staring like the surface of a lake, never closing and not seeing they was dead.

If a cow was anything like a human being, each was outside listening to what's done to the one coming before. There warn't much variation. All of 'em got killt if they was out there in the pen. At the time of one coming in, they was maybe postulating of the future or where they just was, but not much before that, and now they was eyeing the floor and the mess underfoot. What they saw in the barn was never as bad as what they thought it might be. They was comforted on seeing Wilson once they was in. She come out to see them every evening when she came home from Singer. Charlie'd be a stranger but, so long as Wilson was there, there wouldn't be any sensing of nothing upwards of wrong. They was probably thinking right up to getting it that something bad wouldn't happen.

They's probably like people in having a story of how 'em that go in never come back. She bet her sweet patootie it got passed down the line: fence post to fence post, animal to animal, generation to generation. It was in their eyes. They's fantasizing a reward in that barn as they're telling it. A reward so good, returning ain't even thought of. Some, probably, don't cotton to the tale. There's always going to be some what don't take to scheming, so as Dol'd call it, be it from the Bay Area Council or the Feds or she and Charlie.

Last week, one heifer got to thinking, and before Wilson got it in her own head what was going on, the whole kit and kaboodle had been influenced. All of 'em'd follow the one thinking but Wilson's fast noticing, slow as it was, had saved her and Charlie at least a day.

What happened was an old heifer got herself through the fence where Wilson hadn't got the rail back up. Now, a cow ain't one to tear on out but it can get a rail down, and if it stays with a certain line of thinking on something, even with one animal disconnected from the other, she – and then all the others – would get herself free. And this one old girl did. Neither Charlie or Wilson witnessed it but she must've got her snout up and over that downed rail and followed her snout with her stepping hooves and out through the fence she was. Once she was past that rail, she was scooting down the lane fast enough and then, being naturally fearsome creatures, the others'd went scurrying off too, on account of they ain't no different than a person: panic leaks in to the heart, infecting the stomachs and the brain and then off they go. A person, once it dawned on them, would do the same thing. That old girl knew trouble was brewing. Her eyes, gathering same as them minute storms what come up fast at Higgins Lake, set down on the fence line of grey gravel.

She trotted off down the lane, kicking up even that packed dust, scattering it into that December onslaughting wind speared through with winter. Then, them others started their churning too and got themselves around to march out of the gate like soldiers, like in *The World at War*. Wilson took off out of the barn, yelling to Charlie to come and give her a hand for crying out loud they're all getting away. She wrenched through 'em as they was piling up and traffic jammed where the rail'd come down. Hold on.

Then Wilson herself had one of 'em ideas'd come to her that was almost avalanche feeling – she couldn't have stopped it if she wanted to, but before she had the brains to reflect upon it, she got herself in and around all 'em animals jammed at the gate and got ahead and watched her own self like she'd done it a million times before, which she never ever had, leading just one follower ahead of that first girl that escaped and got that follower to block the heifer's way. 'Em two slowed down panting hard, steam coming out of their four great pie-plate nostrils and them two great minds come together, there in that dirt lane.

The two of 'em stood there, snorting. Their snouts still as cement, their nostrils tightenin' and expandin'. The escaping one bucked her head some, whipping it side to side. The other one, the follower, just stood there watching with the patience of Job. The heifer's chocolate eyes, now milky with knowing, clouded over.

And it was then Wilson knew there was some beings put on this planet what just knew from the get-go that they just got to be and there ain't no use in fighting and that was what life was all about, it was nothing but surrender after surrender, giving up after giving up after giving up, and the others, like that old heifer, where fighting was all they knew, where there's always one in every bunch that just ain't going to go along. There ain't no surrender. There's a struggle.

To get 'em cows back in the pen, she had to paint the idea of continuing on the path they was on, separate from the one of being afraid. Fear gets in the veins. If Wilson could get some space in between going on down that lane and the 'fraidness of what was to come, all 'em cattle'd stop connecting thoughts, one to the other, and causing 'em like that old girl to take flight.

Wilson gave in and got all of the cattle out through the fence and then to surround around the one'd got out first. With they was bunching her in, that old heifer couldn't feel her own self. All of 'em ringing her in'll give solace and warmth which spreads her fear so thin she can't feel it in her body. When a heifer's all packed in like that, headed in with all the others, she won't think independent no more. All of 'em, ganged up and circled around her, sweetenin' her up, pushin' her back in line. The antennas in her skin will pick up on all the other cows wanting to go the way Wilson's prodding 'em. Sure enough, then, that girl'll march into the barn like it was her own intention from the start. It ain't been no other story for cattle, or the human race – nor it wasn't neither for Wilson herself, not since she found Dol was her one true love. Having to fight like hell to stay on track what with all the crowding and sweet-thinging and prodding. And fear churning in her own stomach.

Everyone in town treated Wilson as a man. Not 'cause that was what she was, but looking at her you'd guess wrong what was between her legs. Her head rose out of shoulders wide at the base and stumped on top. Charlie said her neck matched a pork shoulder. Wilson had tried in all her younger days, sometimes with the help of Dol, to be more like fancy girls. She couldn't. She made peace with her thick neck, her strong arms and shoulders that a Razorback lineback could do with. Her idea was that God gives all folks gifts yet it's only the smart folks what use 'em. Her arms were thicker than her neck even, and a hell of a lot stronger still. Get a sack of Yukon Golds, you got her gut. Chase a chicken, that's her legs.

She'd out-arm-wrassled three-quarters of the guys on the three o'clock shift. Beating ol' Charlie was a breeze. He had got it in his noodle he was going to beat her this year. Ha, just 'cause he's aiming at targets don't mean he's going to hit a bull's eye. By the time Charlie got himself up for the job, maybe she wouldn't stand for it no more. Maybe Dol would come first and whup her heart. That was a dream worth daring. She'd find out soon enough. Wilson smeared the ring her beer bottle was bleeding on the bar. Twenty-six minutes till Dol's shift started.

Dol led her on. They all did: Dol, Charlie, Julie, every darn one. They had good reason. Wilson could move things where God couldn't. Take Dol. Dol needed his strength to draw that makeup pencil across his brow. It was heavier than she'd ever know, he told her. Take Tanya and Michelle. Where was they going to get reliable transportation to take 'em all the way out there? In what part of God's plan would they be driving that chi-chi, shade-of-midnight F10 truck out past them mountains? Huh? Wilson's part, that's what part. When they was clowning with their five-CD compact disc changer, sporting that remote control, who'd they have to thank? Not Charlie. Charlie couldn't lift a ball-peen hammer to save his life. Sure as hell not that mother of theirs wound up tighter than a bull snake just before she strikes.

Wilson herself never needed no lifting. If she didn't amount to nothing it wasn't no skin off her back. And compared to the dreams of some, compared to the dreams of the girls, compared to the dreams of Dol, say, there warn't no way she wanted. Dol come into her head puckering. A grin cracked Wilson's stone face. She spun her bottle.

Dol's puckers was always meaning something. His was never just lips poofing out. She and Dol did kiss one funny time. Oh, they cracked their tummies over that one.

They went skinny-dipping at the gravel pit in Scott's Woods. Wilson was in her early twenties, and Dol was seventeen or eighteen. Sweat dripped from Wilson's armpits it was so hot. Dol had his rubber bathing cap on and wiped the sweat from his temples. The rocks carpeting the slopes bit into their feet, so they climbed up on big glacial debris holding hands and took deep breaths and leapt out over the water, as if they were Batman and Robin.

Coming up for air, they were surprised by a young man watching them intently on the shore. He unhooked one thumb from his belt loops and tugged at his groin.

'Hey,' he said. 'You two by yourselves?' He winked.

'Hey, yourself,' said Dol, pulling his hair cap down and his one-piece up. 'He's flirtin,' he whispered to Wilson, his breath tickling her weak spot, her ear. Dol held up a finger to shush the man. He put an arm around Wilson, brought her closer and planted a good one on her lips.

'I seen that before,' said the young man. 'That don't scare me,' he said.

It scared Wilson though. She felt blood flooding her cheeks and her tongue swelling in her throat.

'It ought to,' said Dol to the boy.

But what really bound her and Dol was the work they put into trying to be who they were.

Tonight was what'd been pressing down on them during all of their days. A person walks side by side with what's coming, Wilson figured. Tonight was the night Dol was going to fess up and say yes on account that a person puckers on purpose even if he ain't aware of what he's doing. Wilson hung her jacket on the seat of the bar stool, the air too hot on account of her racing heart.

A long, long time ago Dol'd seen it: *p-o-w-e-r*. In junior high he'd seen right through that show. Before anyone explained, five words to Mr. Sloan, their history teacher: *Get in line to disappear*. Though he was only fourteen going on forty-seven he explained how it all worked to Mr. Sloan: *Ain't it no different than history itself? One bunch trying to keep the other'n from being and doing? What was it Pontius wanted from Jesus? Get in line, don't think for yourself. Then, what did the pioneers want from the Indians? Come off the land, give up your claim. What'd Hitler desire of the Jews? Wear a star, get on the train. What about white from negro?* At which point, white Mr. Sloan cut Dol off, probably on account of them Sloan genes carrying a dark pigment.

Wilson's beer was almost done. On top of all 'em cattle getting sick, today, first day back, dagnabbit if that pussyfooter Vincent let 'em know the boom was going to fall – not yet but darned soon. He said Wilson was safe but she didn't believe it. Why her? His 'best man.' Hooey. He said they'd probably get a few weeks before the knife fell.

Then, all of that threat, on top of having to put her sweet bessies down. This made it super important to get married to Dol before her insurance ran out if she did get the boot. She could keep up insurance payments for a bit but then she'd be dependent on Burns. That pissed her off. Burns, who was always needling her about being more of a woman, would twist her and make her beg for care. She could just kick that man.

The end of the road is the end of the road. You can't fight it. A person wants to keep going the way they were. Always. But you got to bend like a stick in the water. You got to learn what happens in this world. Like the cattle. She was lucky to get a few head a couple years back when Pitch Slocum had to sell. All her life she'd loved their bigness and soulful nature, and cattling kept her busy. And now the County was lowering the boom. Them animals would just stand there looking at her before she led 'em into the barn.

Tonight things had to get different. By the look of it, they probably wouldn't because Charlie was late getting here. Maybe he was playing hard to get. He loved to make her squirm. A teaser. That was about the same as what Dol was doing – although he had important business that, he said, did not concern Wilson. That's what he said: 'It don' concern you, Wilson.'

Wilson, however, was not a cow, she wasn't going to line up without using her brain. Wilson kept her eyes and ears open.

Years ago, back when Dol was still with Elaine, Charlie and Wilson were up nailing roof tiles. 'You got to hang on good, Charlie,' she said. Wilson and Charlie had been dancing around each other for a while. Wilson had hooked herself to a large lag screw in the roof of Charlie's house. Her palms were so sweaty up there. She took a lot of deep breaths. She didn't look at the ground. But Charlie was having a field day.

'Let's do laps,' he said. He got up off the tiles and then started running down the slopes and then back up to the apex and then down again.

Wilson felt sick. 'Charlie, can we please just finish and get back down?' She shot the words out fast as she could.

'How come? Don't you want to have a good time?'

'I'm having a great time. I love it up here. I love it so much my hands are all sweaty and I want to boot.'

'Sorry. You seem comfortable enough.' And then he jerked, bein' fancy, and took a wrong step off the roof at the edge of the apex. He cussed and hung there squeezing either side of the apex, trying to pull himself up.

Wilson peed her work pants a little and got down on her knees to get over to Charlie without falling herself. 'Hang on, Chuck.'

Charlie had lost all sense of funning and had her eyes in a vice. 'Don't let me drop. I got weak bones.'

She thought of the strap that tied her to the roof. 'Just a second, Charlie.'

'I can't … '

'Hang on!'

She untied the strap from the screw. She put the one end of it into Charlie's fingers. He let go for a better grip. His weight lurched forward, threatening to take her over the edge with him.

'Okay, get your free hand on the roof and push up.'

When he did this he was almost able to walk up the side of the house.

Staying on the apex, but now on her belly and gripping the shingles hard with the sides of her ankles, she held on to her end of the apex with all of her strength. She couldn't see how Charlie was coming along. She could barely spit out, 'Charlie?'

With Wilson as ballast, he got one leg swung up to the slope of the roof. That gave him enough leverage to pull the rest of his body up. He lay flat on the roof's slope but hanging on to the apex.

'That was close,' said Charlie.

They climbed down and went and stood in the shed. Their hearts were thumping. Charlie said softly, 'I coulda broke my neck or at least my leg.'

The robbins and sparrows were making a racket outside – the wind was quiet. It was time for them birds to head south.

Wilson leaned on the buzz saw. 'We ought to make some of that furniture we talked about,' she said. Charlie had a habit of bringing up good ideas to expand their money earning but couldn't seem to follow through. He was supposed to be raising cattle in Mexico or something by now. She watched him, the muscles coming up from his shoulders and going to his neck and the crow's feet lining his dust-green eyes. Men get better looking as they get older, and the salt and pepper in Charlie's mop didn't hurt him none. He warn't an eyesore in his twenties but these days, in middle age, he never failed to turn heads at the hardware store.

'Charlie, all told, how many times have you gone out on Julie?'

Charlie set his eyes on hers and came closer. 'What do you want to know for? That was real nice and real brave, what you did up there.'

'Thanks for saying it.' The molecules in the shed had begun random collisions. Her stomach soured some. Air pumped into her veins.

Charlie rolled his shoulders to loosen them up and pulled up his pants. 'Yuh, sure was nice of you. You must want some attention from time to time yourself.'

'You ain't answering my question.'

'I'll tell you. Less than twenty times probably but more than twice.'

'I won't never tell.'

'You got the prettiest blue eyes. They're always pretty but get you in a certain light, then they just pop. Ping!'

'Like the ocean down in Puerto Vallarta.'

'Yeah, like that.' Charlie stepped in closer, Wilson couldn't feel her body anymore. He got his face close enough to Wilson's she could feel his breath. It smelled of the spearmint he ripped off the bush next to the shed. Wilson felt removed from her body except that her heart had taken to thumping again. Charlie put his hand on her chest. 'Your heart's goin' at it.'

'I'm nervous.'

'I won't bite.'

'No, but Julie might. Oh, Charlie. Are you going to do what I think you're gonna?'

He whispered in her ear so close it made the little white hairs in her ears shiver. 'Oh, it ain't going to be just me.'

Wilson closed her eyes and waited. She felt the breath on her lips first, and then the pressure. Charlie had gotten her mouth with a warm and soft kiss. It felt like one of those muscle-relaxing hot packs Burns charged her for when she had sciatica.

After a moment, Charlie held back some but Wilson pulled him closer. What she was doing was awful. It felt so good, and she'd never had a chance to fully feel herself with a man – she didn't want it to end so soon. Till Charlie, she'd waited her whole life for a kiss that meant something. She devoured his mouth. She was safe.

After, when they were lying on the tarp pile, she asked him, 'You don't mind my size? My belly?' A cool breeze found its way inside and brushed over the tops of her thighs and her nipples.

Charlie put a hand on her stomach fat and jiggled it.

'Charlie, that ain't a nice thing to do to a lady.'

'Yes, but I like it. I like a woman with some muscle. You ain't like one of them women in Julie's magazines – you don't walk around all hangdog 'cause you got meat on you.'

That was the nicest thing anyone ever said to her. She climbed up, straddled him and he took her breast into his pillow lips. She thought about that now, there at the bar, and was sure she could have the same feeling with Dol. Her mind raced.

Tanya and Michelle meant to stay gone. Their future lay in Hollywood, California, not Bay, Arkansas. There warn't no reason to put off she and Charlie straightening things out, putting one foot in front of the other and heading down their respective paths. The girls weren't coming back. He had to seed the wide-open years ahead. Charlie could put his bad parenting behind him and start again. He wasn't going to do that, and she wasn't going to go loving Dol, as long as the two of them were still fooling around.

Wilson wasn't no better than Charlie, she was duplicitous. But now she had to do what she had to do. God'd be her judge, no doubt about that.

At Avery's, Wilson ripped the rest of the label off her Bud and wadded it into an itty-bitty ball. In spite of how hard Julie had become, Wilson had a soft place for her. These days Julie maybe felt like that close little ball of label she was rolling around her fingertips. All wound up. Wilson scoped the place for someone to throw the paper ball at.

Pitch Slocum could take a joke – he'd like the attention. He had his back turned. Wilson beaned the ball into the back of his head. Pitch half-rose out his chair, scanning the room, squinting his eyes and looking threatening. When his eyes landed on Wilson, she smirked. Pitch, who could always pass for a girl, mock-kicked Wilson from his table. Like Dol, he wore long blond hair with bangs which he kept trimmed and cast over the right part of his forehead. But his hair was real. Strangers often called him 'Miss,' which, to Pitch, was funny the first time.

$$\left\{ \begin{array}{c} \textit{\textbf{Dol}} \\ \textit{6:39 p.m.} \end{array} \right\}$$

You've got to make sure they're sleeping. You've got to tiptoe and peek and keep your fingers crossed. You don't get done half of what you've got to when they're up. You don't get done half of what you've got to. You see them. You can go on knowing they look like that, knowing they're sleeping with their itsy-bitsy minds on God. *You go dream of God. Go.*

'Daddy?' Your nine-year old, Pity, up on her elbow. Squirrel snuggles against her back.

'Sst, sst. Go to sleep.'

'I'm cold.'

'Squirrel's warm, get closer.'

'I can't get closer.'

'Okay. Nighty-night.'

'Is she going to be nice?'

'Who, honey?' Then you get it. The babysitter. 'Yes, she's real nice and she'll be here when you wake up so get under the covers and I'll leave the light on in the other room.' You leave the door cracked.

If somebody would've told you then what they were going to be to you now – you cannot imagine. You cannot think you have that in you. You can't know that. You don't think God would ever give an experience such as this to you. You got Pity and Squirrel – and, with practice, your voice.

You might only hear your voice in secret. Sometimes your body doesn't catch up. Like a, you don't know, like a bad – like bulrushes dragging when you row, like one 'em black vultures swooping down with its arms spread wide, squealing, and your throat is like them crunching talons and car wheels pulling onto gravel and the screeching peeling the skin off your nerves same as those blue plaster dinner plates every time you took to set the table. It is no surprise that Elaine's mother got them for you. She knows that that's what it is to be in between a body craving change and a voice that can't. You've got to practice on your new voice.

Your last doctor gave you a book to practice on but you chose your own because you know better. You got it at the library in Lake City – it was a twenty-mile drive but you took the kids and you went. It's a thin book called *Speak You!* with an exclamation point, by Dr. Jane Peabody Harris, also with an exclamation point. Dr. Jane says your voice is a beach ball, starting at the base of your spine, rolling upward into the *masque* of the face, and on the exhale you can place your voice right where it sounds *like* you. Initially, this was your problem with the book. You don't want to sound *like* you, you want to make *your* sound.

But this was a gross misunderstanding, Dr. Harris advised in an email: you *find* it this way. She says you'll know your voice when you hear it. It'll feel like home. So. If you don't use her way, the closest you may get to using your own voice is to sound *like* you. It's an individual exploration akin to the individual's individuation. That's from the foreword.

You can see yourself on a lecture tour. But here's the doctor's point. Most people use voices they think are their own. Most people talk *like* their mama or their daddy or like the people they see on TV. That is true. Listen to people, you can hear it. You'll see them sitting right there on the couch mouthing the words, then they get up and speak like those voices are their own. Do we not, you think, sleepwalk through 90 percent of our lives? Unconscious? People have no idea that they are not themselves. No idea. And they can't know – how're they supposed to know? Who's going to tell them? Not the people who want you to sound like and be like and live like them. Oprah's not going to tell you.

No, you got to go on that journey all by yourself. Alone. If you look like Tinker Bell and sound like Paul Bunyan you had better go on the journey. And you had better be ready. You don't look or sound like what they want. Boy, they'll come and get you. You know, you've been gottened.

Positive, positive, positive. That is bad, that is negative, that is out of the question, that will not be considered here for you, you will not think this way, you will not. Change your mind, change it, change it. Positive, positive, positive. Oh God, just take this hand, please.

Yes, and this is your dilemma with Elaine. When you are different, very different, from the folks around, you've got to choose positivity. Elaine is cynical, judgemental and closed down. You read interviews online at the library where couples held each other's hands as they transitioned. In some of them, both of the people transitioned. Think about the hope that takes. Think about the faith. You could just cry. It's your great tragedy, not being able to convince Elaine that this could make you a stronger couple. It happens. It's not her fault. You don't blame her. Choosing your thoughts, in spite of your American-ness, is not taught to you. You have to fight to think for yourself. It is a *battle légende*, ladies and gentleman.

That is what happened to Elaine, and you. She is so buried in her beautiful body, you are so buried in your beautiful body. It's not something somebody teaches you to think about. You find it out. In Little Rock, in the unkempt motel when she thought you were with Wilson.

But you weren't, you were practicing. You were all trussed up. You poked your eye with the forgiving eyebrow pencil when she kicked through that door, her black hair yanked back so her face was hermetic, her eyebrows drawn up high to Mount Olympus – all to do a number on you. She was Judgement. You were human. She opened her mouth, and then the edifice of her being collapsed, you could see it, her eyebrows smashing together and her face trembling in and out of focus, like she was a demolition site, like she was scaffolding shivering. For a split second, she gave you no dignity, none, like you were nothing and she was somebody, oh, she caught you, she had you good, but then she just – her whole self fell.

You didn't hide, deny or blink. You looked her straight in those molasses eyes, you gathered her, slick with sweat. Her body shaking, the pitch of her desperation, her smell of Safeguard. A copper hairpin on the sill spit the sun surging in. She's not going to understand. Who could? You can't ask that of regular people, they don't have it in them. They got to get supper, make it to the Safeway before it closes and swallow their whole voices at, in, some office somewhere. She wet your shoulder. When she stood back, she was different. Her eyes could have been the hollow moon, the sweat had evaporated. Her clay skin held the indent of your scented fingertips.

She hit you. Hard. Tore after the stuff on the bed, shattered the tortoiseshell hairband, shredded the blond wig under the desk, ripped the silk hose with her teeth. The rayon sundress, torn. She beat you with a hanger. Then with your moisturizing mittens.

'You are a cliché!' she screamed. 'I am a cliché. You've made me one!'

She kept screaming but Motel 8 didn't kick you out. You held her, then let go. We all got our row to hoe.

'Don't tell Pity, don't you dare tell Squirrel,' she shrieked.

'Don't let the door hit you on the way out.'

She took up Jesus, you took up Mencken. Mencken makes plain sense and you hear your thoughts in him. Christ, he said, had nothing against women. Mary Magdalene was the foreman of his team. Magdalene, a woman who 'worked,' was one of Jesus' closest advisors.

Lift up your mind with your voice. You practice this: 'Jesus Christ preached glad tidings highly favorable to women. He esteemed them socially and set value upon their sagacity, and one of the most disdained of their party, a lady formerly in public life, was among His regular advisors.'

You can always trust Mr. Mencken, Magdalene sits right there in *The Last Supper*. Da Vinci knew. Mariolatry, not a common word by any means, tells of love for Mary, Mencken says. It wasn't invented by popes, which is what all the Protestants would have us believe. The Gospels make plain that women have been knocked from some shaky pedestal. No, what those popes invented is the rule of women's inferiority, and the church, it seems, can't let go of misogyny.

You think that that's what's been wrong with the whole world. You were a man. You know. You know because you're right between the two, you know 'cause you got one foot on land and one in the water, one foot in and one out.

When traversing such tricky precipices, the thing is not to pitch your voice high or low but to aim your words. You don't want an avalanche. In order to keep the team discipline once Jesus was long gone, the popes came up with celibacy and barring them from marriage. To make that easier, women became rotten apples and pits of sin. That allowed hundreds of thousands of boys and young men to, unwittingly, move into the line of fire.

Women calculate. Words're not wasted. They don't squeak like a Power Ranger on speed. No. Words have consequences. If you consider the ramifications of your words, the voice changes immediately.

The result was the deliberate organization and development of the theory of female triviality, lack of responsibility and general looseness of mind.

You got to counter all that. You practice. You got to be you, you got to be the new You. Don't act it, be it. You do what you have to do. There's all kinds of things you got to practice. You've been in another body, you got to make yourself get used to the new one. You will. Cutting doesn't solve everything. You can't stop halfway. But first, you got to get to them tonight. You got to get there and you got to look good and you got to get what you went for. Listen to the man.

Yeah. Now there's one for you.

Listen to the ol' boss man, Avery. He cancelled your health insurance because he says it keeps you sick and afraid. He can't afford it like you can't afford to heat your house.

You got to go. This is your chance. Tonight. Burns hmmed and hawed it out: this Atlanta doctor might give it to you for free or something close. He wants you to help around the office or something. You can do that. You aren't buying it on your own. You aren't.

{ *Julie* }
6:41 p.m.

And I hadn't seen him since. Since Tuesday. Time was tightening in on us. Come on, Charlie. C'mon, c'mon, we're going to settle this. Out of the frying pan and into the fire, Mr. Man.

The temperature was dropping and lulling it to quiet out there. Nothing was coming down yet. The couch seam cut into the flab behind my knees. If I squeezed my eyes and dreamed my arms wide I could plunge, I could jump straight onto my tummy and reach in and tear it out, and then stream into that choked night shaking my bloody hands and screeching. Or I could stay here and straighten Charlie out. Jesus, smell the fermenting bouquet in the shag: macaroni and cheese, meatloaf, cupcakes, cigarettes. The beer he's spilt. Twenty-five years of us: Michelle, Tanya, him and me. Housecleaning never came easy.

That night cowed to the coming storm and I could hear every little thing. What I wanted to hear was if that Chevy Luv door slammed shut. If I could've just seen him or just heard his voice then I'd see progress. But there I waited, in limbo. Looking out the frosty glass, sitting on the couch and clicking the TV on and then off.

If it were to be him in the driveway, I would to have sat right back down so I was the first thing he recognized with them raccoon eyes of his coming through that door. That rush of fresh polar-bear air mixing with the heated-up oxygen inside, stroking a hold of his chin and unable to leak out. The coal lining his eyes comes from not eating or sleeping right. When did speaking to me get so spooky? When couldn't we make a little decision just the two of us together?

If it wasn't him out there then I might as well've got up. My eyes weren't leaving that front door. That sonuvabitch was going to hike in hangdog and sneak into the kitchen. Yeah, and when he was in there he could clean that danged grime piling higher than my nail polish.

When he roamed home, I hoped to profess what was on my mind. I ought to have owned up that I finished with breeding. Then if he romanced me sweet, in his smoke voice, if he'd talk to me and thaw my hand in his calloused one and mould his creased forehead into mine, then, who knows, maybe then another road would show.

He spun that sticky web too, way back when we first was thinking about kids. My feeling sorry for his stony mind let his scheming get the better of me then. But last Tuesday I found my wobbling voice, then my struggling caught myself up like a fly in a web. I unearthed my tongue. But tonight, like last Tuesday, it may be the bite that proves the spider.

We could do a trade-off, couldn't we? This thing was growing in me here, that calf was growing fast out there. In the barn.

When I went to see Father Tibs this morning I compelled myself to decide: peel it off or avail it of my womb. I hadn't slept hardly. My mind was fuzzy. The ballpoints standing in a can on Tibs' desk squirmed in my dizzy eyes like cottonmouth snakes grovelling to a ditch at dusk. Tibs aimed Bics at the can from his desk clear across the room. I dipped into my anger, which helped to clear my thinking.

'Boy … Julie. Got me. You ain't done, huh?'

'I haven't done nothing vicious. Yet. Tell me something smart, something real Catholic.'

'What do you want from me?'

'Being a man, what would you say to me – forget the priest in you.'

He looked at the desk calendar, the clock with Roman numbers, and back at me. 'Still smoking Kools?'

I dug them out of my purse. 'Take them.'

'Hmm. That's good. Quitting means you care.' He lit one, leaned against the wall and sucked a good long draw.

'Of course I care, Jesus Christ, what do you think?'

'They put us in classes for this.'

'Spell it out for me, just Tibs to Julie. Tibs to Julie, what does Charlie say?'

'Not a peep,' said Tibs, still judging the situation.

'Please, steer me,' I said, practically pleading. Not too deep down, I was driving to Burns, already stirrupping up my legs and allowing that Hoover of his to fix me.

'He's a good man, Jules.'

'Well, lock me away and fling off the key.'

'Help him to help you. Is it possible you're not giving him credit where it's due?'

'Tell me one thing he ain't got credit for.' There wasn't nothing stopping me from just going and getting it done then. 'What lines of credit would he apply for with my shanks up in the air? That's the same thing my mama said too. The bane and beauty of our body is to hide things from almost anybody. She said too what you do hide is yours to hold. Not giving him credit.'

'Man to woman, talk to him.'

'I want to. But he's got no appetite for it – he's not there, he sneaks in, feeds that animal, eats at Avery's. I think he thinks that he's just going to show up in June for the glorious arrival.'

'Have you gone over there?'

'Jeez, no, I ain't gone there.' That got me to thinking. I could try there, couldn't I?

'Jeez, Louise, it's a free country.'

'That's what they say. I am chewing this over.'

'Neato.'

'I aim to wrench that calf's throat.'

'Don't do that.'

'I aim to ease him home.'

'Coercion.'

'Is nine tenths of the law.'

'He could maybe not know what words to say.'

'Strange hour to get tongue-tied.'

'There's a lot riding on what he says.'

'Then I'll do it.'

'Do what?'

'Have it. After. I'll do it.'

Tibs offered to come over to yak it through with Charlie. 'He's got to show his face, first.' Ol' Charlie was going to talk like he never talked before.

And, come spring, that crabapple alongside the driveway was going to bloom again.

{ *Charlie* }
6:42 p.m.

Truth is you dont have a say in shit You think you do but on account that its days like this one that show you dont He and Julie didnt have nothin to say to each other She wanted to get rid of it he didnt The man has been completely sidelined What she wants shes gonna get And there wasnt nothin he was gonna do about it You can salute Jane Fonda for that Even his girls believed in abortion *Its my body Hands off my body Dont tell me what to do with my body How would you like it if the government told you what to do with your body* Its my sperm That ought to count for somethin

The bitin metal stung through his pants It was warm in the house He thwapped the windshield wiper cause he could Cause it was probably stickin Cause by the time the storm hit full on it would She was in there waitin for him Gunnin for him Starin at the front door

Eyein him to saunter through and let him have it Twistin that wooden spoon in her fingers Singin her songs Twistin her pine board spoon ready to wrap it around his head Who was he foolin She wasnt makin him supper By his clock he was already fifteen minutes late She couldnt keep a green bean from goin limp if her life depended on it

God his mind wouldnt shut off They werent the same anymore nothin was the same it could be with a new kid thats what everybodys afraid of aint it things not stayin the same Thats not completely true Maybe shes just as afraid of them stayin as they are and all she wants to do is to get it right thats all get it right Aw hell he ought to drop the ring off he could do it and get back to the barn to say nighty night to his baby before he went in That girl was out there and she was the only one he could really talk to he was gonna close his eyes and bury his face in that warm furry furry neck Baby baby baby he wished to hell she would say what was on her mind instead of puttin up that show that she dont want a little teeny baby a little itsy bitsy baby who dont want a baby what kind of woman dont want a little baby There was the top of her head in the window

Oh it made it so his mama come into his mind His mama, the court reporters typist, come back into his head type type typin right outside his room till the wee hours and *hey why dont you get off your can youre the laziest kid I ever seen not interested in nothin but what you can shove in your mouth You dont see me eatin every ten minutes do yuh*

Never leavin him alone always after him never lettin up jest always waitin to rattle him to find a way to get to find him out to find out what he was up to *Do yuh What would yuh say if I whapped you upside of the head If I get half the chance thatll show you what you should be thinkin about*

And oh he remembered that time he didnt want to be at school and when Miss Lily was talkin facin the blackboard he slid from his seat to the floor the other kids gawkin at him but not speakin and he reached out a feeble finger to take the desk leg for to make his point better If he could jest get one finger to that cold steel and after he did he laid there serene as a squirrel shot through between the desk and the radiator And Miss Lily kept on about timesin the digit under the other one then movin to the left and timesin the lower one against the top one next over till youre all the way to the left then on the bottom movin one to the left and repeatin it and then she was sayin now you add and she paused and asked *Mr Ceame whatre you doin on the floor*

Charlie kept up his game of not speakin and jest laid there dead He would be poked clean through for her to hold him and when she floated over and crouched to him and all the other kids crowded heeheein and hawin Her smell scoured him through with a ribbon of scent so like a cloud like what them spirits fade to before the light folds them in and him there prone out flutterin his eyelids and strainin out groanin not too much and not too little She leaned close to him and if he closed his eyes she had the same tang as the fruit bin on Thursdays Apples and dates and raisins and cinnamon came to him from the cotton heaven of Miss Lilys breast where she pulled him to and she clutched him for no reason and told him true he was a good boy and she thought he would grow up to be magnificent

That was what she said *Magnificent*

And she lingered until his eyelids flickered open and wobbled him back in his seat and circled back to her board forgin on

Now you add straight down

She went on as if he had been no problem at all but after school told him she had to call his mama and tell her hed gone to the floor because that was state law and didnt he know all of them was governed by the letter of the law and when he took to boohooin she told him the law had to be respected it had to it had to it had to but she was sure he was fine

That night when he heard the phone ring he knew who it was His spit went He couldnt swallow

Uh huh went his mother *I see Oh Ill make sure hes all right all right Sorry for the trouble he give to you maam*

His mother havin to say sorry He was goin to get it He ducked into a corner in the sittin room bidin his time He heard the hard plastic of the phone crack into the cradle and his mama let her air out

Charlie You wanna get in here

He couldnt move

Charlie Ceame I am countin to three

He turned and dug his nose into the wall

One

He dug his knees into the boards the more it hurt the slower shed come

Two

He scrunched up makin himself as small as he could

Three All right

The lights went on in the sittin room and her shadow came through layin across the carpet like spider legs creepin for the fly He squirmed and wiggled into the corner

Why doncha come here

He forced himself to see her

I said why doncha come here goddammit

His knees were like air His feet wouldnt move

All right goddammit And she come at him and hauled him up shakin him in midair like he was a rag doll and then set him down and he shut his eyes tight knowin what was comin

She whacked him upside the head

Green and pink and blue and red exploded in his head No wordsd come so he bawled loud enough to make her go away and she warned him ifn he didnt stop shed really give him somethin to cry about

She stood in front of him for a long time studyin him Then she went back in the kitchen and after a while when it was quiet shed run the water in there and then turn it off and tell him dinner was ready

Your daddyll be here

Charlie shooed his mama out of his mind

$$\left\{ \begin{array}{c} \textit{Dol} \\ \textit{6:44 p.m.} \end{array} \right\}$$

You study your face in the mirror. You've done a good job with the lines that narrow your nose in fluorescent light. You do look good tonight. Even in the rusted mirror the landlord won't replace and with your cold hand shaking with shivers. You smooth your foundation and think of something else. A girl can't shake and shiver through putting her face on. You imagine meeting the doctor. 'You do look good.' You sing-hum into the mirror. 'Mama says, Mama says … ' You shimmy some.

'You're poetic, aren't you?'

'I couldn't say, I did go to college exactly one semester. Consequently, I know less than I should.' You'd dig one toe into the floor and look over your shoulder.

'You from around here? Yes, you are, aren't you? You're a hot tamale.'

'Oh, stop it.'

'You are.'

You're scared you're going to forget: who you were, the tune of your voice. That unique vocal melody and the giggling cackle of not fitting your skin. But even that. You won't remember that voice teetering on collapse. Say something, make a memory, draw back the curtain. Nothing's been decided just yet. No papers have been signed. Out there in the sparkling fields where ghosts huddle before gathering a storm of memory to sequester us, to lock us in, to demand attention. Out there, cotton snow empties its historical burden on the living. That saying comes to mind: snow like meal will give a great deal. You're betting on it.

You're going to be a different person. Completely different. Who knows if you'll even be 'Dol.' You'll be a renegade like your great-great-grandma, one of the Black Dutch who snuck away from the Trail of Tears, soldiers watching their every move, and hid in caves scared to death they'd get caught but brave enough for the risk. They survived out there throwing stones at rabbits for food and foraging for roots. Then they stayed in the Ozark Mountains until white people would just let them be.

Your eyes in the mirror. Those eyes will never be the same. You may nip or tuck but it's what's behind the pupil. That will never be there again. Stop it. You might want to name yourself different. A loaded namesake like Sandy, Medea or Elizabeth – the first was your dog to whom you proposed, the second because Jason got nothing past her and the third because of her scream in *Suddenly Last Summer* – that piercing cry that wrought the terrible vision of Montgomery Clift being torn asunder, limb from limb.

You don't have to tell you, not for good anyway, tonight. Being Walter is just like being a butterfly. In the cocoon you were Walter, when you got out and could think they called you Dol. Pearl. You could call yourself Pearl. Pearl's good. Oh God, you could be a Pearl!

You cannot forget. You'd better hope that storm picks at your scabby skin with memory. You had better not forget. You forget everything but you better not forget who you were, Walter Walter Walter. If you forget, there is not one person who can remember. He is gone then. You put on your lipstick like this, wipe the edges like this, make yourself pretty like this. You have done this your whole life. Walter is Walter is Walter, a boy in Sheer Shiver lip gloss.

The heat's on in the bathroom but not the living room. Your daddy's wool hunting coat chafes the hotter it gets in here. You should have turned the heat on out there because that sitter's coming. You hope she is. She's late. Wilson's friend's wife. Charlie's wife. One of those hard women. Wilson says she came in once to Avery's when she first moved here but you don't remember meeting her. You were a busboy then. Wilson's going to fix the radiator in the kids' room. Stick your nose in there without a coat, you'll lose what testicles you have left. With Elaine in Lake City training to be a Korean missionary, what's your choice? You need a babysitter, sister.

You can't imagine Elaine in Korea. That is the end of the world. That people've roped her in and tied her up good. Between their salvation and the butterfly you will become, old Elaine doesn't stand a chance. The Elaine you married … But don't go there.

Blend, blend, blend, you're so bad at this, you missed hairs. An epilator. There you go, love that little machine, see, you have to get it right. Them teeny hairs pop right off. The doctor's pity has to be the second thing he thinks of. We want: *Jesus Christ, get that woman a chair! Who's your daddy, honey? May I have the honour?*

Every Joe should know what you do to keep down razor burn. Mr. Atlanta Doctor's going to see to what lengths you'll go for a pipe dream. No pun. You don't make meatloaf with one hand and apply eyeliner with the other unless you mean business. Every goddamned joker at that bar ought to know the effort you put into filling the craters *Glamour* calls pores. They ought to sit right here and watch for one cotton-picking minute. Who the hell would choose this?

You can't trust doctors as far as you can throw them. You can't tell what they're thinking and you can't believe their words so you got to just sit tight and let them mosey to the truth. Truth. Dr. Bill Burnett, the first psychologist – quote, unquote – you went to, he called you a transvestite. Uh, excuse me. This eyeshadow application is *sans faute*. Jesus. Not to pull rank but this is past dress-up, Doctor.

When Elaine was moving out, she was screaming, 'He paints his toenails.' Without the right words, this was a plea for you to keep your penis. 'Sick, sick, sick,' she wailed.

Everyone must categorize you – except Wilson. Everything gets a name, a medical classification. The whole project of the AMA, the NIH and the CDC – not to mention the FBI – is to reduce the whole of human identity to acronyms decipherable only to those with a certificate of approval – i.e., a degree. The acronym is life, the acronym is validity. You can't trust a doctor because you never met one of them who held on to the mystery. Hello? Rich, sweet, grey, not known. You can't turn your head without bumping into mystery, if there weren't mystery you wouldn't have so many dings, but you won't hear that from a doctor.

Tonight, you imagine, you will walk by the table, but you will not give them notice. They will be studying the menu. The doctor from Atlanta will have his spectacles pushed up on his brow in disbelief. Fries, $1.25, jalapeno poppers, $2.25, chicken fingers, $3.50, soup du jour the same but cheddar cheese adds a quarter. The prices are so low. Thirsty Dr. Burns will gulp ice water and study his colleague who is pinching his lower lip and flipping through the fried-snack pages. Burns will pull at his lip and clear his throat. Decorum will prevail, no eye contact. They will be nothing if not gentlemen. However, when they do glance around the room their smiles will be too wide. But you will get to them before they embarrass them-selves. Burns should know better.

'How do you do, gentlemen?'

'Well.' The smiles will leave their faces when they get a good look. Up and down. They eat you up. You will have outdone yourself. 'You weren't fooling,' Atlanta says to Burns, who smacks his always-dry mouth.

'I hate to brag, but didn't I tell you?'

'You're the one?' he says to you.

You'll blush as you are sure the praise is unwarranted. They won't be able to take their eyes off you. Frankly, it's unnerving. You cannot account for a stranger's eyes.

'Why don't I get your stomachs filled, gentlemen, then we can talk business.'

'Got all the time in the world,' Atlanta will say. 'I'm in no hurry. Let me introduce myself to the most beautiful lady I have had the pleasure of laying my eyes on in a long time.' He will stand up from the table. 'I must say that frothy blouse certainly defies the weather!'

You will tuck your dishrag into your cherry apron. It's been a long time since syrup's been poured on your cereal, so to speak. 'I wanted you to know how desperately serious this is, and I am, about possibly working with you.'

'You do not have to tell me. I can see it plain as the nose on my face.' Dr. Blah-Blah at your service. Jumps to his feet, hand out. Sober, determined, he will grip your elbow, shake your hand. He'll seek to put your mind at ease. He'll do anything in his power to ensure that the right body is tugging on those apron strings – if you know what he's saying. 'It is not too much to add,' he will say, 'that the world needs authenticity such as yours. My work is God's work.'

You will grant a smile that says it all. 'You know how to butter a guy up.'

'You are an exquisite creature. What's your name, doll?'

Hah, hah.

You'll have to be careful. You throw on a blond wig and some Magenta Mirror toenail polish and men with money get ideas. 'What can I get you? On the house.'

'On the house? We don't want to get you into trouble.'

'Oh, Avery can afford it. And if he can't, I'll tell him what's what. For crying out loud, I've raised two kids on the bones he throws me and he's not buying insurance anymore, is he? Don't you worry about Avery. In this weather, you don't walk out of the house in heels if you can't take on the slippery spots. You know what I'm saying?'

'You are an impressive specimen. The way to a man's heart is through his stomach.'

'Please your eye, plague your heart.' You'll smooth your lemon miniskirt over your goosebumped thighs. Everyone will be all smiles.

'Are you wearing White Diamonds?' Dr. Atlanta Blah-Blah will ask.

'I am.'

He'll cross his legs. 'This is going to be easy.'

'Oh, yes?'

'Yes. I'll tell you why. It's simple enough. It's clear to me that the ramifications of the work I propose to do with you, the beneficial consequences that will reverberate throughout, well, Western civilization are more than just about you and me and our myopic little personal *poor me*'s.'

You've suspected as much but who could foresee?

Burns will lean in, pulling on his hands and massaging his throat. 'As long as I've known her –'

'Not so fast, Burns.' You'll have to butt in. '*Him*, thank you very much. I'm a *him*. So far. That's why we're here, sport.'

'Oh, him, schim.'

'I understand and appreciate your integrity but it is true,' says Dr. Blah-Blah. He is a smooth operator. 'You need to accept that what you are doing is for the benefit of – you don't mind if I say it, do you?'

'We have to speak freely,' you'll offer.

'Mankind. Simple as that. What you are doing will benefit mankind.'

Dr. Burns will sit up straight. 'A man without guts lives on his knees.'

'I can safely say that your transformation will inform massive social change, as well.'

'It will?'

'Oh, it will mean the liberation of millions.'

'From guilt, repression and self-imposed prison?'

'At the least.'

Burns' brow will be tied up. 'It will?'

'Why of course it will, my man! Look at what we have sitting at the table before us. Lord, have you heard that voice? Have you seen her move, my brother? I got to say *her*, I'm sorry, I'm so taken. She is, please do not let me embarrass you, she, he, is what we have been waiting for.'

Here, in front of the bathroom mirror, the blown heat dries out your eyes as you smudge your eyeliner with a Q-tip.

{ *Julie* }
6:45 p.m.

It was Indian summer when I got knocked up and now it was December. Something had to happen fast. Outside, the wind'd started kicking up some. I heard a few creaks out on the porch but when I looked there wasn't no one there. Goddammit if that – I thought maybe that sonuvabitch was weaseling around out there. What was he torturing me for? I can't do this alone. I wanted to say to him, 'Can't you just come in and open your lips?' If I smashed flat on my belly and gave this larva a wake-up call – that'd've gotten him in here to talk.

Well, hello, Dolly, BASH!

Well, hello, Dolly, BASH!

It was black as armpits out there, I couldn't see nothing but the crabapple branches scratching for the glass. From behind me, the 100-watt bulb in the kitchen exploded a glare on the front window. I used my hands to blind it out, pressing my face against the glass. The frost bit my nose some. Twigs on the crabapple were twitching. Goddarn it. Light at my back shoving me into whatchamacallit's yard-light glare. That overwrought penlight wouldn't let me see past the tree: Wilson. Turn it off, lady. Igniting up the entire state of Arkansas. I couldn't tell if flurries were flying yet.

I ran my finger along the moulding in the living room running into the kitchen. It was plain he ain't never wiped out here neither. I ought to've gone out there. I ought to've gone out there and stood. I ought to've gone out there, seared my eyes into that gravel and stood still as a doe. He'd've talked then, wouldn't he? Oap. That sound. Like a dog scratching. Them cable wires out there.

Light was so bright, I couldn't see nothing. The only thing in this world that don't cast a shadow is a snowflake. All the frost on the windows was like whole little crisscross curlicue universes. Iced up, when it was cold like that, the glass burned and the fresh draft bore in through the pine sill frames. That calf was out there bracing itself against a heckuva lot more draft than I was. Was the heater on out there? Did Charlie turn it on before he took off? Always taking care of Charlie. That animal oughtn't to have to suffer. But I was not going out there. Then my eyes adjusted some. The snow was blowing up close to the ledge this high up and Lord knows what it would have been walking through it. All I needed to hear was Charlie wiping his feet on that mat.

When he first sat out there on the stairs, that first year way back when, there weren't no chokeberry, just a puny stalk crabapple, and the juniper wasn't put in. And he roped me in good. With his pine-painted eyes not leaving mine, he held my hand and told me how he had dreams. How he had his own house, how he was going to get five kids like they were pieces of furniture and how he was going to get a house in Puerto Vallarta. How he'd say it, how the air came slow after the *pw* and before the *do-vie-arta* drizzled onto the *ar*, like it was natural: *pw-air-do-vie-arta*. *Puerto Vallarta*. He was going to raise a herd of hybrids so tender you could close your eyes when you were chewing and mistake the meat for butter. Feed and attitude is all it takes. That is the truth, ain't it? He was ahead of his time, and we were going to be millionaires and retire when we was thirty-five because lots of folks were mixing bovine stock and not a one of them was doing it right, but he would. I bought it hook, line and stinker.

That was the first year. After our fine wedding. At the Veterans place, the VFW. Ol' Selma, his mama, who couldn't hear a shotgun going off on the side of her ear, used to come around a lot back then. Jesus. What a piece of work she was. And his sister. Sue Ann. She never met a beer she didn't like. Real nice people. Not much before, Charlie's dad'd taken a job up in Cadillac and died, boom, due to loving smokes.

Selma was bitter. Real bitter by the time she met me. I was the only person she talked to, though – she'd gone off Sue Ann and Charlie. That voice, like a spade blade in rocky ground: 'I read the Surgeon General's Report that come out in 1963,' she said, 'way back when, you listen to me, I read it, and Leroy can rot in his grave, and I will never forgive that man for loving the cigarettes more than me.' I was awfully far from my own mama so I heard her out.

It is funny how tables turn. My mama and my sister, Tammy, were stuck in Lincoln on what was left of the AFDC at that time. It's so long ago, it's getting to be so's I can't remember what they sounded like. I believe Mama's voice was like if you could hear a wire cutter snipping through sheet metal. I probably blocked it out. Charlie used to send them money now and again, God bless him, but they made their bed and they ought as well lie in it.

Tammy herself came around once too often. All the way down here from Lincoln – God knows where she got the dollars to get this far. She showed up on my porch like she was one of my girls. If she was, she would've squeezed her legs together a little sooner. Or I would've pressed them closed myself.

What I remember is the dangedest thing. Tammy and me was out on the front porch and that teenager that lived next door back then had just got his lawn mower onto the lawn right when we were talking. If I was then who I am now, I would've taught him not to smile at a woman that way 'less he meant it. He had to know what his smile was suggesting. He peeled his T-shirt off, trailing a shadowy path of fine fine fine copper hair from here all the way to there – you could see the muscles in his back twist long when he pulled the start cord, and the peach fuzz coming in over his angel's kiss.

He ran the tip of his tongue around his lips. He gave one last tug to the cord, that old thing hacked and spit till it got going and gave off that sweet grass smell mixed with burnt gasoline. Hoo boy, don't think he didn't know what he looked like.

I had a feeling what Tammy was calling about ever since I heard her rusty-door-hinge voice on the phone. I was a different person then. Very solid in my beliefs – when you get older either what you know sets into place or you see how much you don't know. I don't know which one I am. Hatred filled me then. A baby is a baby. I thought that. The whole country was loose with their abortions. But then Reagan made keeping babies okay. God, he was a good man. I just think of all the things he did right. Still, seems like from when they made abortion legal all the way through to AIDS, the weather's just got hotter and hotter.

We sat out there, I probably gave her iced tea or something to cool her off. All I could think of was my own sister was going to be a murderer. A little baby murderer. But I had the luxury then. What I saw in my mind, to be honest, was that Charlie Manson girl, the one that took that eight-and-a-half-month-old baby out of Sharon Tate, her begging for its life, *Please let me keep it, kill me, let the baby live, please*. Don't never say never. People can do these things. Hanging her from the ceiling. They had the pictures at the library in Little Rock. They threw a rope over a rafter, a beam, and hooked it around that beautiful girl's neck, and hung her like she was – God, she had the prettiest blond hair. They just snapped her neck. Like she was nothing. Like that baby was nothing.

Them, you know, lifting her up, Sharon Tate pleading the way a mother'd do, *Please let me, please let me, please*, the way a mother'd beg, for herself, for her child, and then after, laying her on her side, on the shag, cutting into her. A girl, that Manson girl, carving that baby out of Sharon Tate, exposing that baby to the oxygen and then carving letters into her body. They probably stabbed that baby too. That fetus. Did it feel? Damned straight it did. Was it terrified about what it would lose? No. Life don't make a person, loss does. You ain't somebody till suffering says so. Back then, Tammy's fetus was a child to me. But let me tell you there is a difference. You get to be my age, you raise two you can lose, you know the difference. Suffering separates us from animals.

I thought way back then – this is '81 or '82 – that Tammy was proposing that I should help her to get rid of the baby, and all I could see was Sharon Tate begging. All I could see was that. So I was planning to tell her a bunch of stories to teach her something. So she'd know. When she finally come and I saw her in person, I knew for sure. Tammy's mouth turns down at the corners, in a queer smile, when she wants. The sides of her mouth practically dug into her shoulders they went so far down. She was smiling all right with her legs all twisted together. Like she was sucking on frog leg. She didn't look me in the eye.

'I got to pee like a racehorse but I am just here to tell you I'm three weeks late.' She stood up.

'Oh.' I got up to block her.

The sun spilt over the back of her head watering my eyes. Leaky faucet.

'I am, Julie.'

I had temporarily lost my footing and grabbed her hand. 'You hold it. I got to find the right thing to say. Words'll come to me.'

When Tammy was sixteen they told her that her tubes were blocked and that she would never get pregnant. Doctors shouldn't make claims like *never*, 'cause if you live long enough you come to understand that sometimes *never* don't last.

'What're you gonna do?'

'Well, I haven't done a test yet.'

'Don't you think that's what you ought to do before you come all the way down here hitting us up for money?'

'You are cruel, Julie.'

'I am.'

'Who said I was asking for anything?'

'I am.'

'You wouldn't go with me?'

'Go with you? For what?'

'You know. Go with me, go with me.'

'No. And I will not pay for it.'

'YOU DON'T HAVE TO PAY ANYTHING! IT'S FREE! WHAT I NEED IS SUPPORT!'

'The only time you need support is when you need your brakes fixed or Mama's teeth cleaned or you all can't pay your rent!'

'Who else am I gonna ask? They said I shouldn't drive right after.'

'Mama.'

'I can't ask her. I can't tell her. Doctors up there say they don't have that service or there aren't any appointments available or the doctor is out of town. Nobody's gonna make them help me. So I came down here.'

'Tammy, you go playing around with married police officers, that is your problem. I ain't helping you murder. You come to a funny place to get help murdering a baby.'

'Murder? Oh, now I am going to be sick.'

'Do it right in the chokeberry if you got to.'

'What happened?'

'What do you mean, "What happened?"'

'You moved down here and what happened to you?'

A couple of years earlier, '78 or '79, I come across a whole host of them girls sitting out on the entrance ramp to the 40 West – them all hitchhiking is one thing that happened. I seen them girls, the blood all drained from their faces, heading to Little Rock and the abortion clinic. Driving by, I stared at them, their skin so white. All the blood drained out of them, it was so hot. Them wearing oversized T-shirts to cover, hoping to keep a semblance of respectability, some of them in heavy coats. Them girls cast out. Standing there, the sweat coming off their brows, the thumb of one hand stuck out and the back of the other protecting their eyes from the sun. You know, one of them was squatting on a Barbie suitcase same as Tanya's, she was a doll herself, her hair wrenched back tighter than tight. Them girls in baby-blue T-shirts and jeans so tight they couldn't breathe and with the blood drained out of them by heat. By the womb. I never knew. They were all heading out to murder their babies. To murder their babies, Tammy. I could just tell.

That's not what I told Tammy, though. 'I'll tell you what: salvation by the way of my Lord and that is what happened to me. Beware a door with too many keys. I moved down here and I spent a lot of time by myself, and I figured out what's what, and I sewed my two fingers together at the shop, and now I got a good husband, and a good car, and a good life, and two little girls I love more than anything, and that is the Resurrection. Resurrection. People like you just make me sick sick sick that you would do those horrible horrible horrible things to little babies, I seen photographs of these types of things, and I am not naive, it is the biggest secret that is going untold, the murder of millions of babies just like what they did to the Jews.

'And, Tammy, I know people. I know people that'd take care of you, and you can have the baby, and then you can give it up for adoption, and then you can go back home, like it never happened. Just thinking of that little person growing inside you. Can't fight for hisself. We'll tell Mama you got a job at the Mini-Mart.'

This was Tammy's first visit to Arkansas and to us. I acquainted her with my sad tale of woe and burden, how I got here and didn't know nobody and took that job at Singer, starting out as a secretary which was good enough for me, and more money than I ever made, we never had that kind of money, and worked my way up to Project Manager, and never went out 'cause I was single and didn't want to end up in the position she now found herself. Then I sewed my fingers together and found the God I take for mine now, then Charlie threw hisself at me. Here we are.

Tammy started rat-a-tatting, heel to toe, heel to toe. She stood up.

'But I can tell you, Tammy, the extent I went to to not be in a position such as yours. I went to church every day they'd have me. And I came damned close to throwing myself into traffic out on the interstate, but there is something special about me and God is watching over me whether I want Him to or not. Go pee.'

{ *Charlie* }
6:46 p.m.

Charlie shivered and his balls tingled Gravity had a way of dragging them down over the years and exposing them to the cold Julie was probably in there snuggled up on the couch just on the other side of them windows Warm and cozy Even with this weather a hot flash came over him Perspired around his hairline He didnt want to be ashamed of what Julie caught him doin but there it was Its one of the reasons he volunteered to go over to Lake City tonight and pick up Wilsons ring He and Julie had made such a mess of it he had an obligation to help young love

The day their daughters took off for Hollywood Charlie and Julie waved Tanya and Michelle off standin out by the ditch with one foot in the gamma grass and one in the gravel and when the girls got a ways off he put his arm around her waist but she jerked forward and whacked her dish towel They didnt see eye to eye about them wantin to be movie stars

If you like to be gawked at Julie couldnt see it *They dont know no one out there first of all*

Theyre young

Thats just like you Feedin pipe dreams Young dont last forever She dug at the Ajax under her nails with the dish towel She lit a Kool and aimed the smoke at him just as a bunch of Canada geese squawked over to Rose Lake *Well get a few months by ourselves till their money runs out and youll have to go pick em up on the side of a mountain or somethin*

Youll go with me wont you hon He sneaked up behind her and slid his finger down the back of her jeans

She turned on him *You got all this into their heads*

You got to look on the bright

Thats the pot callin the kettle black She skittled to the house and when she got on the porch she turned around to have a good look at him *My life has been I am cement I cant move cept to get what aint done done Thats what Im sayin Charlie all I think about is what aint done around here If I were you Id pick up your part of that just like Im doin You and mell get along fine I tried to raise em up right and you got em on their way to Hollywood The way I see it I didnt do right by them Thats my row to hoe but dont come lovey doveyin up to me stickin your finger down my pants wantin me to be somethin Im not And that you helped make me to be You arent tellin me somethin I havent thought about every single day for the last seven eight years Just leave me be to do*

The screen door slapped shut behind her

They did not talk much that day or the next When they did it was about where the girls might be Fort Smith Oklahoma City Amarillo and how they might be doin

You think Tanyall remember to check the air pressure in the tires

Wont Michelle remind her

You think maybe by now the potholes from last winterll be filled up

Dont you hope so

Dont you

Then three days after the girls left for Hollywood Julie came home from droppin off old blankets flannel shirts and a couple of jackets to the Goodwill in Jonesboro And from the Safeway Charlie was home alone but in the shed again with the calf Snuggling in some of its hay He wanted to feel its weight and skin on his own and what the fur felt like against his chest It was hot enough to take off his shirt and pants and he snuggled close to the animal Shivers vibrated up from deep within him Safety and comfort feel that good

He didnt hear her drive up

Julie drove up and she tooted the horn a couple of times but he thought he would just let her wait She wasnt goin to be carryin groceries or nothing Even in that heat the high Indian summer was veering towards winter He could feel on the underside of the breeze a slight chill that reminded him that the seasons change no matter what Well and if she did have a heavy load then shed leave it in the car for him to take in

He didnt want no more fights with Julie The two of them had been bickering ever since the girls left And in the last week the silence between em seemed louder than when they were speaking out loud

Outside in the yard Julie hadnt made a peep yet Burnsd told em she wasnt supposed to be carrying nothing It was a week almost to the day Julie came swingin out the back door wiped out and slammed right into that first stair right with the small of her back She said it had dug into her like the blade of a garden shovel would She laid there for a long time and didnt budge quiet as a bullfrog She took off the whole screen door out of its bolts and a bunch of butterweed shed grabbed at Charlie came after a while

He stroked his girls cheek and got a little closer She got herself onto her side and Charlie had to watch his thigh she could bust it without thinking if she brought herself down on it He was doing what Julie had taught him about how to wrap himself around her

He never heard her coming He felt so good feeling the up and down of his girls soft breath Then the shed door scraped on the uneven earth and there Julie stepped inside rubbin her eyes on account of the light change When she could see her mouth kind of fell open for a second and then closed Her arm reached out for the door on instinct but she stopped herself Its understandable she didnt know what to do She might as wellve come in on a handstand

Uh uh uh There are some things that happen you have nothing to say
Like when Mr Mitton down the way had a tiff with the missus and he
crapped on his own front porch

Youre gonna get mites rollin around in the straw like that

He budged

His girl woke up screwed her neck around some and looped her eyes
to Charlie She started pumping her legs to right herself

Charlies jaw locked He saw what it must look like There are some
things innocent as they are that arent for the eyes of anybody else He didnt
have his flag in the air as they say and he had to say Julie didnt look at him
with any judgement She didnt say nothing about it His face got so hot He
stared at Julie wonderin what she was goin to do His mouth was stung
open Not that he even thought about this until later but if he were to end
up in divorce court hed find sympathetic listeners on the jury Julie didnt
have many friends He got to his feet and then got the calf onto all fours
He and Julie couldnt look each other in the eye

Theres a couple of bags of groceries

Ill get em He tied the calf to the lawn mower handle

He and Julie were mute She held the car door open while he negoti-
ated the bags and it seemed that one of em ought to say something they
couldnt just pretend she didnt see what she just saw could they

Julie asked *Uh what am I supposed to think*

Bout what

Bout what

He leaned up against the Cutlass while Julie lit another Kool 100
Charlie studied the thunderheads headin in No words came to him He
tiptoed away to put the groceries up

In the kitchen Julie asked *Is it sick*

Got me Probably not

Dont foot and mouth usually take the whole herd They putting em all down

Yuh

Whats the good of taking one out

On account of we got her in time

Isnt that chancy
Shes quarantined on account of that
What makes you think
Just got to keep her away from
The County dont know
No
I didnt think so You soon as hope word dont get out Arent you concerned about speading the disease to people

Charlie put the Honeycomb next to the macaroni

Next to the Grape Nuts
I aint a pervert Julie
I didnt say it
From what you was seeing Im just sayin
So
Oh come on

Charlie left the kitchen and made a beeline to the bedroom He sprawled on the bed there picking at his buttons with his eyes drawn tight She let him stew on the bed for a while before she followed him She lay down next to him sugared his cheek and then lay on her back watching the ceiling

I got my own faults too

She laid her ear on his heart to feel it thump thumping *Wanna do it* she asked

He drew his finger across her cheek just where fine hairs were coming in

Come on she said *We aint done it in a while* She stuck her finger down the back of his pants *Come on*

Charlie got a hold of her thigh pulled her over and they made love hard and mad enough to keep them quiet for a while more Later Julie roasted a bird while Charlie watched the Razorbacks lose again He didnt check on the calf again until morning

$$\left\{ \begin{array}{c} Dol \\ 6\text{:}55\ p.m. \end{array} \right\}$$

You can get stuffed into manhood only so many times before you take your knife into your own hands and let the emergency-room team clean up the mess. Truth is, you can't tell what this southern doctor'll have hiding up his sleeve. Last year you held your breath for the insurance report. Burns said if being a single man with two little ones wasn't enough to asphyxiate your testicles, he didn't know what was. He'd do what he could, though. The fella he sent you to in Chicago gave Burns, the primary physician, the go-ahead to refer you to the one in San Francisco who would wield the knife. But you didn't get any further. That was the end. Ah, the machinations of insurance companies. Designed to ensure one thing: they don't pay. You're philosophical about it at this point.

Then Avery up and dumped your coverage. Don't you just wonder about this country? Your whole well-being depends on your boss. Your whole health, welfare and pursuit of happiness depends on some little graduate priss perched behind a desk at the HMO, thinking about her mixed-greens lunch salad and can she afford, calorie-wise, sour cream Roquefort ranch or oil and vinegar – your and your kid's welfare an afterthought. We are an insane people. We can't escape the tragedy we created thinking we were doing the best we could.

You tuck the collar of your dad's hunting jacket closer. Smell him. Mildew, Pall Malls, maple leaves, his breath. Rancid, coffee, Clorets. Mom, Dad. The past is snatching at you, rush on. God, please, you hope you are doing right meeting with this doctor. The clock is ticking, and suffering wears you down. The clock has wore you down.

Your mom, your dad. You don't hardly hear from them no more. Not since Elaine got 'em on her side. You are disgusting, despicable.

That night of the worst fight you can recall. Out back, behind the house, your brothers and sisters huddled behind the garage waiting for it to be over. Wilson stood next to you that night. You could barely speak.

Humiliating. You tell her maybe she could go home. Waiting for the shrieking to stop. You are looking in the storm window, through the fly screen, afraid for Mom, you can see over the back of the big chair and what you see grows you up. Dad shoving the couch into her, crushing her into the wall. Squashing her. Wilson crawling her fingers over to yours and squeezing. She is whispering that she ought to go in and break it up. But she don't. She runs back to look after your siblings.

Mom begs him *Don't* and pushes back. You cannot move. The air is crisp so your breath lands on the window glass, flowers up and evaporates.

His eye trawling for injury or accusation. He sees you.

You are stuck.

He snatches at the screen, he's gonna catch you you you, with such a grit in his voice that it is the music of your own bones splintering, and you can run. You zip to disappear behind the garage, to tell your Wilson, your friend, the one who looks out for you no matter what, and your brothers and sisters that you didn't see nothing. You're breathing hard and fast from the sprint. You told them you couldn't see much through the drapes but they were moving the furniture for a change, probably to surprise us, but that you should all wait there to not get in their way. And the whole time you're making it up, you're thinking you'd better make up a story for him, you have to come up with something good to say why you were spying on them. He can see right through you. He knows when you are lying. You are. Why couldn't you mind your own business, he wants to know. Whaddya think, he was going to hurt her? But he was. He was. *You were, you were.* When it gets too dark to stay back there, you go forth quietly. Alone is safer. He can't make you think you didn't see what you saw.

And you sneak like your life depended on it back to the front of the house, and to that crack in the curtains, and you listen before you stick your head up far enough to see, and when you hear nothing you ask God to save you, there you go up, up more, up enough, and it is as if in flame through the glass, the living room blazes oranges right before the street lights come on, you can't hear even what your eyes see, and you wait there a long time to make sure the coast is clear and after a while you've got to risk it, you go back behind the garage where they're all huddling, where the lazy daisies sprout in summer, and take their fingers and lead them quietly in the back door, and up the creaking back stairs, and Jesus Christ she's got dinner cooking, but she's not here, a roast in tomato sauce on the stove simmering and all of you, you and your brothers and sisters, squeak through the kitchen, up the stairs to your bedrooms and wash your hands. Wilson heads home, you wait.

After a while, the walls tick and their headboard knocks one more time, and Mom and Dad come out of their bedroom and go downstairs. You press your ear to the heat register. The groan of the floorboards under the mass of their bodies setting the table. The next thing is they call *It's done, it's on the table, get down here. Do not run. Walk.* Do not see the couch against the wall. She is not there, she is pouring milk. That fight's not important. Do not drag your chair on the linoleum. Pick it up. We take our places. Don't look. Children should be seen and not heard. Look away. Chew, swallow, disappear. What was is no more. What is, is. There is no such thing as anything but Now.

That was so long ago. But this now, tonight, you got to sell it good, sister. You have enough bluebird eyeliner left to punch a good thick line around the eyelids, top and bottom. You take a Q-tip and fuzzy up the edges some more. Get it right. Now your blue eyes pop. Your hair. You tease the lemon tuft falling over your forehead and wonder where that sitter is. You ought to know better than getting a new woman tonight. Someday Elaine will be ashamed of herself. But by then you'll be refilling your Provera, no questions asked, and it'll be raining sitters.

You snap aside the bathroom curtain, pick at the frosted glass, get your eye real close to see if you can see Miss I-Can't-Call-or-Let-Anyone-Know-I'm-Going-to-Be-Late Ceame coming up the road. The garage light bleeds a sick hue over the wheat field stabbing away into darkness. You are poetic. Against the pale of the road and that mask of dog and arrowwood on the far side, you can make out some flurries coming down. She has left you in a pickle. Of course, you never know. Maybe her car didn't start. Maybe her makeup wouldn't go on. Maybe.

You check your phone. Buzzing. Dial tone. You'd think she'd call. God, this is the height of irresponsibility. People have jobs, people have lives. Jesus, lady.

Her number is somewhere. In the purse. No. By the phone. Shit. Huh. Think. Wilson wrote it out in pencil. You put it. You put it. In your back pocket. Nope. It's a $1.30 to call Information. That's a quarter-hour of babysitting right there. No wonder she ain't here.

'Five, five, five, one, two, one, two. Bay. Arkansas. Ceame. C-E-A-M-E. Charles. Great – Oh! Wait! I need a – No! Wait! Oh, for cryin' out loud.' You redial.

'Hello! … I just called Information … Information. But I didn't have a pencil and then the guy hung up … Hung up … Can't you see the call on your screen? … Well, I just made it … Well, I know but you are the phone company … Who are you, then? … You by Knoxville? … Oh, Mumbai? … What's it doing there? … The weather … It is? It's a blizzard coming … It's when the wind's going pretty good and the snow comes pretty thick. You don't have them, I bet … Very cold. Listen, can you not charge me? For when he hung up on me or this one? It's $1.30 and he did hang up and I asked him to wait … Can you give me the same number? … But not for free? You can't take it off my bill? It's $1.30 … What's that matter? … Whyn't they let you see the screens you need to to help me? … Oh, I will.

But I don't have time now … Yes. Well, flip me over and let me take it like a man … Oh, thank you, thank you, thank you! … You have a good night!'

Seven, eight, five, three, four, eight, one. Seven eight five three four eight one … 'Hello. Um. I am calling for Julie Ceame. My name is Walter. Wilson arranged for you to sit my kids tonight but I haven't heard from you and I have to leave my house very soon. You might've known me by Dol, some folks call me that or – Charlie, are you listening? This is for you too. It's me, Dol – listen, it's almost seven o'clock and I have to be at work by seven. It is very important. I start at seven. P.M. Call me. Let me know. Geez, I, uh. I – thank you. Seven eight five - my number is seven eight five nine six two four.' Hang up. Explode. Practice. No people other than Americans, Mencken writes, are so 'violently the blowhard.' Except for the English. Americans cut a ridiculous figure in the eyes of other peoples, we brag and bluster so incessantly and never rely on facts. Since we won the war, we think it's our duty to lead the world. Mencken.

Put thawing hamburger in the fridge. Wipe down grimy counter-top. Check fingernails in the fluorescent light. Grit your teeth. Take off your treacherous patent-leather high heels. Find slop snow boots fast. Look out frozen window one more time begging. Admit it, she's not coming. You've got to get the kids in the car – hoo-da-la. Wake up the sleeping and sluggish kids and drag them quietly out to the – A plastic scarf to save your hair from the breezes chattering your teeth and the flakes unhinging from above. Squirrel whimpers at the sting from the icy belt buckle. Get it off him fast, he falls back to dreamland. Pity sits up straight with soldier eyes.

'Go to sleep, hon.'

Squirrel's head has rolled onto her shoulder and she elbows him. You catch him and caress his fragile head like down.

'Don't wake him up.'

Pity's jaw is set. She stares at her own greasy fingerprints slathered on the back of the front seat.

'Go to sleep, hon.' You rub her brittle head, telling her Daddy will get her tucked in soon, and he's sorry she and her brother got their sleep broken up, and she is Daddy's big girl. You soothe her. Ready for combat, her eyelids lead, her head lolls back and her mouth opens. She is asleep. Shut the door. Navigate to the front, crank the engine, it growls, growls, growls, it starts. Clunk into third gear, ease back, a three-point turn, that's right, crunch snow, and not too far back, mind the ditch, brake easy, don't slide, and good, stop – oh oh oh – pump the brakes. Good, head out, the rear end slides away into a fishtail, pump the brakes, easy gas, veer from tree, turn lights on, tires spit snow, get to Charlie's, and land fishtail sideways in the driveway two inches from the stinking goddamned oh my God garage, leave the wipers on. Heard of salt, Charlie? Sand? Lazy, Charlie. One word for it. Lazy. Shovel your driveway. Read the papers, the Ice Age is here.

The house is dark. Even though it's stationed way out across the fields, Wilson's shed light catches the snowflakes collecting on the siding way out here, a half-mile off. The kids are conked out in the back, so you leave the car running and creep your way out of the car, up the slick front steps, kick the branches grabbing at you, rescue your caught coat and ding-a-ling the doorbell. It is so goddamned cold, criminy, the skin cells on your legs are freezing, Holy Crikey, no one is answering, that is not possible, oh Jesus Mary and Joseph, already, it's not possible, your rubber soles are hardening in the cold, the ones good to minus forty, it is not forty below, is it forty below, you don't have a decent hat on. You hope someone is here. Snowflakes drive into your cheekbones and melt.

She wouldn't just leave you here, would she, and maybe she would, you don't know her, and maybe she's the type, and she didn't call, or maybe she did call and hung up without leaving a message, or maybe she was trying to get out of it and she called and got no answer and hung up thinking she was off the hook. Well, she is not off the hook. She will sit tonight and you better believe you are not being let down tonight. You are not, you are not, you are not. You can't believe she is making you do this. Why? What purpose does it serve?

Holy Toledo, the temperature has fallen. It's cutting right through. You look in the smudged windows but can't make out anything. You lean out to see if the kids are okay, and they are, and, holding your hair in place, you rap on the dirty windows again, anxious and hard, and maybe the gummed-up glass will break, and well that would just be their nasty luck wouldn't it, and that would just be what a loafer gets for leaving you out here, and what kind of people are these criminals, who do they think they are.

Oh. What if the Ceames are at Avery's? Close your eyes and feel the glass with the pads of your fingers. You hope you didn't crack the window. You back away. It's okay. We are meeting at Avery's. You bet that is where they are. Oh, you foolish girl. They are sitting there right now, Charlie and his wife, they are nibbling jalapeno poppers at Avery's right now twiddling their thumbs waiting for you to appear with the kids to take them home and tuck them under the goose-down duvets they have purchased specifically for this occasion. They are sweet people and they are probably sitting right across from that Atlanta doctor. You bet they are. They're all lounging right there, eyeing each other, checking their watches, wondering where this crazy M-to-F is and when is she's going to show up and who does she think she is, making them wait. You idiot, Walter. Go there. Go there now. Get in the Dart and get going. That is where they are. That is why they aren't here. Get back in the car, don't slip, for heaven's sake don't wake up the kids, and oh –

Ah! This is not possible. NO. Your high heels are at home. You do not have time to go back home now, oh, that is just perfect, that is too perfect. Now, what are you going to do? Be late, be late. You have to be late, what else can you do? You are not going in there in clod-hopping snow boots, you are not. Not if you have to squat right here in the snow and stitch a pair out of dashboard lining. In the back seat, Squirrel is slumped onto Pity and she is still down. It occurs to you.

You hurtle back up the porch stairs to the door. Plywood frame, tall window. Close enough to the door. Check the kids. Sleeping. Back up. Take off the boot. Cover the face. Smash one teensy corner of the glass with the boot. Right hand, reach in. Find the – For godsakes, don't cut yourself. There you go. With left hand open door. Replace boot, compose self. Breathe.

'Hello? Hello? Hoo-da-la, it's Walter!' You sing it to make the break-in go down better. Whew. A little carpet deodorizer'd go a long way. Okay, upstairs. You get up there. You find the light switch, you – Ah, closet door open. There are pumps right there. Black, leatherene. Huh. They'll do, Walter. You force your feet in. Ow, they fit, sort of. Go, Walter, go, turn, turn off the light, back downstairs, shut the door behind you. Step carefully down the stairs. Oh my God, what have you just done? Get to the car. Oh my God, oh my God, oh my God! Sing it! Get in, back out. Oh, to heck with her for twisting you up. She can arrest you if she wants but they won't be able to arrest you 'cause you'll be on your way to Atlanta by the time they find you you'll be somebody new, Walter who? Get on to Avery's. Who is Walter? Your lips fly in the rear-view, your voice mute.

YES, we have the same catacomb of memory, YES, we have the same birth certificate, but there is NO WALTER anymore, Walter is gone, Walter has taken flight, he has lifted off, brothers and sisters, oh God please let me lose Walter tonight, please let's abandon him to the lakefire of human forgiveness, let's put him out of his misery, he hurts, Lord, he hurts bad. Sing it, baby. YES.

{ *Wilson* }
6:56 p.m.

Wilson first got back up on her bar stool but then jumped down to get a look at the weather coming in. She put her fingers on the frozen glass. The snow was coming down now, innocently. At this time of night, she could make out the individual flakes dropping like quarters. It should've been warming up out there with the snow like that. Soon it'd be roaring through like a freight train. She hadn't eaten, her stomach was gnawing at her.

Julie had that. That gnawing. The two of 'em had been in each other's lives as long as Julie had been in town. Julie was still smarting from that first meeting, that one time she ever went to Avery's and she met Wilson. Julie still, after all these years, had it stuck in her craw 'bout takin' Wilson for a man and gettin' all cozy with her. Like she was a Wilfred or a William. That woman don't take well to a misunderstanding. She wants her men and her women drawn out in black and white. We ain't all that easy to draw.

Seems at every union barbecue since, Julie couldn't do nothin' but provoke Wilson. Last year, Julie planted herself in front of Wilson and eyed her up and down.

'I don't know. What doesn't make a woman?' Wilson answered.

'Don't get fancy on me.'

'Julie, I don't want trouble. Let's just sit here and drink our beers.'

Standing there, Julie's lips cut straight across her thin face. Her eyes squinted to Dirty Harry snake slits. She drew air circles with her vodka and lemonade. 'I ain't drinkin' beer, that's a difference right there for you.'

'A difference?'

'Between you and me. Mister.'

'I don't want trouble, Julie. Whyn't you have a seat?'

'Mister.'

Julie squatted on Wilson's knee, rutting ever so slightly with a breath of vinegar. 'Feel like something you recognize?'

Julie was referring to her lady parts but Wilson wasn't playin'.

'Fine.' Wilson ought to have stuck with the guys in the driveway. She couldn't see Charlie over there.

'He's gone.'

'Is he?'

'Oh, yes. Charlie always gets while the gettin's good. Tell me what a woman is. Tell me what a woman is and I'll have a seat.'

'Julie –'

Julie meant to get Wilson in trouble. You wouldn't call her drunk, but you wouldn't call her sober. It was quiet.

'I don't know why you have to get so worked up. We're just havin' a little discussion.' Julie chewed her ponytail. She hauled up a lawn chair under the silver maples and landed herself into it. Her jaw hung slack and she rolled her eyes. 'Hoo, shade's cooler 'ere, huh? It's been a long time, hasn't it?'

'Not long enough.'

'Aw, come on. I'm not worked up, let's talk. I know who I am. You and that buddy of yours down at Avery's ever figure out who you are?'

'Dol?'

'Is that his name? That's a funny name.'

'He likes it.'

'What's it stand for? Donald or Danielle or Liberace?'

'That ain't nice, Julie.'

'No, it's not, is it? I don't like feel like bein' nice to a grown man with two kids whose name is Barbie.'

'His name ain't Barbie.'

'Well, it ain't Ken.'

Boy. She was a tough nut to crack. Ungrateful. Unfair. Rude.

The screen door thwapped as Charlie walked back into the yard. He froze. Julie. Wilson. Talking. He shook his fingers at both of 'em. Then he hid his head under the hood of the '68 Delta for sale.

'Pussy.'

'Don't call him that.'

'You gonna tell me what I can and cannot call my husband? Hah! You are mucking my husband.'

'If I said no, Julie, would you listen?'

'Sure I would. I'm as more fairer than Carter has peanuts.' The liquor was seeping in.

'No. I'm not.' But she was.

Julie nattered on, her voice sucking what little oxygen was left on this humid Saturday. The sugared smell of steaks and ribs hung burdened in the air, unable to move. Julie fought to form her words and stay awake. ''S you. Or that Christian insect excuse for a woman. Elaine Be-Little.'

'Julie, Charlie ain't diddling Elaine. And he ain't diddling me neither. He don't desire no one but yourself.'

'Yeah, yeah. Who do you think you're talkin' to? You're doing it with somebody. If it ain't Charlie, then who is it? My nose don't lie.'

'Your nose?'

'I can smell it, you Maytag. You can get out of looking like a woman but what's sittin' 'tween your legs is what's sittin' 'tween your legs. It's a freshly hoed row.'

'You're a delicate peony, ain't you, Julie?' The polypropylene lawn chair made Wilson's thighs perspire. She sipped her Bud.

Charlie peeked up from under the hood of the Delta.

Wilson held the beer up to him, mouthing: *You owe me.*

Charlie ducked back under and the sun glinted off the chrome.

The chair webbing got hold of the hairs on the back of her thighs and the silver maple leaves hung limp.

'Don't you want any friends, Julie?'

'What for?'

'You're as lonely as the night I met you. Twenty-six years and I ain't ever goin' to get out of your doghouse.'

A breeze rustled through the maple leaves and Wilson lifted her armpits to let it cool the dampness there.

'Whew, is it hot, it makes me so drowsy!' Julie fanned herself. 'Nah, you ain't in my doghouse. Charlie, though, is in my doghouse. And if he ain't, you can bet he'll find his way there. Now ... '

'We ain't gettin anywhere 'cause we don't know what a woman is.'

'You don't know what a woman is. We sure can agree on what I am. Ask any of these people and they'll tell you what you are.'

'What do you think they're gonna say? I gotta pee.' Julie got herself up pushing on the arm of the chair. But the legs on the other side went up off the ground. She didn't make it. 'Help me.'

Wilson stayed put.

Julie fell back into her chair. 'I can hold it.'

Wilson sipped her Bud, then gurgled it. 'Charlie does like the way I look.'

'I'm not surprised, you got big bones. Like one them ol' big-barrelled crank washers. See right there ... ' She jerked up, pulling on Wilson's belly. 'That's a roll of rollers right there.'

'Easy.'

'I'm as skinny as Twiggy's toenail. You ought to try Kools.'

'You got to tell me what makes a woman.'

'It's like when Elizabeth Taylor throws a fur around her neck and says ... what does she say?'

'Got me.'

'She says – You know those pictures for the fur coats?'

'Nope.' Wilson changed the subject. 'You say lady parts don't make the woman.'

'Yup.'

'Okay –'

Julie lost her hold on the armrest and slid down further. 'It ain't that simple. If it ain't breasts –'

Julie scrunched herself over, holding tight to the chair and whispering, 'Titties are titties, you know what I'm saying?' She pulled herself back and wagged her finger, sighing, ''Ceptin' you got some real boogeroos.'

The sun slid west until it was facing the silver maples, landing in large patches on Julie's face and toasting her perspiring cheeks.

'Woman's what we do. The way we clean up after the kids, the way we put men in the doghouse, how we talk. You never seen no man talking like this.' She lifted her wings and waved 'em wide as a crow. 'By the looks of your neck, you ought to think twice about that next beer.'

Wilson took a pointed sip of her beer. 'We're right back where we started. You don't think much of what a woman is.'

'Oh no. I have the utmost – I know what it is. To be a woman. Getting. The equipment. That's the nothing part of a woman, look at your … friend. He can do it in his bathroom. Nah, it's the stuff your mama teaches you. How not to take up space. Look away when a boy gets a look at you. Spend every minute of every day of your life thinkin' about how other people see you, every minute of every mucking day thinkin' what somebody else needs, and when you get an extra minute to yourself, you can just think about how that's affectin' other people!'

The sun's heat bore down on Julie and her eyelids fluttered. She shot a flaccid finger out. 'You just go. And think on what … I'm … sayin' …' she mumbled. Her head fell back on her chair, exposing her pasty velvet neck. Red lines defined the loose skin there. Her arm, holding her drink, flopped.

'Let me get that for you.'

Wilson took Julie's glass. Her head fell to the side, leaving Wilson to puzzle her out.

Four months before Julie's girls left, they told Wilson in secret what they were planning. Wilson howled right at 'em. She couldn't think of a single thing she could do to help, she didn't know no movie stars. She came across the four-by-four in the Lake City notices and got it on account of what else did she have to spend money on. She drove it around herself for a while to make her story (she bought it for herself but then didn't like it much) stick. Then while the girls were looking for a car they could buy, she drove up into their front yard, put a note on the windshield, threw the keys in the front seat and moseyed back to her place. Like they said, she was the best aunt they ever had, and they said they would repay her when they got their first TV show. She told 'em it'd be fine enough to let her soak in their Jacuzzi. And to not forget her. She paid extra for Keith Emory to go over the engine with a fine-tooth comb to make sure it would not only get the girls to Hollywood but would run for a while in that dry heat they have out there. Helping 'em was helping Charlie. Still, it killed her to watch Tanya and Michelle head out to I-40.

It killed her also because that was when Charlie stopped petting Wilson's ear. When they first were getting together, he'd stroke her earlobe with his fingertip. Although he never put his hands where he shouldn't unless she wanted him to, she always felt wanted with Charlie, and safe. She went on a couple of dates right out of high school but there was something about her, she supposed, that made men want to show her what they were made of. And she'd had to put them in their place. She never hit a date, but if they'd pressed on she wouldn't have hesitated.

First one was Hammer Gould who, when he was saying good night, thought he could take a hold of her breast. If he'd asked first, and hadn't grabbed it so hard, she might've said yes. But he didn't. She got him around the neck, opened his driver's side door and shoved him out of the car. She got out and walked home alone, right through downtown. She'd never wanted to shove Charlie but the whole thing had changed. She'd gotten past thirty-seven, and she didn't want only the physical anymore. She wanted to share all the joyous corners of her heart and the fear and the worry and all the normal things two people inspire together.

The distance between Wilson and Charlie had been a long time coming. If she was going save herself, she knew she'd better lay tracks between what was, what is and what should be. And doing for Tanya and Michelle was never only about Tanya and Michelle. It was about doing something for Charlie without directly doing something for Charlie. Julie being the landmine she was and all.

'Em girls were like they were her own daughters, like they were hers and his, and some of that love ought to rub off on Charlie. Wilson loved Charlie back then and she loved him now. She had a bad feeling, though, that the walls of the whole world were like a vice scrunching shut. But if she got off her high horse and did a thing for herself, if she did a thing on account that it was what her heart told her to, if she did it on account that it was more wrong not to, then 'em walls could stop closing in like those drifts banking up with the wind.

She never told him she loved him. She never got to it. The truth was she felt sorry for him more than she loved him. That ain't the way to treat a friend so she wasn't going to feel that for him no more.

She should've known better and now, sitting at the bar picking at her beer, she knew she'd lingered too long over her attentions to Charlie. Tonight she was bringing forth a real Love. For Dol. When he got here, she had to tell him. She had to give him the ring and make a stand.

There was one good reason she didn't have her own family, there was one good reason she felt like she lost an arm when the girls took off and there was one good reason she was sitting at this bar mooning: she was a hmmer and a hawer.

After she'd taken in a couple of beers, Charlie would come in with the ring, and she'd lay down the law. She could do it right here. Quietly. She'd thank him for the ring and set him straight. Yes, straight as that calf of his standing up on its own four legs. This is how it ought to go. She'd pop him open a beer, cheers him and let him have it.

'Charlie, it is high time you and I cooled off.'

'Whaddya mean, buddy? On account of?' He'd sip his beer.

Hmm and *Haw* were Charlie's middle names too.

'You know what I got to say.'

He'd chew on the skin flaking off his thumb. 'I don't know nothin'.'

'Let me say it.' She'd hold a flat palm up to shut him up. She'd appeal to him as a husband. 'Charlie, this ain't workin' for either one of us. Now you know Julie is … is … she ought to be more than she is to you.'

'Oh, now.'

'You are neglectin' her.'

'What?'

'I'm makin' a change. A big change. You're goin' on back to your wife … '

'Back to my wife?'

Wilson'd put away thoughts of that barbecue colouring in. 'Who is a fine woman, probably just about the best I know, and I'm … You're … gonna make your own way.' Mostly. She couldn't leave him high and dry.

'Oh,' he'd say. Charlie would lean forward. 'Dol, huh?'

'What Dol?'

'Dol, Dol.'

'Don't go all Dol-Dollin' me. You don't know nothin' about Dol and me.'

'Well, I know enough to drive to Lake City and get you a ring!'

Wilson's cheeks'd get hot. 'You don't know nothin' … ' She'd pick at her beer label.

'How you know he wants to take a walk down the aisle with you?'

'How you know he don't?'

'I'm going to be makin' myself scarce, Charlie.'

He'd feel sorry for himself. He'd puff his lower lip. 'I just … I … you're right.' He'd cup his hands behind his head. 'Okay. I wanna be a dad again.'

'Tell Julie.'

'She don't listen like you.'

'If we didn't spend so much time, I don't know … you'd find words for Julie and I'd, you know … ' The weight of saying too much bore down. 'I want to make my own family, Chuck.'

She and Dol had never even messed around. If they were goin' to, Wilson ought to get it started. All their dealin's, over all these years, since they were kids, were nothing but clean and proper. She ought to be grateful.

A week ago Wilson spied on Dol and his nine-year-old, Pity, through a hole in the dining room shade. Pity had planted her feet flat in front of the bathroom door. Wilson couldn't see the whole thing, but Pity was pulling on the doorknob, humming at her reflection in the full-length mirror, gummed up with water spots and toothpaste. And when Pity tugged the door back, singing like a cat when she'd got its tail. Dol was there in the bathroom putting his face on.

'Honey,' Dol said, 'whyn't you learn a good song?'

'Daddy, you sang to me when I was in Mama's belly.'

'Times change.'

Pity sang anyway: 'I'm crazy for you , touch me once, and you'll know it's true, I feel it in your kiss … '

'You don't feel nothing in nobody's kiss, young lady.'

'I do too.'

Dol came to the bathroom doorway. 'Whose kiss you feel something in, sweet thing?'

'Yours.'

'Aw, ain't that nice?' Dol needed the mirror to get his eyeliner on right. 'You kids didn't clean behind the stool.'

'We traded and that pig-eyed sucker won.'

'Your brother ain't pig-eyed.'

'You looked at him?' Pity stuck her arms out to her sides preacher-style. 'I'm crazy for you.'

'Pity, please? The swinging on the door – I got to see myself.'

Pity pulled the door shut so Dol could have a good look at himself.

Wilson could see Dol's reflection. He had piled his brassy blond hair on top of his head, put on the leather skirt Wilson had got him when he first told him he was going to get all his work done, and lilac eyeshadow thick enough to butter bread.

'How you think Daddy looks?'

'Let me see.' Pity stuck her head in around the door. 'Pretty.'

'Pretty is as pretty does. You're just sayin' it.'

'I ain't.'

'Yeah, y'are. But I'll take it.'

Wilson could hear Dol putting his red, blue and lilac pencils along with his other doodads back into the medicine cabinet.

'See you at ten-thirty?' Pity asked.

'You see me, little girl, tomorrow in the a.m. I'll come in and kiss ya.'

Wilson's cheeks flushed and she stepped back from the window. At her feet, dried-out broom sedge hadn't been mowed. All summer. It clumped all yellow and tangled, looking to be a lot of hell come spring. Under that scrub tree next to the shed, a family of rabbits were watching her with their brown softball eyes. Somebody ought to be out here pulling the weeds up and seeding it through – no reason it shouldn't be her. She could take care of Dol and his kids, Pity and that little porcupine, Squirrel. Just then her period come in on her leg and she doughnutted out of there.

{ *Julie* }
6:57 p.m.

It was getting to seven. I didn't hear a thing outside. Them ceiling pipes had leaked clear from here in the living room all the way to the kitchen. The way the light came in, in a square, the kitchen looked like the doorway to a spaceship trap door – yawning wide such as in *Close Encounters*.

'You open yourself to God's grace and you cannot do yourself no harm no more. Just get back here and listen to me. You can pee in a minute.'

That's what I said to Tammy then. She lay flat back down on the porch. 'You ever thought of takin' yourself on the road?' she said.

'On the road? As a what?'

'Uh, a preacher.'

'Me?'

'You don't ever shut up.'

'Hey, I shut up plenty. I'm married. For example, I never told the story of when I first got here to Bay how I met Charlie's friend. That was an eye-opener. She's a girl, you know that? Well, back then, I thought she was a fella. They was, there was, oh my God, I cannot tell you how my head went spinning.'

'Good, Julie, listen – '

'There's another one at that bar, he runs with Wilson and Charlie, but his skirts are better'n any one you and me'll ever have. Wilson took me into the restroom under false pretenses and that's when I found out he's a she. I admit it, I flirted with her on account I thought she was a he. It kills me to even think about it.

'Julie, is this going to be gross?'

'I came this close and I cringe at the thought.'

'Close to what?'

'Close to what-do-you-think? To this day, she's in my doghouse for not saying nothing. And that other one is a he. God, I always draw 'em to me too. Like you. Like flies.

'All that to say, sister, that when I was with you and Mama in Lincoln I didn't know about the rules of the world. I had a hunch about them. But I didn't have no one to tell me like I am sharing with you now. Now we're sitting here on the porch and you want a vacuum hose to suck out your insides and that little baby, and I call it a baby, it is a baby as much as the day is long, and I can sit here and tell you there are few rules anymore, a man can be a woman, a woman can be a man, all that don't mean a hill of beans to me, but I can tell you sitting here, having been away from home for seven years now, in another state even, and not knowing nobody, and having two of my own, that what matters is that person that's growing inside of you, that's all that's in it in my book. I'll get you set up so you can have that baby. You don't have to take it home.'

Poor Tammy, poor me. Me with the big mouth has got myself into a pickle. I had one foot out the door to hook myself up to an Oreck myself. Cole's mama, Beulah Little, did get Tammy set up with a group of right-to-lifers who were going to keep track of her but then she took off. Tammy must be holed up somewhere. She called before Mama's service to say she didn't have the money to come from Colorado or somewhere. I wouldn't take the phone, Charlie talked to her. I didn't want to. But she would've told us then if she had had that kid.

The phone peeled off ringing. I shut my ears to it.

I'd given my life to that man and I was forty-six and I'd be goddamned if I was gonna spend another eighteen chasing up and down those stairs after another kid. I wouldn't have even been in this Vlasic jar if it weren't for that calf. Wilson could have kept it and it could have stayed where it was and got blisters and liver failure with the rest. So we really saved it, did we? We brought it over here, fed it and made up the shed to keep it warm. And it got us off track.

If Charlie wanted a kid so bad, he could spread his own legs. A vision came to me: Charlie's puss moaning, a tornado siren and baby blankets coming through the front door.

The phone kept ringing.

The answer came to me. It would be a flat exchange. I'd birth that fetus, I'd have his child. Or, I'd leave that cow's blood on the gate. Nothing's passing from me into his heart, unless it's from between my legs. He would stroke my face with the back of his hand. He'd hold me on storm nights. He'd take off his shirt and lie so close behind me I could melt in the fine chalk of his chest. If not, we'd see if he could taste my boot heel in the back of his throat.

The machine clicked on. I had turned the speaker down. I wasn't talking to Charlie on no phone.

I moved quickly. To the back door for the car keys and my purse, coat off the hook, one arm in one sleeve and the other in the other, back over to the light switch by the dish rack, take the good buck knife, put my boots on, open the door, shut it behind me, take the rising wind in 'cause it'd got colder, breathe in breathe out, hold on to the rail, one step, two steps, three steps, four. Step over what's left of the sweetspire bush, one foot in front of the other. I'd make sure he talked to me, I'd make sure he was delivered to my door.

{ *Dol* }
7:10 p.m.

When you get there, you turn off the wipers, leave the Dart idling and the kids in the back seat. You go have a look-see in Avery's front boxy window. You take the presswood steps one at a time. No one's put salt out here either. On the porch, with your back against the wall, you peek inside. You make out the faces.

Wilson.

No Charlie. Shoot, where is his wife? Don't see Avery neither. He must've ducked out, leavin' the place to you. Crowded, but just regulars. No one in particular.

Oap! There's Burns coming out from the john. He sits with a stranger. You can't swallow for the lump in your throat. It's them. The stranger is got up like a bumblebee – yellow polo shirt, black polyester slacks – scratching under his arm.

A snow devil bursts off the parking lot and nips your calves.

Burns squints at the customers while the bumblebee – oh, he's the Atlanta doctor. Drumming his fingers on the tabletop. He'll never like you enough to help you. You can't go through with it, you are not what he is looking for. Why should he help you, what do you have to offer, oh, what is all of this about, you shouldn't've come here. You shouldn't've. Go on now, get out of here. The Dart sputters, your future unravels and the past rushes you. You might as well go turn it off, get a look at that sky, wouldn't you know it, tonight's going to be a doozy. You exhale, watching your breath fall – when smoke descends good weather ends.

You take a step down off the porch. And then another. And then another, until you are back on the ground where you belong. You slink to the car, open the door to sit on the brittle vinyl seat, and then, and then the wipers've stopped halfway, catching enough freeze and flurries to stretch their worn rubber membrane. You rub your shins and calves hard to get the blood going.

Ifs and buts butter no bread. Why not you? Bullshit. Give me one good reason, who says. You're just as good as another. Better. He is never going to find another like you. Never, never, never. Not as long as he lives, and a person in your position ought to see a good thing when he gets it. You finish with a get-over-yourself and get in there. Only poets and pigs are appreciated after death, brother.

Sister.

He can pick you as easily as the next guy. And he's come all the way out here because he must think you've got something to give him. He knows you're willing, he knows you'll do it, he knows you're serious, he knows you mean business. You kick those boots off your feet and slide on the leatherene pumps. You get the extra key from under the car and lock it up, leaving it running so the kids'll have the warmth, and you get yourself inside.

'Lady Marmalade' comes on the juke, you remove that PVC hood of thorns, toss your buttery curls back, plant your hand on the knob and swing that door open. One foot in front of the other, you wait until half the eyes in the room, and every eye at Burns' table, is on you. But you know where you're going. The door shuts behind you. That click feels just right. You put one foot ahead of the other because your life means something and *entrer*.

You walk straight to the jukebox, pose till the song's over, unplug it and then plug it back in. You don't even have to look. You choose C49: 'You're the Reason Our Kids Are Ugly' by Conway and Loretta. For Wilson and her skunk-tail hairdo.

You take Wilson's elbow and usher her off her stool and behind the bar. You've got something to say to her.

'Now, I know you approve of me getting my change. But you get huffy when I do things on my own. Please don't make a scene tonight. My future is sitting on that chair over there with Burns.'

'I won't.'

'I's always so proud of you on what you did for me when Hinkle made me play football in Phys.Ed. And you wrote a letter to the principal on my behalf. That was so brave and strong and let me fly without squashing me. I want you to be that tonight.'

Then and only then do you turn the sides of your mouth up and condescend to grin. You take in all the eyes, let them get a good look at you. You walk behind the bar, take off your coat, shake out your locks, toss the coat, flip open the refrigerator, pull out two beers and walk over to Dr. Burns and that bumblebee. The bee is scratching his armpit – the beard does not make the thinker.

'Good evening.'

He hasn't stopped staring or scratching since you came in and don't think you don't know it. You walk to the table, knees rattling. Don't blow it.

'Walter, it's –'

'My friends call me Dol.' You extend your hand, letting the bracelet of gold lace hang like thread from your elegant, slim wrist. The light, unflattering as it is, shows off the Merlot nail polish. Wilson flicks a look, Burns and the bee follow your gaze to her. 'These, gentlemen, are on me.'

Bumblebee jerks to his feet, takes the beer, offers a moist palm. You gauge his moistness by the erratic clusters of red bumps along his hairline. You weren't expecting nervousness on his part. His Arctic parka drops off the back of his chair. He wipes his hands on his thighs. You soothe him with a handshake and a finger to his chest.

'I'll join you shortly.' You inform him his coat's on the floor.

You make sure Wilson's watching and make a face. 'Dr. Burns, cat got your tongue?'

Burns is thinking far away, watching the flakes that're coming down now outside, ignorant of the dandruff flakes on his friend's shoulders.

'Dr. Burns?'

His mouth is jagged as if the lips were cleaved one from the other. Or as if he's just swallowed his pride. He nods.

'I'll be right back.' Everyone in the place has a drink in front of them. Every table is talking. You've got ages. You disappear into the storeroom and just then Wilson rises up off her stool towards you. You kick the door shut. Today is that tomorrow you thought about yesterday.

You squat on a case of Bud and pull the Tia Maria off the shelf, crack the wrapped cap and take a swig. The syrupy drink nips at your esophagus going down. Inhale, exhale. Nice. You warm the cool, penile snout of the bottle with your hands and catch that loathsome fishing rod between your own legs. You practice your breathing exercise and picture a quiet pond with a couple of peacocks on a rock nearby. It calms you. You never did have much use for that thing. Conway and Loretta're skipping: 'You're the reason I changed, You're the reason I changed, You're the reason I changed ... '

You put your fingers under your skirt and a lump the size of a meatball rises in your throat as the disgusting testicles nestle against your thigh, and you pull so hard at the cock it could come right off.

{ *Wilson* }
7:13 p.m.

C onway and Loretta went over and over at the jukebox.

You're the –

I –

You're the –

I –

You're the –

I, I, I, I, I, I, I, I –

Wilson knocked. She couldn't hear a damned thing in the storeroom. 'Dol? What's wrong, hon?'

The floorboards inside creaked.

'The jukebox is going at it.' What was she going and hiding for? 'There's folks out here need beers, hon.' God, what an awful racket. 'Listen to 'em, hon. There's a bunch of 'em.' Folks was pulling out chairs, crashing beer mugs too hard and going on like the deaf.

Wilson got fed up. She didn't appreciate being ignored. Her stomach clenched, then soured. She turned her chin to the right, then the left. She thought, she cradled herself, she kicked, she stomped off, stomped back, knocked, kicked again, turned herself in a circle, banged her head and pounded her elbows into the wall.

Take a man with no hands, that's probably how Dol felt. Like a no-handed man, like a stump man, like she had a bloodsucker stuck to her and she couldn't get it off. Would it be no different for a no-handed woman? At the bar, she picked up her beer. Dol wasn't planting gladiolas in there and where the heck was Charlie? Wilson's throat itched and fear trickled like a greasy, leaky stream right down into the pothole that was her belly.

Well, Dol just might say no. So? Dol might make fun. If she's gonna, she's gonna.

When they were younger, the two of them used to go hide in Wilson's bedroom and practice. Being only twelve and an expert already, Dol was working real hard to get Wilson to uncover her tool box of woman-self. Dol said, 'As a boy, you have to throw your cocky shoulders side to side and you never look at nothing nor nobody but what's ahead.' Wilson shook out her arms, then her legs, and rolled her shoulders. Getting herself in the full-length mirror on the far wall, she lurched towards it, throwing her shoulders.

'I never seen a man walk like that,' said Wilson, being seventeen. She was pretty sure she had more experience studying men than Dol did.

'You watch, they all walk like it.'

'Cole Little don't,' Wilson said.

'Yes 'nd – '

'Cole Little's a slug.'

'And girls walk like this.' Dol leapt off the bed.

Wilson picked her ear.

'A girl's got her shoulders back, she's got a straight line across from one shoulder blade to the other.' Dol showed a line from one deltoid to the other. 'Then, watch.' He put his right foot in front of his left and took a step slower than molasses.

'Cher don't walk like that.'

'Cher ain't a woman.'

'She is!'

'She ain't. She's supernatural. See? With boys you got the shoulders moving when you walk and with girls you got the way you walk and your waist going side to side. I'm going to be a girl when I grow up.'

'Oh, you can. I seen it on *Donahue*.'

'Well, I will.'

'How come you want to? You don't like what God gave you?'

'No. No, I do not. When I touch my chest, I imagine that there are breasts there. That they're full and plumped and that this thing isn't between my legs. And it's not even just my body. I see things like a girl. I don't like wrasslin'.'

'Oh, Dol. Do you touch yourself?' Wilson covered her face and whispered through her fingers. She almost didn't want to know. But she did.

'Not down there, I don't. Here's something,' said Dol. 'Girls don't look no guy in the eye. Boys look at you. But they look at you like you're not there. You watch. If a girl likes a boy, she looks down, at a wall, at her fingers – '

'Damn!'

'Yeah, that's how you know if a girl don't really really really like a guy she'll look all in his eyes, straight on – to make him believe what ain't true. The boy ain't gonna see nothing in her eyes.'

'What do boys do?'

'They can't take their eyes off parts of girls. They see the girl. But only 'cause she's attached to what they're really looking at. You could put two titties, a twiddy-twat, a fanny and a pair of lips – hang them on a string in the air and it wouldn't make a bit of difference to a boy. If she's playing real hard to get, he might notice her hair. Other thing is that what a boy sees when he looks at a girl is his vision of hisself in her, and then he sees if she fits into his future, he puts her in his picture and all but it's a picture of him. She fills in the spot next to him. The girl can hitch herself to him or not. You watch, you'll see I'm right.'

'I look people in the eye.'

'You ain't a good example.'

'On account of my mama I am.'

'That's your mama. If I was you, I'd tell everybody I was a girl. You just got to broadcast it sometimes.'

'You can't put a dress on a person and expect her to act human. They're the dumbest thing ever come up with. Mama come once and give me this Easter dress that reminded me of cat piss. I held it out in front of my coveralls and my mama stared at the ceiling and chewed her lip like she does on account of she don't like something but won't say it. And when she did, she said my coveralls might as well be a pair of a hobo's old socks and that I's gonna wear that yellow dress if it killed me. She meant it too, she had her hands on her hips, and she was diggin' in so deep her knuckles were white, and her chin was out to here in front of her.'

'Wilson, your mama loves you and is just tryin' to help her little lost cause.'

'I could just see on her face what she was burning up to say: "Look at the way the collar comes to such a nice stop, here at the throat, the dark yella brings out your eyes, don't you think? And you'll look like you're just floating on a cloud with that pretty, pretty lace hem." But she didn't. She changed her tack. She said, "I wanted you to be happy. I wanted you to be satisfied. I wanted you – it's too much to ask for you to be the prettiest girl, but I wanted you to be as much as you could be on Easter Sunday. Everything I do I do for you and your father, I ask for nothing for myself, nothing, I don't take nothing and what do I get out of it? Do I get to look pretty-pretty? I don't want to, I make do just with what God give me."

'So I pinched that slippery dress between my two fingers like it stank to high heaven. I couldn't barely look at it so I tried to bribe her. I said I'd wear it. But, come Easter, I would wear my beaded hippie bracelet to church!

"'I don't make deals," she said. "And I'm not leaving this bedroom until you are in that dress." She made a sound like poppin' the tab on a cap of pop. Then I got smart. "Huh. Don't know, Ma. We got to come to some sort of agreement."

"'Don't get smart alecky with me," she said. "You are not walking into the service in that getup. Not when I got an airy Easter Parade bouquet."

'I squinched my eyes, lowered my head like 'em bulls Mr. Slocum has. I was getting mad. I tightened my mouth up. Since she didn't want me to have on what I wanted, I wouldn't have no control at all. If I could've I would've peed right there on the carpet. Since I didn't have to go, I let go of my shoulders, let my belly and arms slack too, and threw myself on the bed, right where you're sittin', which is what brought it to mind in the first place. Couldn't bounce 'cause of the springs. I sat right there looking at myself in the mirror. I'd'a called myself pitiful. But, Dol, then it was like I never seen myself before. Like I was asleep my whole life and then I woke up on account of Mama gettin' after me – I seen what you all see. My eyes're little slits like a pig. My teeth stick out too far. Look how far my ears stick out, and to top that one ear is higher than the other. And I told her: "You give me one good reason why a person who looks like me oughtn't to wear holey overalls."

'Her fingers dug into her hips and she wouldn't look at me. She got the fat on her hip bones between her thumb and forefinger and then dug her chin in her chest. That means she ain't sure if she won. "You're so pretty," she says. "I want you to look pretty. How come you don't want to look pretty?"

'"Mama. I never said I don't want to look pretty. But there ain't a dress out there that can change what God give me."

'Oh boy, then she jumped. "Well, it sure can help, can't it? Look at me. You'll never catch me in slacks."

'I did look at her. Mama ain't ugly but nobody never called her pretty 'cept Daddy.

'She walked herself to the mirror, took out her lipstick and wet her lips. "It's an art, really, hon. God isn't a designer. You got to dress up what He gave you."

'"I ain't pretty."

'"Country people say *ain't*."

'"I am country."

'"That's right. But you don't have to look like it!"'

Wilson picked at the foil *Storeroom* sticker on the liquor closet door. What in the heck was Dol doing in there? Ain't nothin' to put away in there.

Down on the linoleum, on her hands and knees like the dog of love she was, Wilson couldn't see nothing but the grime stuck at the door jamb. And Dol's shadow walking quickly back and forth. She was probably nervous and was in there getting her gumption up. Wilson squinted, backed her nose up, used one eye then the other. She got fed up. There was a shadow, then it shrunk off. Heck if she could tell. Dol couldn't stay in there forever, what about all the customers? What about that Atlanta doctor old Burns brought over?

Dol's trouble went this way, Wilson thought. What if, when it comes the time of life when you notice what's down south, you got what you ain't supposed to have? Nobody can kindly tell a person what they're supposed to have 'cause only they got all the mirrors on this planet in their heart, only they been in all 'em times when they don't belong, only they know the end of being in the wrong body. They look down there and they got the ears of a giraffe. Them ears don't belong to 'em. No. They're different than a giraffe. They can't be born a giraffe if somebody else, or even themselves, wished it. They got to do something. They damned well will start doin' whatever they got to so you can have 'em ears taken off. Wilson wondered how come she was thinkin' about giraffes. A giraffe is a giraffe or they ain't. If you ain't, take its ears off.

Dol said having a penis was like having a penis. God don't care if you like His biology, and He don't care what earrings you got in your jewellery box neither – if Wilson understood correctly what Dol meant. Until opportunity knocked, you had to roll with what He gave you. That's what it was with her and her penis.

Wilson watched sneaky Burns coughing into his sleeve. That stranger, got up like a yellow jacket, fixed his gaze on her, pushed the table away from him, yanked his sweatpants back and forth and set out towards her.

'Could you just tell her – ' he pulled on Wilson's sleeve and squinted in some strong breeze ' – we want to talk to her?'

Wilson jerked out of his grubby mitts. 'You ain't dressed like a doctor.'

'Dr. Castor Cummings at your service. You'll excuse my dress. I jus' flew from New York City to St. Louis to Jonesboro. From Geneva first. You know where Geneva is?'

'That –'

'You can call me Cummings.'

Wilson sized him up. 'Doctor. Cummings.' She chewed on the name. 'So. How do?'

Cummings held out his paw to shake. 'Good 'nough.' He poked at his armpit.

Wilson tapped on the door. 'Hon? Dol? This gentleman –'

'Cummings.'

'Dr. Castor Cummings wants to talk to you.'

A cardboard box was scooted across the floor inside.

Then, pretty as pretty can be, smoothing his hair and tugging down his skirt, Dol opened the door. 'I heard about you.' He put a finger on the doctor's chest and tapped it. 'Didn't I tell you I'd be with you shortly?'

That finger travelled from Cummings' stem to his stern.

Dol squeezed between 'em without excusing himself, hurried to the jukebox, whacked it to stop the skipping and curtsied to a round of applause. He strutted behind the bar, dragging his finger across Dr. Cummings' chest again as he did.

'Don't taste every man's soup, you'll burn your mouth,' Wilson hissed.

Dr. Cummings sighed at the end of the bar.

'Oh, he will be with you when it suits him, Mr. Cummings,' said Burns.

Dr. Cummings harrumphed and rolled his eyes.

'Well, it suits me. Give me one little minute,' said Dol. 'Go on back.' He shooed the doctor away with his Merlot nails. 'I'll be right there.'

Dr. Cummings folded his arms. Wilson got curious why his fingers kept scratching under his arms. Cummings turned his back and Dol turned on Wilson.

'Why you gotta always be around? Don't you have something to do?'

'Dol, God gives food but does not cook it.'

'I can take care of myself.'

Dol just made her so mad. Wilson slunk to a table. Dol held up a steaming-hot beer glass and started to march around the bar.

'An ice-cold one, please, on account of it not bein' too much trouble,' said Wilson.

And just get a good look at the wet, cold skin of Dr. Burns. Shaking his wrist at the jukebox and blocking the view of the snow that was starting to come across sideways out on the porch. *The length of a snake can't be told till it is dead,* Wilson thought.

Isn't Dol a pretty bee-bopping thing? That sonuvabitch Atlanta man was cooking up a nasty. Oh, she could just feel it. Something fishy, something not good, something he and his forked tongue dreamed up.

And Dol gobbled it whole. If that rattlesnake Burns didn't have something to gain from snookering then he wouldn't have done it. Maybe it'd be a fair trade and maybe it wouldn't but one way or another Wilson'd find out. All it took was for her to dip one long finger down into her hidden well of secret powers and his skin'd peel off, exposing him for what he was, but good. Burns ought to know himself what kind of female he was playing with and, if he didn't, he sure was tipping a glass towards finding out.

Folks hung their heads, some snickered.

Dol held up the glass with his fingertips, locked Wilson's gaze and let the glass drop, crashing into the trash tub. Never taking his eyes off Wilson's, he curled his lip, hardened his eyes and walked real slow to the cooler. Polite and dainty as an organist on Sunday, he opened the cooler, removed a beer glass and brought it to Wilson.

He set the glass in front of Wilson. 'Don't start with me.'

'I have started with you.'

Dol flounced to the corner of the bar and huddled with Dr. Cummings. Wilson turned her back and fiddled with her beer, peeking at 'em now and again. On his tiptoes Dol led Cummings over to a two-top by the bar. Wilson slid to a stool at that end of the bar. Dol pressed his lips together and squinted hard at Wilson as he sat. He raised his eyebrows. Wilson picked at what was left of a coaster. A skunk was loose in the kitchen.

{ *Dol* }
7:33 p.m.

You sit down. Across the table from Dr. Castor Cummings. He taps your side of the table, sips his beer and claws his pit. 'Cheers.'

'Back at you.' You try your best, but you're sweating. It's like twirling for the Veterans Day parade. A girl gets nervous. Get yourself together.

Cummings speaks first. 'You look better than a ripe tomato or a cold beer in July.'

'Oh, my.'

Burns and his water glass've disappeared. You cast your eyes wide. By the front door, Burns fingers the jukebox, eyeing the sky.

'Dr. Burns is easily distracted,' says Cummings.

You say you wouldn't know. 'You know him well?'

'Well 'nough.'

'I forget how thirsty he is.'

You ask what music he likes.

'I like that quiet when strangers have so much to say but won't say none of it.'

'Who sings that one?' The dumber you are, the further you get on.

'Where there's no silence, only sound remains.'

'That's a long title.' The whites of his eyes have a dirt sheen to them like porcelain in a grungy sink. He reminds you of Stuart Krassen, the politician who sold the Dart to you and Elaine on a song and dance way back when. He wasn't doing you any harm, per se, but he wasn't doing you any favours neither.

'Sound is my thing. Listen,' he says. 'You just try it. Go on ahead and listen.'

You do, you listen. But what you hear is Wilson rolling her glass on the table, chair legs scuffing the floor, Keith Emory hacking up phlegm, Vernita Lee clicking those blue acrylics longer than Rototiller blades.

'Listen now.'

The sorry old Carpenters' opening to 'Please Mr. Postman,' the wind poking into the roof and that machine-gun hum of liquored-up conversation. A chair scrapes, syllables rise – you can't make them out.

'A bunch of –'

'Go on, keep listening.'

One sound, the *plink* of a piano – it comes rolling right out of some snort. It comes tumbling right out after, like they were produced intentionally to come one after the other. Then a chair not picked up, scratching the maple laminate but drawn out, extended. Then, for your ears only – you can follow it back. That one chair-leg scrape reverses, looping into a *plink-plink*. Then, then – there it is. What comes first is the quiet, outpaced by a second *plink* shaking itself out and opening wide. That sound is what's left from the smothering silence, subsuming and subtracting. It is absence itself imagining, and then permitting, vibration.

'Hear that?'

You heard but you can't say so. The last thing you wished for tonight was metaphysical discovery. You cannot say so, you cannot. He picks at his dry bevelled cuticles. Picking at his hands, what does he have in store for you? Pinball. You are that speeding silver bullet, shot into the dark ring – steel, shiny, ripping into the light. Inertia forces the leap – it is the very state in which you find yourself now. Spinning. And then jammed. Caught and slamming against the glass, eventually landing back in front of the flipper to be whacked back out to the maze.

Your penis is the creator of your womanhood. The hatred of your penis is the root of your femininity, it is your noise rooted in silence. Can who you are be created by who you are not? The rush of sound is the truth of becoming. Sometimes you've had visions of the spongy, chicken-skinned flesh peeling away to fall into a crystal-clear stream in the mountains, like what there must be out in Colorado or L.A., the way it must have been when man first got here. Hatred for your penis wears the stone on which it falls, leaving a concavity for your sex. What is left behind is a hollowed-out space for you – woman. Although it was not always so, your sex is made clear by what it is not.

You turned to Elaine for a time. When you had just started in with her, she would draw one long finger along the side of your face and then down the line of your spine. It always worked on you. The first time she did it, you lifted her and lay her on your bed. She moved her shoulder on account of the springs practically raw beneath her. When you found a place for your knee on that tiny mattress, her lips were chapped some as you lay yours upon hers and then you entered her, delightful. Her muscles clenched you, drawing you in further, releasing and drawing in again. You held her shoulders, her legs clasped your torso, her ankles dug into your back before she flipped both of you over to ride you, and in that miraculous moment, which you always thought was Pity's conception, the biological imperative rooted in the union of male and female crystallized in your body.

You'd like to share all this with Cummings but you keep your mouth shut.

{ *Wilson* }
7:47 p.m.

A layer of smoke hung under the ceiling and the windows were fogged up. The doorbells tinkled and Vernita Lee strutted back in, seesawing on her collapsed arches and brushing the snow off her head. She scooched herself in between Pitch Slocum and Keith Emory and put her sore feet up on a chair. She'd been dancing on the porch while getting some fresh air. At the table, Dol's curls'd fallen and he flipped them on account of showing off his neck.

Wilson clutched the bar but Dol drew a zipper over his lip. Wilson clenched her jaw, Dol whinnied. Wilson squinted her eyes, her head wobbled. Dol stood up to twirl around in his not-much-more-than-a-band-aid tube top and bump-and-grind skirt. Dr. Cummings tucked his arms around himself and gazed up at Dol.

Vomit rose, Wilson blinked. That Dol wouldn't know shame if it were a gold crown. Stomach acid burnt into Wilson's throat, so she gulped her beer. The bile got washed away like blouse straps. Like that scarf passing as a top, this whole place was taking on the air of a two-dollar brothel. Dol ought to know that a shirt that size has not one iota of decent.

And sure enough, all the folks were gawking at him. Crouched at their tables, they averted their eyes like they was crows looking for what was edible. They leaned forward to whisper while pretending not to ogle. When Dol crossed a leg, heads turned. When his green eyes glanced, eyes fell. He flitted his gauze skirt up and let it fall like dew. Pitch Slocum spilt his beer, Keith Emory grinned like a python. They rubbed their bellies, Vernita massaged her feet. It wasn't two minutes before she was shaking her titties too.

That would not be the first time Vernita acted up to protect herself. Take Pitch Slocum. Take that photo hanging over the bar, all faded to pink. Take Pat Boone. He marched in one afternoon, probably in '85 or '86, on his way to sing at that Choctaw boat. Paint him black and call him Anna if he wasn't in head-to-floor mink. Pat Boone isn't the first star that comes to mind, but when he does, he don't come in a mink coat. But there he came. Shimmering. The bleached mink so shiny-shiny it must've been shampooed with glitter. And he was sour.

First thing his eyes landed on was Pitch Slocum and he ordered him to bring a Diet Coke. And Pitch ordered Dol. But when Mr. Boone sipped his drink, he caused a to-do. There wasn't a lime on the lip of his glass. With a hand on either hip, Dol set his second pop down and, with some sugar, let Mr. Boone know two things: first, Pitch Slocum never told him to put in a lime. You got to ask for yourself if you want something. Second, they never did have limes at Avery's. If they did, he'd sure as shit put it in his Coke. Dol stuck his nose in the air and turned his back on Pat.

Mr. Boone's mouth twisted, his lips peeled back, showing his fangs, and he closed the mink around him. He shivered and turned his back. By now Avery's was packed full of folks all staring at Mr. Boone and waiting for him to show his alligator shoes. But with his panties in a bunch, he just folded his arms and stared at his Diet Coke. No lime. He didn't say a word. But that weren't the worst of it.

One of the folks who come in with him, who didn't have on nothing more than what could in some quarters be called a halter top and shorty shorts, whose rear seam had the power of one of those flute players blowing at a basket of cobras, got up on the table behind Mr. Boone and put on a show. She got a hold of Pitch when he was passing and whispered her name to him. He announced, 'And now, ladies and gentlemen, I am proud to introduce Vernita Lee!' The crowd clapped and Pat Boone slid down into his chair. Vernita spun a bestial web with her lacy fingers – when she danced her feet were not sore. Mr. Boone slumped, Pitch Slocum weaved. Mr. Boone didn't blink, Pitch was spellbound.

Wilson put a quarter in the jukebox for 'Turn Your Radio On,' a real old-time foot-stomper. She had to see this.

Pitch was a known dancer, and the audience's feet started in tapping. Vernita leapt off the table, pushed Pitch before he reversed. She snatched at the fluorescents, Pitch at his toes. They circled first to the right, then left. One step forward, two steps back. Three steps her way, one step his. She poked, he jerked. Hip roll, knee hike. Mouths open, lips wet. Fangs bared, Pitch focused. Sweat sprayed, lungs caught. Bent back, titties to chin.

Her taste-of-joy titties hung so far and shook so much that Pitch's eyes shrank to the squint of Moses on Sinai. He lunged and shimmied. His ankles sprung wide, his belly sank crude. She got the seat of his pants, he got her calves. Vegas showgirls couldn't bop wilder as they swung into chairs and scattered the customers.

Wilson set forth that Vernita must be Pat's daughter, Debbie, behaving worse than a you-know-what. 'Maybe "Vernita" is a disguise.'

'It's not Debbie, I'll tell you that,' stated Keith Emory. Dol wiped the bar. 'You understand?' asked Keith. 'I know Debbie Boone. Debbie Boone don't look like that.'

'Do you? You don't know her.'

'Well, I know enough to know when I see her. I seen her on TV. "You Light up My Life."'

Later, Vernita told the story of how she was walking from Bakersfield to Memphis to see Sun Records in person and her collapsed arches were killing her. Pat and his people come up and Vernita had her thumb out.

Given Mr. Boone's circumstances, and the blessing of his may-or-may-not-be daughter Debbie, when she didn't act like a skitter bug on horse pills, and a mink that could've paid close to a year's rent in Bay, he could've been in a better mood. It wasn't like he came to town every day. Dol said he probably just wanted to get away from it all and go somewhere where he could be honest and real and blow off some steam without ending up in the newspaper. That's how it is with famous people. They're just real people when it gets down to it.

'That Debbie must be a disappointment,' said Dol, poking Keith with his acrylic thumbnail.

'It ain't Debbie,' said Keith.

But Wilson didn't see how they could be so sure. Especially after what happened next. Debbie or not, that Vernita took Pitch Slocum by the chin and led him into the men's restroom. The jukebox played on, 'Over on the Hallelujah Shore.'

Nobody came out and nobody went into that bathroom for seventeen minutes. The song ended. Nobody put money in the jukebox. Some folks huddled at the restroom door. They pressed their ears to the jamb, cast their eyes upward, roamed their fingers on the wall to feel the shaking. They listened. The folks what didn't dare be nosy stared at their tables or picked at their beers. A few chewed their ponytails and others their fingernails. A rooster howled. A lawn mower cacked. A semi sped past. Pat Boone rocked in his chair. Forward, backward. He'd seen it all before. When the door finally squeaked open, every eye in the place was trained on Pitch and Vernita. Except Mr. Boone's. He wouldn't look at all.

Finally, Vernita and Pitch came out wiping their hands on their jeans and avoiding each other's eyes. Pitch, taking the high road, said, 'She made me do it.'

They planted themselves at a four-top. Some kind of pride and shame must have been in 'em because Pitch never said what was done inside. Vernita held her head high, chest out, and eyed the gawkers. 'I ain't sorry,' she said. She seemed very pleased with herself. No one except Wilson thought Debbie Boone would carry on that way.

When he got up to go, Mr. Boone didn't tip. And Dol noticed that little bit of stinginess. He got his Polaroid from under the counter, slipped it to

Pitch and then called to Mr. Boone to lift his fancy-schmancy coat off the floor. Vernita plunged towards him, trying to get him to sit back down. When Mr. Boone flipped her off, Pitch got all three in the picture.

Going through the door, Mr. Boone put his hand right in Vernita's face. She stopped in her tracks. He pointed his finger right into Vernita's face. 'I am sorry I picked you up.'

Then Pat Boone blew the snot out of his nose with one finger the way the farmers do, saying if he had to see this town in Heaven, it'd be too soon.

'Can't say he ain't a poet,' said Dol.

Vernita slunk back against the wall, watching what little future she might have had drive off. She gave up hitchhiking and decided to stay in Bay. She'd been running the laundromat ever since. And Pitch still claimed it was all her fault.

Wilson spun slow in her stool, taking in that old Polaroid. On the left, Mr. Boone's finger had bled into a pink cloud and Vernita's arms had purpled on the right. Just the faded line of Dol's eyeliner could still be seen there. Wilson put it out of her head that the one in the middle always dies first. 'That's an awful tale folks say to liven up picture-takin',' she told him.

Time and remembering had taught her that there wasn't a stone's throw of difference between Vernita dancing on a table and Dol curled up in that chair over there, his legs tucked beneath him, showing himself off like a *Solid Gold* dancer in heat. He had to flip the edge of his skirt up. He had to tip the strap of the camisole. He had to giggle, then turn grave. Wilson would have given her left arm so Dol wouldn't have to. And now, with Wilson, Dol could have a real shot. He could use her insurance. Hormones for his breasts, lessons for his voice. The beauty shop for his beard and back. A cut for the penis that hung around him like a criminal record. But Dol had to take her ring. No insurance company in the South was going to pay unless they were husband and wife. Even then it wasn't guaranteed.

Wilson had proposed already. To Dol. Two years before. Dol said yes. He'd get Wilson's benefits. So would Pity and Squirrel.

But the insurance company representative, meeting her for a bite at Avery's, said it would be a cold day in Hell before he ever approved his company ponying up for that work. 'People don't fix God's perfection.'

'I'll tell you about perfection.' Wilson kept an eye on the rep, who drank a glass of milk. 'And I am a Believer,' she said.

First, how about that custodian at Singer? Her fetus had an extra chromosome. It was dying. Inside her body. What did they do but force her to keep it. Even when it died at six months.

'A nation that kills its own children has no hope at all,' declared the insurance representative. 'You got to let things take their natural course, and you don't dodge God, and cutting things up and making everything artificial just 'cause you don't like His decision – '

'Eyeglasses ain't real. Neither is driving a car. Or that fat in crackers for shelf life. That'll kill God's creation.'

'Transfats. You got it, lady.' He shook his butter knife at Wilson. 'Love the sinner but not the sin.'

'Jesus wants all 'em people to get sick? And to stay sick?'

'I don't claim to know what – '

'Now you don't. Now you don't claim to know. You know you got a whole family what ain't got and ain't gonna get to see a doctor. What do you think of that?'

'The Lord giveth and He taketh away.' He ripped open a pink packet of sweetener.

'Oh, He does, does He?'

'I don't make the rules, I spread the Word.' He toodled that the truth was everybody did have health care.

'What?'

'Sure as Heaven ain't on fire. Everybody, in every state and in every city. I'll give you two words. He pressed his tongue into his teeth. 'Emergency rooms.' He put some honey on his cornbread.

'Oh. Emergency rooms do gender-reassignment surgery, cancer treament?'

'I can't account for perverts!' The representative pressed his hands on the table. 'We're talking health care!'

'Me too.'

'Not for people like that. Truth is –'

'Truth is he's the damned best daddy you ever saw and if you had one iota of a Christian heart you'd –'

The rep held up his hand. 'You know, if it was me, I'd okay it in a heartbeat.'

Wilson threw up her hands.

'What do I care? Really. I'm a salesman. I got no stake in it. But you got the Board of Directors looking out for the share price, and what's going to happen to that if the company gets allied with people –' he hunkered down into his chair ' – like your ... friend.'

Wilson got hold of his chin. She squeezed. Hard. 'On account that people in your business are so ... slippery.'

The rep talked through his teeth, trying to pry her fingers off his face. 'Now why you want to be like that? God don't have to be fair, and it's up to us to make sense of Him.'

When Wilson threw him out, he hit the front porch. Hard. Being nothing if not practical, Dol turned Wilson's proposal down flat.

Cummings wiggled his nose. Sniffing for fear. Dol wouldn't blink. The two of 'em were closer than paint to drywall. Cummings scratched. If they breathed a little harder, the varnish'd peel right off the walls. Sucking in, blowing out, sucking in, blowing out, sucking in.

Wilson set her mind on figurin' out what Burns was getting up to: shares in an HMO, a position in a health-care something or other, a degree to hang around his neck?

Bottom line trumps people. Wilson thought some more: Okay. Up prices, cut coverage. Got it. Down service, blame cost. Maybe he'd got himself in with one of them HMOs.

Lower access, pool doctors. Now he's dragged in some bozo from Atlanta. That's what all this was about. Something in that pooling business. And Burns had done it all just to get this this this – whatever it was – up and breathing. That's what it was. Absolutely, positively. Getting a small-town sucker, a small-town boy wanting to be a girl, just like so many what come before and so many what're going to come after to buy into something. Wilson didn't know what yet but it was something. Dol buying in, whatever it was – Burns' ticket to a white beach and cool breezes somewhere. A snake in the grass – she had his number. She reached down into her hidden store of secret powers. She aimed her X-ray vision and fired at Burns. He didn't flinch, so she sprung into her comic-book mind.

She leapt off the stool so the wind caught her cape and the rafters came down close. She thumped her chest, howled, her flying-high arms reaching for Burns' slippery neck and then sinking. Folks gripped their tables, eyes bugging out as they ducked lower, dropping their jaws and shaking with the shivering fear of barely escaping a cannonball. Wilson had powers all right.

Two months ago, Vincent, her supervisor at Singer, wouldn't pray Jesus. She intended to use her powers for conversion. Now if she thought about it, Vincent was responsible for her entire plan this evening. Out of nowhere he had become her angel. The most decent thing Vincent had ever done was yank Wilson aside one day to sneak her some inside news.

Light in his loafers, Vincent covered his face like a show pony wearing blinders, he stood up straight, proud of himself. 'I don't have to tell you this, I want you to know, but I got to 'cause I am sure your heart is just breaking.'

'What – ' Wilson stood sideways to Vincent. She looked over the notices on the bulletin board.

'And I want to ease your suffering, so just be quiet and listen like a good girl.' Vincent twisted his arms tight. 'We're changing insurance companies, Missy, and I think you'd want to know that this new company is a little more inclined to think of things your way and – '

'What're you tellin' me for?'

'Concerning Dol. I am talking about your little plan to help Dol. Which I think is so sweet as to be unimaginably romantic and noble and beautiful and probably something Burt Reynolds would have done for Sally Field if she'd've let him and wasn't so concerned about her career 'cause you know that's what it was that broke up their True Love romance and that's why she couldn't believe it when she won her second Academy Award and was so overcome when she – '

'You pussyfooter. What you got up your sleeve?'

'I'm just saying I'd do anything to make a dream like that come true. Love is love is love.'

'I got no time. I can't fix nothing, and I ain't working overtime.'

Vincent's eyes were wide and moist. 'How come you don't trust?'

'Oh, now you're a crybaby over it?'

Vincent dabbed his eyes with a handkerchief.

'I do trust. I don't trust you,' said Wilson.

Wilson leapt off her bar stool, and when she landed a rain of Hell came with her: beer and bulbs, forks and fixtures, assholes and asbestos. In her fantasy, her hands got that slimy doctor's neck and she twisted. She twisted till he saw yesterday. Or so she wished. Actually, she just stood there with a few customers shootin' looks at her.

Dol cocked his drawn-on eyebrows and bared his fangs.

Wilson stuck out her lower lip and picked at the gunk in the plastic pine bar. She puffed up her chin, *Go ahead then, Dol. You just suffer, you're just the flower in the bud, ain't you? You're just the, the syrup in the maple, huh? You're just the, the, the – oh, for crying out loud. You made your bed, Wilson, lie in it. And when you're done, Walter, and through and crying your eyes out, who'll just be here, at the end of the bar, waiting? I will, you know it.* But if she could bite her lip and get up, maybe Dol'd chase after. She thought once, and then again, about that, before loping across the room, vibrating tables, earrings and glasses, and squeezing in between folks who thought too much of themselves to suck it in. She snatched her jacket.

Dol covered his fangs but didn't budge. His lips were shamelessly puckered and his eyes were wider than the Speedway racetrack. At the jukebox, Wilson tapped Dr. Burns on the shoulder so he'd look the other way then punched p1, 'Turn Your Radio On' by Mr. Albert Brumley. For Pat Boone's sake. She hissed at the python next to her. 'Ain't you rubbery, Doctor?'

'Ain't I what?' Burns thrust his thumb in her face. 'You –'

'Spit it out, you fork-in-the-t–'

'Better not go out there with me, Fr–'

'Be very careful about your next two syllables.'

He bleated the next like a goat. ' – an-cine, if you know what I mean.'

In a side-by-side world, Wilson leapt up, did a somersault in mid-air and came down fists up. She swallowed. 'Corruption finds a dozen alibis for its evil deeds. Don't live it up so high that you can't live it down.'

Don't. Step back. Go outside. Bite your lip good. She balled her fist, she didn't punch, she didn't speak. She bit, she swallowed, she marched. At the door. *Think.* She didn't want to go, she had to. No, she didn't. Her atomic brain crunched. She could talk to Burns, he could fill her in – how come she couldn't just say what she wanted, what was she afraid of? Wilson planted both feet on the porch and stepped into the cold.

If that was the way Burns wanted to be, not telling her what they were all getting up to, she'd go outside and freeze her sweet patootie. She'd go into the weather all right, she'd head straight on into that horizontal wind. She'd catch pneumonia. You betcha. That'd teach 'em. She'd get so sick it wouldn't matter how good her insurance was, she'd die anyway. On account of she wanted to, on account of she chose it, on account of what was life for? She'd suffer, she'd call it quits. She'd die.

That sorry excuse for a doctor, Burns, couldn't fix a bee sting. That hussy in there, Dol, 'd get a fine plate of Just Desserts. Done right, love leaves you cold. Dead. She saw how her mama and daddy ran around on each other. She with her Brooke Tyler romance novels and highfalutin' ideas, he with his insurance widows and that secretary he had for so long.

When Wilson was good and cold and buried and gone, Dol would stand at her grave crying his eyes out over not seeing the love what was just waiting for him. His tears would nutrify the earth with coulda-woulda-shoulda but it warn't going to bring Wilson back. Not that time.

The screen door was slow to thwack behind her, so Wilson kicked it shut. Slivered flakes scratched at her cheeks and neck. She pulled her collar up and batted at an icicle, and then another one, and then the whole row of popsicles. The air dug in, her nipples stiffened.

The weather. Oh. Why, that's exactly it. It gets cold, folks don't choose how their nerves react. Do they? The air chills, goosebumps come up. Inhale. Goosebumps ain't chosen. We haven't got a thing to say about them comin' up or goin' down.

Bending away from the leaning gusts, Wilson lit a smoke. She thought of her whole history. She thought of Dol's. History was like the cold air, it was like the weather. The weather changes you. Whether it's your history, your memories or your sex – they all shape how we move through our days. We bundle up against 'em or get into the fold of their cool shade. Dol was just reacting to the weather in her life. The same with poor old Julie, whose Charlie wouldn't even say boo to her, rutting there on her leg, in her head. She could still feel it and squeezed her own legs tighter.

The body changes, oh God, there's nothing more to what's between the legs than what you remember, what years make you into, on account that it's cloudy, sunny, foggy, rainy. Bodies are born and then pitied. At that union barbecue, Julie had jerked up from her passing out sayin', 'Woman is borned, then woman'ed as she grows.'

Wilson watched the smoke linger before a zigzagging gust snatched it first to the east then to the north, until only the sparkling sky remained. Three blinkers hung like the straight edge of a windowsill. She licked her finger and covered up the middle star. The one in the middle dies first. The wind, blasting from Memphis, dried the spit from her fingertip. The snow was coming in good enough from the east to have to squint looking into it.

Wilson would forgive Dol, even though she wouldn't treat a dog the way he treated her. His horse was pretty high tonight but he ought to stay put with the folks that cared something about him. Not strangers who roll in from Atlanta before a snowstorm selling pipe dreams. Very few folks around here cared what was between his legs.

She turned her back to the wind and flicked her ash. When it was all out in the open, they'd go to Lake City, to a real restaurant with menus, to a movie or to a sit-down ice-cream shop. They'd go on a date. That's what people do. They'd take a walk by Rose Lake down by where they sucked out the swamp.

They'd talk it straight: how come Dol didn't tell her how much he cared for her, how he felt he couldn't, it was true maybe that Wilson's passions and the depth of her heart, the pits of her feeling, were too far down, were just too powerful to risk it, and Wilson'd say yes, 'cause Dol knows her better 'n anybody and that was right Holy Toledo you know me better than I know myself and I wish to heaven I could've been there to help you to sit with you and to check out this guy because you know my dear we really don't know him from Adam he's just some guy Burns brought in and do we really want to trust your future, and Wilson would take Dol's hands in hers, *our* future to an utter stranger? And from Atlanta, no less? She had to keep from being too serious, Dol never liked it when her worries got the better of her. Well, she'd say, you got to be careful. Look about what they did to Elaine. Huh, think about that. And. And, and, and.

Wilson cupped her hands into blinders and breathed on the window. She scratched at the frost. She couldn't see nothing good. Dol with his arms folded. Maybe covering his titties, maybe chewing his nails. Cummings was yakking. Nervous Nelly. Won't get Dol that way, fella.

And there goes Dol, scooting his chair out. He's had enough of this. *Me too, sister,* thought Wilson. *Stand up, go on. Yes. Whoop.*

Cummings yammering. Now he's up.

Sit down, Dol, let him go. Shoot fire.

Cummings had his arm. *Shoot.*

Dol sat down. Oh, he folded his hands and pulled his hair back and took in what was said.

Keith Emory rapped on the window glass. He waved, Dol glanced.

Wilson hit the porch floor in a quick faint. As her heart slid back into place, cold soaked into her toes. No clean socks in the drawer, that's what you get. She crawled further on under the window to the end of the porch, banging her toes as she went. When she looked up, a bunch of looky-loos with too much time on their hands were looking at her. Had to be just about every person inside except Dol, who probably had his face in his hands.

{ *Julie* }
8:02 p.m.

I drove around for a good while. Taking my time, tasting the moment. Them fields lit by the spill of yard lamps. Them drifts twisting back and forth like sand dunes. Them parked cars, none of 'em Charlie's. I circled past Avery's a few times, which wasn't hard on account of how large and spread out the roads were. I was giving ol' Charlie time to get in there and get some beer in him. All over the area, roads squared off wide, drift-bearing fields, like the threads binding quilt patches. I'd make him have to call me. Finally, that Luv truck was parked in the lot. A pig always comes to his trough.

Sneaking south on Niles Road a half-mile on, I switched my lights out, leaving little more shine than what Heaven could spare from its place up so far, at such a distance, with the task of overseeing a storm, and me rushing straight on, and letting me slip through since that way witnesses maybe couldn't say they seen me or place me there or at such-and-such or so-and-so, so I coasted off to the shoulder and did a graceful stop so a cacophony of stones wouldn't spray and that's when I turned off the ignition. And swabbed my neck. I was perspiring and wanting to gun the gas in reverse. It's a scary thing what I was doing. Sweat reappeared back there, seeing as how I was mostly not myself, and through the windshield sulked a sullen ocean of Arkansas night plain with the fomenting sky exploding down upon us the way these spells do these days, and the blistering sincerity these winds carry egging on the spring flood waters which ought to scare the bejesus out of one of these generations, but they're going to keep on until the water don't have no place to go except basements, and then way up in those elm trees the pale branches carried on waving, distracting the weather with hysteria, whipping down and up, swooping back and forth and praying to be let free, back and forth calling for these blizzards to move on past, or so at least that's what all the Storm Warning reports pumping from the Jonesboro stations been saying with all the snow getting dumped on Bay, and heavens to Betsy I was prepared, for all the good it did me, but I swear I was sitting there with my dearly beloved's camouflage hunting coat, the one with the blue-red flannel inside and the cotton canvas outside, broken in, he's got the new one, I mean if they ever did a csi on me, if they were going to come over and look for fibres they got me, I am sure the universe is littered with my fibres, and I just bet he's looking for me, he probably is right now wondering if I'm coming back.

At that point, I had to be slicker than the dark – beyond Scott's Woods and on the other side of a fallow snowfield, two barn lights cast the tree trunks, and me, into shadow, so I had to be smoother than the ice. In front of me the gravel caught the mica castings and brightened the shoulder to the side, and the limp leaves flickered faster and faster in the westerlies heavy with the hours ahead, and beyond, stars broke through in the effortless nuclear fission of nothing ventured, nothing gained.

Over there, a barbed-wire fence clenched the ditch, and the engine ticked, and I could beat the storm to Charlie's tires, I knew it, and he would have to talk then, so I breathed in to the count of five, and my breath emerged, four, as gaseous ropes unspooling, three, as I wiped the back of my neck, two, and zipped up the overlarge coat and, two again, climbed out the passenger side then the frozen mud, one, broke under my boot but I held on to the door, and the snow biting into my cheeks coming sideways, and just past where the gravel ended the ditch went down but I leapt that in a fell swoop landing on all fours but holding on to the bull weed sticking out from the drifts, and then glomping like hell up that slippery slope, and what there is of a fence there held me when I got to it. I. Heaving. Leaned there. Kool cigarettes. Not good.

Christ. The Cutlass was too close to the road side of the shoulder.

Jesus. I leaned out, covering my eyes to look, and lost my footing and slid back and I snatched the fence post tearing my finger through my glove shit goddamned mother-mucking jesus christ forgive me because I have sinned goddammit. But the car wouldn't be there long so it wasn't at risk of getting towed off and who was I fooling to begin with that I wouldn't be found out?

I just bet ol' King Charlie Glorious himself was keeping a stool warm at the bar with Wilson and making excuses about not going home 'cause that little chickenshit ever since Tuesday he's only come home after I was in bed because he's scared of me, so he's sneaking back in, sleeping on the couch and easing back out soon as the sun comes up and, well, boy, he was going to get stopped in his tracks tonight. I got myself back up to the fence, even though I got caught on that stiff bull weed never mowed since June. You'd think with the taxes they charge they could swipe a weedwhacker down through here now. Just get one of those illegals out here with a scythe. It'd take him an hour, I said to myself. I heaved my boots up out of the snag grass and got a foothold on the rail. Holding myself high and exposed, I gripped the post with both hands – it'd been a long time since I'd jumped a fence, but tonight the sun had set on the limits of patience. That sonuvabitch was going to talk to me or he'd walk the long way home and I had the knife in my pocket to make it happen and so I hoisted my foot over the fence and sat down on the top railing, feeling the gusts shoving me before pushing off onto the ground and down to the other side so to speak.

Temperatures'd come down, my cheeks tightened. I snuck along the treeline. I could hear voices from the bar. Avery's cast a glow on the woods across the road there and laid a square of light on the blacktop. Then, an engine. I froze. Gunning up. It couldn't be Charlie. Charlie wouldn't even be finished with his second beer. A car pulled out of the lot, the whack of its wipers following. The headlights cut the tree trunks coming my way. I pressed to the wire. The headlights lifted up from the road. The car came on, lighting up my boots, revealing my face. By the time I let my breath out, it was back into the black of dreams. Up past the weather, the night must've been spitting diamonds. That's the same as what it does in Nebraska. Same as it used to be there where every sound is eclipsed by the burden of snow and the second sight of storms.

A steep hill lay closer to the parking lot. I stopped to listen as I gulped the cold draughts stinging stinging my throat. I thought I'd sneak along the ditch edge and take cover by the pines, and from there I'd make a beeline to Charlie's truck. Climbing fences wasn't as easy as I remembered but once I got over the first one, the second was pretty good and I landed right behind the parking lot.

That slippery-as-all-get-out hill cut down below me. The jukebox was loud even way over here. I scooted down on my rump and landed in the dirt parking lot. I looked up. I was seen. A little thing, no more than ten, stood there. First I laid back on the hill, pretending I wasn't there or that I was dead, pressing my eyes closed against the flurries driving into me like steel shavings, thinking I wouldn't draw no attention to myself, but the little sugarpuss wasn't having none of that. She took a few steps my way and I waved her off, but it didn't get rid of her. I brushed myself off. I was up to no good but I didn't have to look like it. I knelt down and dug a bit in the dirt and snow at my feet. Stupid. Nothing a ten-year-old likes better than dirt and mud. I just dug my hole. Froze in the mud, in the slush. Now my hands were soaked.

'Go away.'

The girl sprung at me. 'Did you find it?'

'You shouldn't be standing around in a parking lot, young lady. Where's your mama?'

'I don't know.'

'You lost out here?'

'No, ma'am.'

'Get on home, then.'

'You can't tell me what to do.'

'Well, I sure can. And I am. Get! You'll freeze to death in this weather.'

'You don't scare me.'

'Who's your mama?'

'I don't live with my mama.'

'Get home to your daddy, then.

'He's working.'

'You go wait … ' I was wondering where I could stash her. A little thing like that. I could put her out back. There's got to be a dumpster. She could sit tight and safe in it, stay warm. I could give her something to play with in there. She could get run over out here. Right there was Charlie's red Luv pickup to her right and behind. 'You go wait back there.' I pointed across the parking lot, and to her left, by the wall there. 'Then I'll get you back home.'

'Did you find what you were looking for?'

'There wasn't nobody looking for nothing, now get over there before you freeze to death.'

People stepped out onto Avery's porch, thwapping the screen door. I ducked and dug in the dirt again.

The girl took a couple of steps towards me.

'I seen you at the Piggly Wiggly.'

'No. You haven't seen anybody.'

'I have.'

'No.'

'I have too.' The girl squinted. 'What's your name?'

'I'm busy, okay?'

'What're you busy with?'

'Don't be nosy.'

'I ain't.'

'Go over and stand by the wall. You're going to get yourself run over.'

'You can't tell me what to do.'

'You want to get slapped upside your backside, keep on. We're going to go find whoever owns you or is looking out for you.' And as soon as I said that, I knew who it was.

'Supposed to be a lady, but she didn't come.'

My macaroni-and-cheese dinner turned over in my gut. 'Well. Some people are not responsible. Get used to it. Oh, Christ. Go on over there.' I pointed to the back wall of Avery's.

She didn't budge.

I ignored her and snuck right up in between a Dart and Charlie's Luv.

'What you want with my daddy's car?'

'Shh!' I dropped and grit my teeth. This girl was going to get me caught. 'Hey?'

'Yes.'

'You want to help me?'

She raised and then dropped her eyebrows.

'Look over there.'

'For what?'

'For a minute.'

'What for?'

'Nothin'.'

'How come you want me to look then?'

'Missy, you're making this – '

'Let me come with you.'

'Just look over there. Please.'

The girl turned to look and I scooted around the front of the Dart to the side of the Luv and got out the buck knife.

'Hey, ma'am?' The kid come after me, sloshing between the cars.

I hid behind a tire. Her boots dragged through the slush and gravel. I holed up behind a tire, pinching my earlobes for warmth.

'I won't tell no one, lady.'

Her whisper had fear in it. I bit my lip and as I did it sunk in further. Oh, for Jesus H. Christ: this was the kid I was supposed to sit. There was two of them, weren't there? Heaven only knew where the other one was.

Maybe there was only one. I didn't remember. I never called that Dol back to say I couldn't sit. Absent-mindedness is going to be the death of me.

'You got me all wet – don't leave me out here. It's cold, lady. I'll find you.' The girl began slogging between the cars towards me. 'Oh!' She fell and started crying. 'How come you all leave me? You all leave me!'

I jumped up, but then thought better of it.

'Help me, you!' bawled the girl.

I scooted over and took hold of her paw. She wiped the snow from her eyes and went stock-still. Somebody close was smoking 'cause that perfume undulated to me in the gusts. I turned that little caterpillar around, nudging her to the back end of the parking lot. Out there a stand of Jack pine butted up against that field. She could shelter herself in the trees and I'd be good and gone by the time she made her way back.

'Where you takin' me?'

'Nowhere. We're goin' to put you back here with me getting us out of the wind in the nice trees.'

'My daddy says there's snakes in trees.'

'Darlin', there's snakes everywhere. Arkansas snakes don't come out in winter. They don't want nothin' to do with you.'

At the edge of the parking lot was where that stand of pine sprouted up. The snow'd stuck up between the boughs and the drifts, yawning out a hollow in them so as to provide a wind break.

'Oh, dagnabbit.'

'What?'

'I have – '

'What?'

'Lost something.' I patted at my pockets for effect.

'What you lookin' for?' the little lady asked.

'I'll tell you what, you stay here and I'll be right back.'

'No. You're gonna run off and leave me.'

'I won't. Why would I do something like that? Now you be a big girl, I'll be right back.' I stepped off and that little fly come right with me.

'I ain't staying.'

'Okay, then.' And then, God, finally shining a bit of His glory my way, brought a bunch of bunnies near the base of one of them Jack pines. There wasn't shine to see all of them but there was a big one and some tinier ones. Hallelujah. The inside of their ears was catching the light from the parking lot lamps. 'Hey, shoofly.'

'What?'

'Come here.' I led her back into the Jack pines. Now you be real quiet,' I whispered in her ear, 'and I'll show you something.' And we crouched down and she caught sight of them little quivering things and was spying on them, mesmerized like a spider before she strikes, and when she turned around, I was gone.

{ *Dol* }
8:13 p.m.

What would Mencken say? In milli-, no, nanoseconds you you you rifle through the pieces you know.

'Did you hear it?' A reptile in the underbrush, he sits there. Inert, taut and waiting.

'No.' You lie, you giggle. What you heard was the front door rattling in its frame. 'You've taken my breath away some.'

'Huh.'

'I'll try it again when I get home. It's quieter there.' But, truth is, you heard it. You heard it. Now what? Now what, sister? You want to clench your teeth and hold on to the chair. You don't, you lean back. You wink at Cummings. 'What's the music you like –'

'You asked me that.'

'Right, then – I'm antsy.'

'You've got a lot on the line.'

You sure do appreciate his coming all the way out here.

He says you ought to come to Atlanta since you're ready to deal.

'Atlanta? Oh, Lord.' You went to that snakepit once.

'Did you like it?'

'Well, it was in my experimentation phase and let's just say, sure. It's a big city, lots of people.' That was the trip that put you on to Elaine soon as you got back. You went to Atlanta all right and got lost in poking your head through the looking glass but good.

This man wearing a Kojak hat picked you up in his tiny red sports car and took you to his white brick house but it was a orgy house of amusement. There have to be ten or twelve men there, all falling on themselves, tangled up on the floor, purple dish towels spread out on the furniture. You recognize that fellow from the Braves. He has the longest hairless legs, down on the floor leaning up against the couch, and his legs, which are quite spread, stretch from where he is all the way over to up on the back of the other couch across from him. There is some fellow squirting Mennen on him. All of them are loving on each other but gander at you like a siren's just gone off. In Bay, men just pat each other on the back, but they are doing a whole lot more than that in Atlanta. You shift on the inside. You become an anthropologist. They're finding here what they can't get elsewhere. Their teeth are grit, their eyes wide open, their muscles clenched. But you don't feel nothing. Nothing. It is like standing in a waterfall but not getting wet. You aren't one of them. You wish you could be. In this world, ain't nobody has it worse than the gays. Nobody. 'Cept fat people and trans-people. It would be easier for other people if you weren't a sissy. Who wants a straight sissy?

'Different in Atlanta. Different than the same ol', same ol',' you say.

Cummings rubs his armpit on his ribs, humming 'I've Got You Under My Skin.' He wants to know what you do for a kick around here.

'Not much.'

'You could do worse. In Atlanta, we got Jane Fonda. Trust me, I am not bragging. You know, in a year, you could have your whole business wrapped up.'

You didn't think he'd just come out and say it like that. Like it wasn't anything you and he had to talk about, like it wasn't something you had to plan, like it could happen, like the two of you could make the money come. Jane Fonda is a good reason to move there. Your penis tingles, you suck in your tummy. 'What, do you own an insurance company for people like me?'

'No.'

'You'll forgive me and I'm trying real hard to contain my excitement but Burns didn't tell me exactly how you could help.'

'Your whole life you've been waiting for a guy like me to sit across the table from you.'

You nod, because the same-old, same-old's been one thing after another for you. For instance, you're lying on the landing looking at the gold walls and watching your mom get ready. The landing is narrow and there are doors on all three gold-fabricked walls. Your legs are on the top stair and your back is on the landing.

Now you can hear your mother not speaking. Nothing. But then the silence did not feel like creation. It was barren. Sterile. She never spoke to you. The silence produced only tight-teethed growls or torrents of the impossible. She did not hold you. She did not touch you. After Scouts, she did not believe you when the quartermaster pushed you against the wall and stuck his pine-cone cock in your face telling you to lick it lick it lick it two years before you egged him on to hump you in a field at Rose Lake, and three before your brother left him naked in the snow saying *If you ever touch my brother again, I'll kill you. Just forget about it,* she said. And when Terry Frank's boyfriend lifted you up off your feet, shoving you into the lockers, she refused to say a word. The last time you got touched by your mother was on the trip through her vaginal cavity. At six days past your birth, she went back to work.

You are sure that watching your mother step out of hot baths was a formative experience. And you always could. The door was never closed. Your mother had gone nuts, shattering the mirror and speaking in tongues when you and your brother were little. Your father broke down the bathroom door to get the two of you out from behind the toilet. She was diagnosed schizophrenic but refused treatment because no one has a right to poke around in anyone else's head. So there never was a lock on the bathroom door. Cringing, crapping or crying, you were always watched. To ask for privacy was to trigger a *Who do you think you are?*

Lying there on the top landing, you see your mother step out of the hot bath and towel off. Her teeth are clenched while the creases in her neck bloom and fall under their own weight. Her legs are ribboned with purple and scarlet veins and crowned by toes flushed with blood. You stare up from the *National Enquirer*s or *The Star*s she insisted on buying, even though your dad harangued that she was nickel-and-diming you all to death, as she dries her dripping auburn pubic hair and wraps her Clairol Sunshine hair in a towel.

You want to be the pad of her finger fondling as she powders. You see yourself in her, you see yourself as her.

'Your hair's nice.'

She sneers because she knows you want her to see you so she steps over you to her bedroom and what you see is the outer folds of her clenched labia.

Then again when she returns to the bathroom to talcum herself. You see yourself in her. You see yourself as her.

She pushes the door open further to let heat escape and, as it does, the air burdened with steam thins with the astringence of her Corn Husker's lotion.

She leans against the sink and into the mirror, the fat on her hips filling out the dimples in her thighs as she applies foundation with her third finger. The junk pouch of her belly mirrors her bottom's protrusion.

Your family's all tits and fanny.

On the carpet you angle around so that you are facing her. And it isn't hard to not be seen since she is so focused on her own eyes. When she does look up you look down, reading stories about *I Dream of Jeannie* and Michael Ansara, Ol' Blue Eyes and Barbara Marx, and the romance coming between the Six Million Dollar Man and Lindsay Wagner. In those magazines there are blond women holding tape measures around their waists grinning because they've lost five inches in fourteen days. There are sleepy cavemen found buried in Irish peat bogs dumbfounded by the modern world and there are miniature vehicles capable of flying you down the street and into homeroom if you only had enough money to buy them.

You were thirteen, still praying for and expecting breasts to rough up your skin – you'd spot Sick Don in the hallway with his nipples swollen bigger than peaches ogling all those girls marching like doomed Indians to the locker room, not knowing the treasures dangling from their clavicles. You prayed for the same, you stalked them too.

They stuffed everything into powder-pink tees and electric-orange tube tops complaining how their breasts ached and boys didn't look them in the eyes no more, and they had no idea of the power they had, and for that brief moment in the river that is their life, the sway that is sex was never more truly seen or revealed naked to be plucked if they could only see using your eyes while you hunkered down by an open locker door while getting a good look, but for reasons different than that of Sick Don and the boys running past the secretary's office.

Cummings paws at his shirt seam. You tell the doctor that, yes, you have thought about it for a long time. You run your finger along the curved ledge of the two-top.

The doctor follows with his thumb.

{ *Wilson* }
8:13 p.m.

Headlights flooded the porch and the Luv's engine ground down like a backed-up septic tank. No use even turning around. In the cab, Charlie turned the high beams on Wilson, lying there.

'Turn 'em off, you sonuvabitch!' Now she couldn't see nothing but blotches.

The high beams switched to low. Her eyes cleared.

His shit-eating face glowed behind the dashboard and the flurries streaking through the beams. He waved at her, honked twice and turned the lights off.

'What are you, trying to blind me?'

He gripped the truck door, winked at her and jumped to the ground.

Her stomach wiggled. She got to her feet. Downy and smokes came to her on the breeze. Her throat closed up. She sucked in her gut and jammed her hands into her pockets. She looked at the ground. Stop it. Stop it, stop it, stop it. She was going to marry Dol if it killed her.

Charlie threw a snowball at her.

'Did you get it?' His hair got all kicked up in the wind.

'Yuh.'

He had to go and wear his tight jeans that showed him all, tonight of all nights. She didn't want to carry on with him but that didn't cool the warm ache in her tummy. 'Let me see.'

'Hold your horses, it's freezing.' Charlie stepped carefully on the icy stairs. 'Ain't Dol supposed to salt the stairs?'

'You let me take care of Dol.'

Charlie sighed big and clapped his hands. 'It is co-old.'

'How's Julie?'

Keith Emory rapped on the window and waved at Charlie. The rest had gone back to their seats. Charlie waved back. 'Fine, I guess. Looks warm in there.'

'You haven't talked to Julie yet.'

The cold damp got to Charlie's joints. He did a knee bend. 'I'm going to do that when I'm eighty. Can we go inside? I want a beer before I head home.'

'Whyn't you just talk to her?'

Charlie tugged at his shoulder. 'Whyn't you just get me a beer? Shoot, it's colder'n a well-digger's grommet.'

'When you show me what you got.'

He pulled a square velvet box, smaller than a cigarette pack, from his pocket.

'It looks like a tooth.'

'Okay, buddy. You ready?' His teeth chattered.

'Only for the whole rest of my life.'

But Burns popped out, the screen door snapping in the wind. Charlie hid the ring box.

'You couldn't figure out the jukebox?' Wilson asked.

'Wilson, just, okay?' said grouchy Burns.

They stood there.

'What do you got, a party going on out here?' Burns had the voice of an outboard motor chugging up after being stuck in muck.

Wilson mimicked him, growling. 'A party going on out here?'

'How's that?'

Wilson crunched Burns' head in the fat of her hand. 'Burns here is up to something, Charlie.'

The doctor oozed out.

'Afraid?'

'Now, Fra–'

'I wouldn't say it if I were you, Doctor.'

'I was just going to inform you that even the devil was an angel at one time. I need one of them smokes,' croaked Burns.

'I got three words for you,' said Charlie. 'Cancer, cancer, cancer.'

'Cancer's a girl I threw out twenty years ago. She took almost everything I got, took my saliva glands. I can't … spit even.'

Charlie dug at his shirt pocket. 'All I got to say is visits to your office sure have been paying off recently. For some anyway.' He got Burns in a playful chokehold and knuckle-polished his head and said if they were going to stay out on the porch he was going to the car for his coat. 'Some people got a whole new generation to think of.'

'Every man knows best,' Burns swallowed, squeezing out his sayings. 'When his own shoe pinches.' He wriggled free and rubbed his hands together, eyeing Charlie's cigarettes.

Not all the snowflakes'd fallen from the clouds. Wilson studied the sky slung low and swollen. Something terrible was coming. 'Y'all're slippery.' She whacked the doctor upside the head.

'That calf's gonna be my date tonight,' said Charlie. 'That shed'll be warm enough.'

'You'll freeze,' warned Wilson.

But Charlie jackknifed off the porch, bolting back to his truck.

'He's … lucky man.' Burns followed his evaporating breath.

'Oh yeah?'

'Yuh. Fatherhood, his age. A tree is is known by its fruit, not its leaves.'

'Early ripe, early rotten.'

'What's that meanin'?' asked Burns.

'One bad apple spoils the whole bunch.'

'Well, an apple a day.'

'But you can't always make out the worm eatin' away at that apple.'

'Pluck your fruit … faster than the frost, Francine.'

Oh, she could just hit him. She bit her tongue.

Burns scuffed the ice, admiring how the icicles grew down from the overhang, sparkling. Charlie got his coat, horse-snorted and got blown skidding all the way back.

'Whoaaa! It should snow around here more often!' He had on a flannel military tent coat.

'My advice: watch all that jumping, sport,' advised Burns. 'You damage yourself you ain't gonna be a healthy daddy.'

Wilson knocked one boot into the other. Charlie bounced up and down. Burns' sneaky eyes crawled from Charlie to Wilson.

'So,' said Charlie.

'Yuh,' said Burns.

'It's coming down now,' said Charlie. 'I took the long way around up from Finkel Road over to the 48 and come up.'

'The 48, uh, was pilin' up. When I went by there I cut off, come down by Paxton's,' said Burns.

'See, I was goin' to, on account of I thought about the Paxton's but you don't ever know if they got it clear. The 48's always clear.'

'On account you got the County and on account of you know who, J-U-L-I-E, might be coming along on that same road,' said Wilson.

'On account of that, maybe. Least they're using our property taxes for something.'

'How you thinking about when you go home tonight?'

'Well, I got the Paxton's Way or there's the 48 again.'

'I'm … taking 48.'

'Why chance it with the weather?'

Wilson's face burned. 'You tell me the mole-thing you are up to, Dr. Burns.'

Burns blew cooled smoke in Wilson's face. 'I … can't tell you.'

'Is that right?'

'Patient confidentiality.' He drew up his hood to cover his bald head.

'Oh yeah?'

Charlie shivered. 'So, the 48?'

'That's what I'm thinking.'

Wilson stomped away, then leapt back. 'Whatever you're cooking up, Burns, pitch it out. I aim to marry Dol.'

'Oh, if that … don't beat all.' Burns poked his Catholic fingers into his neck. 'You know, 's a fine man. Uh.' He got a hold of Charlie's shoulder to be friendly. 'Uh, you know, got a beautiful wife, two – almost three kids, huh? A beautiful family, hey. And then, uh. Now you, you know? Then you got Dol and Wilson here, who are aiming to twist the laws of God and Nature. That's fine by me, I wouldn't want it for myself. Ain't nobody that can live … bifurcated.'

Wilson didn't know what bifurcated was but figured he was making just this side of a crack-handed comment. Boy, wouldn't her fist like to kiss his jaw.

Burns dug his heels into the porch and faced Wilson. 'Who the blankety-blank-blank knows what you are? And I'm saying that with, you know, a medical professional aspect to it. You just don't go into regular taxonomies, do you? '

'You got to go showing off with your big words,' said Wilson.

'You got you and now her … well, she ain't a her yet.'

'He ain't a her.'

'And what are you? A him?'

'I'm a her!'

'That don't mean the state is going to validify … the two of you strapping on gold bands, prancing the Hallelujah chorus, singing all the way to City Hall.'

'Why shouldn't they? I'm a woman, he's a man.'

'So far as that'll get you.'

'So far as that'll get us, that's right. And we're going to get hitched before that changes.'

'Ah. That's what this is about. Charlie, you got to talk to your friend here.'

'Charlie don't have to tell me nothing about it!' Wilson shook her fists. 'He don't know nothing and you don't know nothing. There's no reason Dol and I can't get married.'

'There is if … he's a she,' corrected Burns. 'Not if he don't change his birth certificate.'

'She ain't a she!'

'Well, did you ask her that?'

'What's 'tween Dol and me is between Dol and me, not you, not Charlie.' A pressure elbowed in on Wilson's sternum, her blood vessels constricted. 'What's Dol up to in there, can't you just tell it?'

'You … tell me.'

Charlie reached out and gently pulled the end of Wilson's mullet shag.

'Oh. I know. You are such a mighty snake in the grass. You don't want Dol to have his change.'

'Well, I do,' said Burns, defending himself. 'I want her to, whatever she wants.'

'No, you don't.

Burns slopped his cracked lips with his dry tongue.

'Why you got to go and put a whole bunch of secrets into everything, you lizard?' asked Wilson.

'I'll tell you what, Francine Marguerita, it's you who don't want Dol to finish her change … because then you just be all alone, huh? You don't have prospects. No man in this town wants … is going to climb in bed with a, a, a flatbed truck. Nobody around here wants to spend the rest of their … is going to spend the rest of their lives with a freight train. That's what you are, Miss Wilson. Nobody wants … you can't have a bull rutting on top of a normal person.'

{ *Julie* }
8:21 p.m.

Those folks were still on the front porch and Charlie's Luv was just past them, closer to the road. I made my way behind the building along behind the trash cans and through the drifts alongside the dark next to the building. That flag wire at Maple Elementary was snapping its pole, sounding off like sonar on *Jacques Cousteau*. Past the screen door, I peeked around to get a gander at who it was on the porch – goldarnit if it wasn't Charlie and that refrigerator and Burns shooting it out there.

My sinus pressure forced itself in. I could trudge back the way I came. I couldn't let Charlie and them catch me. I'd freeze to death if I just stood here in this frozen world carrying on. I got down in the snow and let the piles up against the porch hide me. I snaked along there on my belly, not hearing nothing but muttering. The red hood of Charlie's Luv was through some birch ahead. My husband had a way of drawing out and volumizing *on account of* which is what I thought I heard. After a minute of lying there listening, I wasn't sure if I was actually hearing Charlie or the tapes in my head that never let up. I peeked up through the porch railing.

I was going to be sick. Charlie had his arm around that Maytag, his fingers pulling at the strands of her hair. My sternum just about collapsed at how gentle he pet her. Like she was, like she was, like she was. I ducked back down. Like the lizard I am, I scooted between the birch and elm and out to the Luv's tires. And not a one of them saw me turn my face into the raging weather and ease the sharp side of the buck knife right into the rubber.

It didn't give the first time, it was so tough, so I got hold of it and held it just like a psycho-killer slasher and stabbed at it until it gave, and the air hissed out, but like cancer in the early stages you wouldn't know what I done unless you were paying attention to the truck going lopsided some. I could feel the cleansing air on my cheek it was coming with so much force, and the front end sank. Oh, he was going to be stuck now. Now he was going to have to call me to pick him up and I would make him talk to me. Who's got the bigger knife now?

I sat out there on my haunches for a good minute before I got to thinking I had better get on home or I was going to get caught with my pants down. They were still there out on the porch talking and smoking, but I couldn't tell who it was now for sure – I was afraid to look and I didn't know where my anguish ended and real life began, and it didn't matter anyway, if they'd seen me they'd have hollered or come after but they didn't and there wasn't any way I was getting closer now that I got this far, so I snuck off, forgetting all about that little girl waiting for me with them rabbits.

It says something about me that I could leave that little girl there, out there in the cold, but I am not apologizing. I had been driven to the edge of my seat and goddammit if I was then going to be held responsible because some she-man who does not know his rear end from a hole in the ground cannot find a babysitter other than myself. I held on to that knife for better or for worse, and I could feel the weight of the blade against my tummy, and I climbed back up that hill, went along the treeline, back over the fence, slid down the ditch and then up the slope back into the Cutlass. I did it, I made it, Hallelujah, and there I was, of all the people in the world, putting my regrets right out there for the whole world to see and for the blizzard to hit full on, and saying to the world *See, you handed me a man what won't take me straight enough to look me in the eye and a fetus taking root inside of me that I got to rip out fast or the rest of my life is sunk, and I don't want that, I just want to be with my man, and I want to rest and* – I got back into the Cutlass and all that worry over leaving the car there was for nothing because I got back into it and onto the road shiny as linoleum, and I don't think another person had even drove by probably on account of the weather and I got on home without one person ever knowing I had been gone and I was pulling in our driveway when an idea hit me.

In the gut. Oh. Jesus. The snow peaked into dunes over on the east side of the yard. That notion, what came to me the second I put my foot on the porch steps, drove me into those drifts coming around the corner of the house, and from there I could see the lip of the drifts glittering, the way whip cream does sitting in the dark on the counter, like them fields I was looking at before I cut them tires, in the thin glow of Wilson's halogen a ways off, and I understood that I couldn't escape the throw of that lamp if I wanted to, no matter what was said, no matter what was did, no matter what was nothing, and that the yards of snow between where I stepped just then, the kitchen to the right and more and more behind me, were lit white on white since the nights were so pure in winter, and that that illumination inside of me seeped forth like the halogen out through my skin, through my pores, my blood vessels, and that light spreads twice as far in the cold when the weather is freezing and nasty and won't give up for nothing, and I was glad for it even as all the same the path ahead was icy, and next to my skin the blade had gotten cold.

Three months ago our own yard halogen exploded when Charlie was getting a ladder and backed into that shed he's come to take for a barn, and this is – let us not forget – just before the calf came and so you know the good Lord was conspiring against me, and boy do I have His number, and forget about Charlie replacing our bulb, no no no, Little Mr. I-Can't-Open-My-Mouth couldn't bring himself to climb up on a ladder, and the fact that it was *our* bulb that needed fixing, not Wilson's nor any other goddamned light bulb in the whole entire county, the whole entire state, the whole entire country – our bulb was nothing that would reflect upon his oily self because that is what counts when you come to think about it, the reflection, not the source, no, not what creates the light, and if he was really going to get seen, I mean *seen*, it would be on my watch, on our territory, and I'd see him all right, but if that bulb had burnt out anywhere else on the planet he'd be right up on a ladder to replace that bugger. But because it was ours, no.

I couldn't see nothing but the inside of my own rear end then, but I was fighting. I was fighting to distinguish my *me*, my self, because here I am, *I* in *we*. I was fighting to pull *me* from *we* and these two don't come apart. I could pull and pull and I did but it's a tug separating a yolk from an egg. A yolk ain't nothing without the white. That's the pull between *us* and *them*. That's the *I* and the *you*, the *he* and the *she*. When my sister Tammy said she was pregnant she said she felt like the world wasn't just about *her* anymore. Of course she felt that. The world had always been just *her*. It's no mystery. *Us* is our *self*.

At first, the night was cold. Absence sunk in through my coat. If I was in outer space, it might've been that cold. Wilson's yard bulb glittered up the path for me. Ahead, the very tips of the drifts stretched, fingering this way and then that. I kept standing there and the cold did change.

A part of me wanted to trudge out into that mute snow between where I stood and the drifts spiralling upwards out into the fields and out past the shed. The dry freeze lay onto my skin, coating me up and wanting me to stay, fastening me to the earth with nothing changing. After some time, if I were to root, I would spin off over those unsounding mounds of December, seized. What if they chanced upon me tomorrow, after I'd been blown off the path pushed by ferocity? They would light upon me the next day in the brittle sun sticking out of the snow, out there in the back forty, like a popsicle scarecrow, melting freeze pooling at the tip of my blackened nose, and that fetus inside of me pruned up, still clutching its face.

Me and it'd be buried together, me its coffin like Sharon Tate was the coffin of hers, and that terrible story of Barbara Eden in *I Dream of Jeannie*. That her baby died inside her at six months, and she had to carry it to term or she would have died, and God, I thought, that beats all, that just beats all, that poor woman. Yeah, I got His number. If I died out there, I'd be holding it, protecting it from the earth and the groundwater that can't be drunk no more. I'd be protecting it from the fingers of boys and the despair of men. I'd keep it from silences so loud they hush it all and that goddamned harangue that begins with the sun going up.

The idea came to me when I landed my foot on the porch. I bore down on my feet to make them move, one after the other, up the stairs. A pane of glass in the front window had a hole in it. Goddamned kids. I'd go inside, get them lights on and then head on out back. If it's a break-in, tonight is not the night a burglar wants to come across me. I slid the knife out of my pocket.

I turned the latch and tiptoed in. There wasn't nothing disturbed so far as I could tell. The throw pillows were on the couch just the way I left them. No extra lights were on. 'Anybody here?' Then I said it again in case they were in the basement or up in the closet. 'Come out. I won't call the police. Anybody here?' Nothing.

My task at hand leaned down on me. It took time to gather them thoughts in the snow-swept yard. Then in the house, down them tricky back steps, around the side of the house and getting caught in that veil of illumination and opening the quote-unquote barn.

I had to cut quick and not pussyfoot, the calf should not suffer.

$$\left\{ \begin{array}{c} \textit{Dol} \\ \textit{8:25 p.m.} \end{array} \right\}$$

The Smokeeter groans above and the bumblebee smirks, saying how he ought to buy the joint and get rid of this old tin roof.

'What would you do with it?'

'You could run the place, couldn't you?'

'Well, yeah, I could.'

You grin back not because you like the offer but because you're not sure if that is the offer you are here to discuss. Is that the help he's offering? To keep the job you already have?

He jerks his thumb up at the Smokeeter then points over his shoulder. 'That old thing could be replaced, along with those ceiling panels – you know, they're rotted through over the bar.'

'I know.'

'Wouldn't cost – '

'No.'

'I ought to buy this place.'

'Huh.'

'I might.'

'Okay.'

'You know – '

'You don't want to get involved in a place like this.'

'Oh?'

'We're so far away from anything.'

'A half-day's plane ride.'

'A half-day's plane ride.'

'An hour of that is getting out of the Jonesboro airport, a half-day of it if you're coming from Little Rock. Which is good sightseein' too.'

'What? You going to make it into a resort?'

'See?'

'What?'

'You could run it.'

'Run what?'

'A gambling hall.'

'You're going to turn it into a gambling hall?'

'Life takes plans, baby, I'll tell you. Even with a stop at Clinton's birth-place you could put a tour package together for less than a thousand dollars a week. Then I'd know that, after you come back to Bay, you're going to be okay. I don't want my handiwork going to the dogs.'

Your eyes are opened now.

And before you can stop him, your dad thunders down the basement stairs after screaming *For goddamned crying out loud can't I ask you to do anything and can't you just for once do it right all I asked you for was to find a goddamned Phillips-head screwdriver is that so hard?* And, Yes. Yes it is. Yes it is yes it is yes it is. There you are staring at what you know now were drill bits but back then you had no idea maybe they were for chipping at paint it's not like he ever taught you how does he expect you to know everything no you are trapped by not knowing. No doors, no way out. And he's coming at you and you back up the closer he gets because you cannot run he will find you and then you'll really get it *you stupid sonuvabitch call you a son of mine* but here he'll just wallop you one maybe yank you by the hair to get you out of his way and then you have the idea to get out of the narrow workbench get out get out get out but he is coming and if you can get out fast maybe he won't get you but your legs will not move they will not move move move move you are stuck what is wrong with you you surrender accepting and your breath empties ready for the strike and when he gets here it is as if he is still on the stairs but he is here and he's got your neck pushing your eyes at the row of screwdrivers next to the wood chippers, now wobbling in your gaze like heat rising up off the tar on that summer road near Lake Waterloo and he tells you which one is the right one and puts it very close to your eyes explaining about its four prongs like an X or a cross that any idiot could tell it before pushing you out of the tool shed and *Now get the hell upstairs and outside and watch how I'm doing it.*

'I'll bet you could get three to five hundred flying in per week.'

Your eyes are wide, wide open. 'Huh.'

'Yeah, see?'

'I do now.'

You put your straw between your lips, the Coke crawls up to the top, spills onto your tongue, wetting it.

Cummings watches.

You drop the straw back into the glass. 'Oh, I do have plans, by the way.'

Cummings blushes.

You got him.

'You ought to get yourself to Atlanta, is all I'm saying,' he says.

You lean back in your chair, letting the front legs come up off the linoleum. You flutter your aquamarine-eyeshadowed eyelids and sway some to the music. Cummings gets a good look as you roll your fine, narrow shoulders. He covers his bug eyes by squinting. You flit your fingers across your throat and extend your snow-white breastbone. Cummings has the shiny stare of someone who has seen it all.

Wilson says your breastbone is one of your best assets and, if given half the chance, it would support, her words not yours, some real humdingers.

Cummings screws his mouth up.

You fold your hands in your lap. Oh, Atlanta. 'I would move there, believe you me. But what would I do in a city that size besides get lost? I've never been out of Arkansas except to go to college – two semesters. And that Atlanta trip.'

'What was your major?'

'Cosmetology.'

'Really?'

'No.'

'Oh. What was it?'

'Guess.'

'Got me.'

'Try.'

'Microbiology.'

'Not exactly.'

'English.'

'You're warm.'

'History.'

'Cool.'

'English history.'

'Cold.'

'History of English.'

'Oh, for cryin' out loud.'

'Literature.'

'Heating up.'

'English literature.'

'Boiling –'

'American literature.'

'On fire. I took this American essays class. If I ever went back, that's what I'd do.'

'You want to be a writer.'

'Oh – no. I couldn't write a shopping list. No. I could just wrap myself up in H. L. Mencken. You know him? That's okay, you can Google him. Essays are my blanket. All the things folks think of.'

'I don't know anything about them. Like what?'

'Oh, let's change the subject. Atlanta's so big! Two years ago I drove to Little Rock to find where my ex-wife had run off to and I got lost, lost, lost. But I was always going to get out of here.'

'So do it. Then, someday, you can come back and get yourself a little piece of heaven.'

'That's a little thick. We're just this side of heaven.'

'Listen,' says Cummings. 'I'll set you up in Atlanta, put you to work, and when you're settled we'll start in fixing you up. We'll get you started on yams ASAP.'

'Yams?'

'Just a little joke I repeat too often. Progesterone comes from yams. Of course we'll have to do testing to ensure that's the right hormone for you.'

He hunkers so near to the tabletop that his breath produces a vaporous pool there. It blooms and withers as he speaks.

'Yes, and leave your kids with your folks or – ' He pokes at the air towards Wilson out on the porch: 'That fella there. You're buddy-buddy with him, he'll look after them.'

You titter, real hangdog, and say how much you can't stand being away from Squirrel and Pity and shake your head. 'She don't know nothing about kids, let me tell you. But I'd leave them somewhere.'

'She, eh? If that don't beat all. She ought to stay out in the fields. She could pick some cotton. Okee-doke.' Cummings launches up from the table – he's gotten serious, his jaw is tight. 'There you go, that's it. Interested or not?'

He wants you to beg. The colour is draining from your face and you lunge for his arm and tell him no, no, don't go. Okay? You'll have her or somebody look after the kids and you were only kidding, jeez Louise, don't be so sensitive, she's wonderful, fabulous, please don't leave, you're the one chance I got in this life, please. You'll do anything. You bury your forehead into his knuckles. If he doesn't help you, there is no help. You are not above making a spectacle of yourself. You press your forehead further.

The blood flowers in his cheeks. 'Your insurance is gone and I want out of my HMO. We can help each other. You are the key to an important part of my own transition. To corporate independence. But it is going to take a lot from you. HMOs are good for HMOs, corporate for corporate. For you and I, it's got to be tit for tat too, so to speak.' The doctor has gone crude.

You aren't above joking. You nod your head to show how eager you are.

'You come and work for us in exchange for our services. Your services for our services.'

You have been delivered. You can be a secretary, you can take care of the books – you did that for Avery, and although you couldn't type straight through with no mistakes, you are nearly good with the people on the phone, and even though you're from Arkansas you do know the alphabet and and and you you you can file.

He picks at himself saying, 'Uh-huh. Well – '

You know those women working in doctors' offices, sitting behind the counters, all they do all day is roll back and forth on their chairs, pulling files and peeling the plastic wrappers off candies. You ask the doctor if he wants another beer.

No, no, he doesn't want more beer, he wants to know if you two can do business. He doesn't need a secretary or an accountant.

'Well, what do you need then?'

And then he tells you.

'You wouldn't have to do much, bear in mind, and only now and again when we needed it.'

And when you ask what activity is it he tells you that, well, you're going to be dealing with their investors, there's a lot of cash pumping through the health-care system right now, Big Pharma just has loads of it, and a lot of MDs are getting fed up with the system, 'cause they are stymied so often when it comes to helping patients.

'So we're looking to go independent, looking to be entrepreneurs. There was a young woman, twenty-seven or twenty-eight, pregnant, cancer – I could've treated her. You know those Teabaggerin' folks say people like her should go to ERs. ERs are going to treat her? It's not a broken arm. Treatment takes months, sometimes years. She went to free clinics, she got consults with six different doctors – all of whom said they wouldn't treat her without insurance. She had a cervical tumor as big as the day is long. I heard about her from a patient and called her. We did the consult and got her scheduled to start radiation and Cisplatin. I got a hold of my sales rep and asked him to throw me a bone. While it was too late, he agreed to get me the chemo drugs for nothing and I talked to the hospital about treating her. But she passed before we could do much. And there's thousands of those stories.'

Cummings was on a roll.

'Nobody pol wants to fix it 'cause they get so much money from Big Pharma and Big Insurance, so doctors are looking outside the States because the only way out of the managed-care system is to go independent and support yourself and there's enough doctors with us with all our expertise including gender dysphoria that we will get you reassigned and with your assistance keep the stakeholders settled.'

You ask, well, you tell him that you understand his predicament but that you're still, well, not sure what it is, how it is that you can help him, and then he tells you, he tells you you'll have a place.

'A fine condominium, bear in mind, with all the amenities. And there you'll be for when the investors need relaxation.' He gestures like Vanna White showin' a slew of letters.

And, when you were eleven, you crawled side by side with Jay Horn through the blue stem rounding the rim of Rose Lake. Everyone was playing hide-and-seek. He was older, you looked up to him. He paid attention, you were someone. High summer. Dusk. The milkweeds stretching out, one stuck to the other. The light's thick. The two of you lying low in the snake grass. You're lying there, not sure what to do next. You're both listening for the others. A teeny red beetle makes his way over a dandelion bloom. For no reason at all, Jay eases on top of you. He is rubbing and thrusting through your pants. You don't resist, your thinking is all mixed up. You close your eyes, wonder where your brother is. And Jay presses himself into your fanny. You want to fight back now, you don't know why. It feels good and awful. An ant trots to the end of a stalk and, realizing there is nowhere else to go, hurries back from where he came, again to the point of the blade and then to the underside and then speeds all the way to where the stem plunges up from the earth, and though it is now hard to see, from time to time in between your hard exhales you catch a glimpse of that ant climbing up one side and down the other side of clumps of field dirt.

You're scared but too much to cry. Your throat is closed. The chill of the day leans in to the evening.

You haven't thought of that night since the first time you made love to Elaine who had, it turned out, the same indifference to your feeling. To your self.

And you can hardly believe what you've just heard. You don't believe it. You ask again. 'Relaxation?' The bottom falls out of your stomach. 'Huh. For whom?'

Cummings looks at his lap, jamming his thumbs at the skin under his shoulders, and argues but but but you get your gender reassignment and all the Provera you can get your hands on, and you scrunch up your brow because Burns never said nothing about relaxation, and you wonder did he know ahead of time, but he never seemed like that type that would be involved with no malarkey like this, and you even take Pity and Squirrel to him, and then Cummings goes on and says if it means making your dreams come true is it too much to ask and how else're you going to do it, and you don't know, you don't know, you don't know if there's anything else, and you ask are these investors men? And when he says, yes, of course they are, you want to fold up and die, but who is dolled up here, and who egged Jay Horn on, and you're the one with aquamarine eyeshadow, lounging in a gauzy skirt and, come on, that's what you're good for. That's what they see looking at you since time began. A thing to shove up against the wall, a fanny to hump in the field. How is Cummings supposed to know you're just, you're just, you're just like he is, you don't … how was – Burns ought to know that. You are a divorced father of two.

'Excuse me.' You stand. Get your balance, right your heels. Get away, get away. One foot in front of the other now. You look back at him. He scoots up to the table scrunching his shoulders. A betting man, he winks. You tell him you'll be back. You grin, dip your chin and hold a finger up. One little minute. You've forgotten Pity and Squirrel, Wilson has disappeared, the storeroom is ahead.

{ *Wilson* }
8:29 p.m.

Charlie and Wilson found a two-top in a corner of the room. Burns was at his table, his head on his forearms. Next to him, Cummings cast anxious glances from his perch. Lord knew where Dol'd got off to.

On Charlie and Wilson's table lay a ring box, blanketed in velvet.

'Burns don't need to see this,' Charlie whispered. He pried the box loose on account of the sticky table. 'Don't she wipe off these tables?'

'*He*, Charlie. Dol's a he, ain't he?'

'Got me, what's he say he is?'

'I don't think he never said. Only what he wanted to be.'

'If he says he's a he, he's a he to me.' He opened the velvety preciousness.

Gold rays rushed out of the box and flickered in her eyes. The band swooped down and around gentle as one of 'em drifts. Wilson gasped, threw her arms back and punched Charlie.

'It's like Christmas lights.'

'Well, buying this ring, you did bring some beauty to this old ugly world.' Charlie turned it this way and that.

'It's like a, like a itty-bitty bird.'

'Go ahead, take it.'

The tip of her finger was too big to get a hold of it so she got it with the pads of two. Her hands had been shaking all day. So much so that she had to ask Charlie to drive to get the ring.

'Oh my God.' Reaching for the ring, her fingers wouldn't steady. The metal felt soft and warm to the touch. If she squeezed too hard, surely it would dent. In the stone, she saw triangles laid upon Egyptian pyramids upon more crisscrossing cut, and way far back, all the way inside it, even more still. 'It's like the Superman Krypton island.'

'Is that going to do you?'

'I never seen nothing like it, Charlie. Nothing.' A panic came over her. 'Where's Dol?'

'Ain't seen him.'

Burns came out of the restroom, wiping his hands on his slacks. He pulled up a chair like nothing had happened.

'Where's that ... girl of yours?' he asked Wilson.

'Don't know.'

'I just wanted to ... tell you –' Burns noticed the ring. 'Nice.'

Wilson put the ring back in its case. She snapped it shut and put it in her pocket. 'You don't need to be looking at that.' And she tapped his chest so he'd know better. 'You don't say nothing to nobody.'

Burns dragged his chair closer, put his elbows on the table and held his face in his hands. 'Things aren't ... the same since I got bought out.'

Wilson folded her hands in her lap. 'Charlie, tell us what the song says to that.'

'Cry me a river.'

'That's right, cry me a river. Cry me a big ol' river.'

'Goddamned HMOs. In case you don't know, Francine Marguerite, those are Health Maintenance Organizations. But you can't get any old health care in an HMO, you can only get the treatment the insurance company says you can.'

Wilson snorted. 'Goddamned doctors, goddamned HMOs.'

'It isn't doctors. I told Julie, I'd ... you know.'

'What?'

'Take care of, or, you know, do what she thought she wanted done. She wasn't exactly sure yet.'

'You got a big mouth with some things,' said Wilson to Burns.

'You saying that I spoke out of turn?'

'Uh,' Charlie sputtered. He brought his chair in and lowered his voice. 'Can we not talk about that, that we are gonna … we're having it.'

Dr. Burns dug at the floorboards with his shoe.

He knew more than he was letting on. Maybe Julie had got on and got to his office.

Burns thinned his lips. 'Platinum won't let me do … it either way is what I'm saying.'

'It's the law,' offered Wilson.

'Yeah, well, state law this, state law that. I know one or two who's trying to … get around state law, Miss Francine – I am much more sympathetic to your plight than you think.'

'I will – '

'They got a state-funded museum that says dinosaurs … lived at the same time as … cavemen! So now, when you're talking health care, the provider can decide.'

'Ain't you the provider?' asked Wilson.

'No, Platinum Dominion is.'

'The HMO?'

'That's part of them.'

Charlie stared at his flat hand.

'I used to be a provider but now they … got a different board of directors and them from … Kansas got a controlling interest and when they yell the Board jumps. They just made a ruling a couple of weeks ago … that certain services were not going to be offered within their catchment. A while … back there, that's why Avery got rid of his insurance. You know him, he didn't want to lose any of the … folks that come here. He's a small businessman, and Platinum made the premiums so high. He and Dol'd just wait for health care, until thinking and fair … play come back and the curtains were pulled down to show the Jesus freaks for what they are. Of course that's … not what he told Dol or anyone. He's not stupid. That's why Dol don't have insurance. That's why I brought Dr. … Cummings here. There's no good reason Dol or Julie shouldn't get what they need. It's inhuman, it's it's it's it's a witch … hunt on the poor.'

Charlie lost the blood in his cheeks. He was thinking maybe Julie had gone and done it.

'You know,' Burns croaked on, 'I am old … enough to remember when being white was being closer … to God. It's all set up for the high class. You never know, maybe we'll get … all that socialized medicine like Canada. We need … it.' He held his face in his hands. 'I don't know.'

Charlie ventured trying to read Burns' face. 'You know anything else what I should know too?'

Wilson's head was swirling. Burns wasn't about to tell Charlie if Julie had done something she hadn't ought to.

'I don't know nothing.'

Wilson knocked her boot on the floor to get the ice off it. Charlie put his chin on the tabletop. Burns blew salt crystals to the floor.

Wilson meant to get this party going.

'Well, so,' said mouthy-mouthed Burns. 'Now I don't know details of Dr. Cummings' offer. But he's a part of a new organization, Syndicate something, that could let me out of the arrangement with Platinum Dominion. A doctor's faults are covered with earth and rich men's with money.' He turned to take a look at Cummings sitting alone at his table. 'I don't know … him that well. They sure were talking a long time. I don't know where Dol … is.'

'How come the change on Platinum Dominion?' Suspicion got Wilson. 'You said we should be grateful they bought you out. Just on account that some holy rollers climbed on board?'

'Holy … Toledo!' Burns slammed his mug down.

Charlie lifted his chin and customers raised their eyebrows.

'Now I think … you, Francine, are taking advantage … of a good man – Dol is a good man – when he is down. But. But that ain't more … my business than … what it is. And that … is not fair play.'

'How come you want to say that?'

'That ain't the … kind of Jesus-type love I know and if it is I … don't want to know it. They came in … here three years ago and sold me a song and dance about how they'd lower medical costs, keep me in business … and my patients would be able to afford me and they wouldn't have to go to Little Rock. Well, it … hasn't exactly been like that, has it?' By the time he stopped yammering, Burns' fists were squeezed tight and his mouth shut and opened for air like a lake bass in a dry bucket.

He squared off to Charlie.

'Have you … seen the bill for Julie's visit? Have you? I gave her a bill on Tuesday, probably nears a house payment.'

Charlie stuttered. 'No, but ain't it covered?'

'Not if they don't approve what they call a reproduction consultation.'

'But –'

'No, and that is the point. They … ain't going to pay for nothin' no more and at the top of that list are certain activities which … you two are playing with. I'm not a shyster. I'm a doctor, I help people. Under their … thumb, I cannot help people. Bob whatever-his-name-is sits on the … board of Platinum, and then sits on the board of Conquer Care.'

'Conquer?'

'Analgesics, pharmaceuticals. Deciding … not only what I can do, but how I get to treat it and … what I get to treat it with. And they didn't … quite explain it like that. I can't make a man a woman, for cryin' … out loud, but Jesus Christ I used to be able to get my patients to someone who could.'

'Is that what this Atlanta man is about?'

'Hell yes. I don't want to … talk no more. I'm heading home.'

Wilson collared Burns' arm. 'It won't happen?'

'Well, hell no … it isn't, no, I'm talkin' too soon. Cummings might work somethin' out.' Burns sat back down at the table. 'Thing is, see, well, he's got this other syndicate, how do I know if it's better than the … Platinum nonsense? I don't. But he's … got these folks and they think they can … pool enough resources, make them an offer to buy us back from Platinum.'

Wilson furrowed her brow. 'What's it got to do with Dol?'

'I don't know, not the whole … story. And he swore me to … secrecy on pain of the … whole thing falling through.' Burns lifted Wilson's hand from his forearm, gently. 'We just have to wait it out. Sorry, I ain't been back to my office, Charlie. I can't tell … you nothing more.'

He got up and moved sideways through the chairs, landing at Cummings' table.

Wilson clasped her hands.

Charlie stared at his.

She pressed her palm to the tabletop. First thing she ought to do is to find Dol and see what Cummings had to say to her. She was probably digging something out of the storeroom for somebody. She got up.

'Chuck?'

Charlie didn't answer.

'You ought to go home.'

'What'd she go and do that for? Oh, Julie.'

'You don't know she's done anything.'

'I know enough to tell me what my stomach says.'

'Your stomach ain't the facts.'

The pelting'd collected in the window panes.

'I got to go home and feed the calf 'fore it gets too much out there.'

'Go on, then. I got my hands full tonight.'

'A girl's gotta eat.' Charlie put his finger to the dripping glass and drew a stick figure. 'It's cold.'

'Maybe you ought to just go home and say hey to that iron-ore wife of yours.'

'I'm no good for her.'

'Compared to Him there isn't one of us what measure up.'

'Okay. So I'm going to head on out.' He took his coat off the back of the chair. 'Come over later if you want to see how Julie's and my little talk went.'

The storeroom door stood closed. 'Maybe. I got to see what's happening.'

'So, don't cause trouble.'

'Don't you cause trouble.'

After Charlie shut the door, the doorbell tinkle faded and conversation increased. Wilson headed straight for the storeroom door. Dol's purse was open on the bar.

{ *Dol* }
8:31 p.m.

You can't believe it. You can't believe it, you can't believe it, you can't believe it. You can't believe it, you can't believe it. Go, get up. Where? That doorknob. Get in the storeroom keep it in keep it in keep it in keep it in keep it in keep it in. Get inside shut the door believe you're safe. You repeat, rapid-fire, Mencken's advice that no man ever completely believes another, there's always a sip of doubt that is half from animal nature and the other half from logic – the trouble with the world is that we display our inner sentiment even after we have been betrayed. Contrary to popular opinion, women are much better able to keep their sentiments to themselves.

Mencken. Bring it home. Cut you open, cut you bare. Pour it out, flood the street. Go, went, gone. Fly, flew, flown. The mind clears, you clench your fists. Oh, they, your hands, were getting so tiny, so reedy, so grass-like, now they've gotten fat and these thick calves bearing unbearable bulging muscles. You catch your finger pads on the unstoppable stubble punching through already.

God, God, God. You press your forehead into the door. Pity and Squirrel are asleep in the car, their faces, the texture of their skin, the fight to yank the day their way, your rescue sits with them, you have no clue.

There is a plan. A plan, a plan, a plan. The plan was, the plan was. Bring it home, bring it home, bring it home.

Now you know, Jesus Christ, you know now, Holy Jesus Mother of God, Archie Betty Veronica. You think you picture it okay.

'Dol? Hon? It's me.'

Wilson.

'Dol? Your purse is just out here on the counter. And that handsome preacher is snoopin' around askin' about you and the kids.' You pop a bottle of Freixenet.

You break into low-slung song. 'The Wichita Lineman is still on the line, I know I need a small vacation – '

'Dol?'

'But it don't look like rain – '

'Dol, Dol?'

'And if it snows that stretch down south won't ever stand the strain, and I need you more than want you – '

'Come on, hon.'

'And I want you for all time, and the Wichita Lineman – '

'You're crazy.'

'Is still on the line – '

'You want me to just leave your purse out here on the counter? I can. I can just leave your purse open out here on the counter. If you want.'

'And I need you more than want you and I want you for all time.'

Here's what's ahead for you.

You look like a million bucks. You've gotten yourself dolled up. You wait. Watch a battalion of stratocumulus slink east to home. You cross your legs, admire your calf muscle that flows to the thinnest slip of an ankle. Silk hose poured onto creamy leg. Goddammit. You're worth it. You sip. The champagne nibbles at your cheek. You know exactly how it will go. You are frozen. You are in a dream.

The doorbell dingles, you voice-activate.

'Yes.'

'Ms. Heyer?'

'Yes.'

'Ms. Heyer, there's a gentleman here to see you.'

You stand. Move to the window where sunlight cuts the Veuve Clicquot into twigs of light twisting on the pale lime carpet. You empty your eyes. Down there, people are ants.

'Yes.'

'He's ... '

'White?'

'Yes.'

'Balding?'

'Yes.'

'An American flag?'

'In his lapel.'

'Yes. Am I on speakerphone?'

'No!'

'Don't you know who your senators are, Dennis?'

'Should I send him up?'

'What do you think?'

'What should I tell him?'

'I don't know, Dennis.'

'Yes, ma'am.'

'Say what's right, Dennis.'

Dennis signs off. You swallow, check your lipstick. Your hair is swept up for a letdown. Your backside's firm, your stomach sunk. Show your teeth.

Undo your blouse, open the door. In comes the senator. Eyes bold with Blefora, he goes straight to the windows. He shakes one drape, then the other. His infrared vision traces the balcony, the doors and the living room pile. Lifts the sofa, puts it down. Turns the tube on, turns it off. Bedroom doorway. Scans the spiced-peach rug, fondles the closet door. Closes his eyes. Uses fingertips to scan for microscopic microphones. The Plantation Princess sleep set.

'May I remove this endearing canopy?'

'Is this foreplay?'

Climbs on the bed, jerks the canopy.

'Excuse me.'

'I'm not saying you'd sell dirt on me – it's what I've got to do. In a position of power.'

'Do what you have to do, tiger.' You fold your arms, lean against the door jamb. You admire the flags of the G8 including Georgia and Arkansas and Texas that Madame Wong painted on your nails.

'I couldn't take anything for granted as CIA, don't ask me to now.'

'Wouldn't dare.'

'We don't mess around.'

'Got it.'

'If you know what's good for you, you won't try to pull anything on me, I tell you. There was more than one swamp I swam, knife in teeth, target in sight.'

You fold and unfold your fingers. 'That is so interesting.'

'Yes'n I'll tell you. My life is not so different now, sister. Brother, sister. The only reason I got out is there's no dough.'

Kitchen. He's turned the nuker to the wall now. He watches you watching him. Tap on, tap off.

'Got anything in there? Eh, little lady?'

'You tell me.'

He slides up to you, arms stretched, belly spilling over, hair stickier than yours. Aquanet.

'Okay, let's do this,' you throw out.

'Bend over, baby.'

Your mind wanders. Madame Wong, sugar, fingers, pecks.

The senator dreams too. About appropriation, which wets his eyes, about chairmanship, which scares him stiff, about what he'll do when it's all over.

You comfort him with a finger in his backside. The thumb, the U.S. flag – he's a patriot. Poking in rhythm.

You. You know Pity and Squirrel are going to need. New. Clothes. For. School. Squirrel has walked. All over the cuffs. Of his pants. Fraying them to nothing. Got to be. Replaced. More food goes on him than in him. He's going to need. At least two weeks'. Worth. Of T-shirts. And whatnot. Pity. Is in. Terrible shape. She doesn't pay any attention to what impression she's making and by her age she ought to know better.

The senator's a patriot. He's close and, before you know it, done.

After, you shut the door, feel the cool drywall, your shoulder chills.

'Dol?'

A whisper follows a knuckle rap.

'Dol?'

A fresh cut of meat to burn.

'I was on my way by. The kids're out in the car. Dol? Don't you think it's cold out there?'

A distracted voice, monosyllabic, paternal.

'Who do you think you are, bothering me this way?'

'Well – I –'

'You what?'

'It's Father Tibs.'

'I know who it is.' There is a long pause as the patriarchy shoves itself in. 'I ain't Catholic.'

'Yes.'

'I ain't –'

'It's cold out there. And I was driving past and saw all that exhaust your car was making.'

'Mind your own business.'

'I think you ought to open –'

'Bet you do. Mind your business, padre.'

'Walter –'

'Don't.'

'Dol. The kids're –'

'I'm not a puppy.'

'Right.'

'So stop talking to me like a dimly lit chihuahua.'

'Right.'

'Whoever you're trying to impress by showing up here –'

'I could take Pity and –'

'Uh, they're fine where –'

'Walter –'

'DOL!'

'Dol. They're freezing to death out there, ain't they?'

'They know how to work the heater.'

A pause. 'Well. I've kept a lookout for you.'

'Ho, ho! Don't strain yourself.'

'This community is the fragile butterfly I hold in my hands. It's my duty to protect it, to nur–'

'What horse did you ride in on? Who elected you?'

'I ain't –'

'Y'aren't!'

'I am not going anywhere until –'

'Mister –'

'You can call me Father Ti–'

'I don't bother you at your work, don't bother me at mine.'

'Right. So come on out.'

'I have work to do.'

'You can do it with the door open.'

What a piece of work. Clam up. Sit on Tia Maria and Jim Beam. Close your eyes.

'Dol? I've got a mind to take the kids –'

Enough. You swing open the door. 'Father, I do mean the disrespect. Have a good look. Now. What do you want to say, what words of patricidal malintent would you like to say that you haven't already said? That you are compelled to drop into my lap because I've locked myself in a storeroom?' Out of the corner of your eye you glance to see if Cummings is still sitting there. He is. Your purse is on the counter behind Tibs, you point to it. 'Hand that to me.'

Father Tibs clamps his pincers on the purse. 'We have excellent childcare providers –'

'Well. Good. I'll – '

'I could call one of them now. I have a friend who – '

You have got to be let alone to think.

'You know what, Mr. Tibs? That is great. For a Catholic you sound like a good one. Someday I'll take you up on it. Okay? Thanks.'

'I just wanted to make sure – I could – '

'I am.' Trace the grain of the pressboard with your nail. Flip off the light switch. Pitch black.

'Wilson was – '

You step backwards.

' – concerned.'

'Yes, well. That's the story.' The black folds over your shoulders, your chest, and you disappear.

And the darkness inside is like sliding under that seething organic blanket that others call *you* or *Walter*. You can hear the padre moving off after a moment and while you are lingering there, as smell picks up for sight, as touch tentacles out, the mind opens to knowing.

It is not just the blindness of people not seeing you. *You* has always been seen yet *I* never has. *I* herself has only peeked out of her grave. Up to now, physical sensation let *I* into the world for just the teensiest instants. She has never been seen nor never known. Not by one person. Maybe by the dogs or Grandma or God. Maybe.

When you were little and your father would drop you off at your Grandma's, when your mother would be under the weather, a cloud-covered Sashabaw Road would rope around you and the oxygenless blue universe, tying you into the '72 white Impala, as Grandma's low-slung white ranch would backslide into view, the oak trees lining the ditch between you and her dropping away, and once you pull into the driveway, the automatic garage door climbing with a titanic purr, the sunlight, then, bleaching the Pennzoil-stained cement backfiring with just-cut grass into your face, flooding your nose, and then, when the rattling door got high enough, the torn screen door with the bent pine frame whacked back against its hinges, and Grandma leans out, gripping the moulding in her no-sleeve blouse, the skin from her arm flapping when she sees your dad holding back, not climbing out, and then you, the blood rushes to her face, seen even at the distance between you in the driveway and she at the door, waving you to her, and the skin flapping faster even as she swats flies away before, as is the way, hiding the flush of your faces in each other's necks, and having admitted in that glance something safe before burying it, lunging past her into the bacon-soaked kitchen, the screen door now whacking shut, the garage door grumbling down, something to not be spoken in front of the whole family.

And later they are all gone to Farmer John's and you call the dogs in, lying on the floor, your huskies around your ankles, and you put your fanny near their snouts to sniff to exist to lick to feel, and they stick their tongues in and their noses are cold, because your life depends on it, and it is here that you glimpse, for the teensiest instant, your eyes shut tight, your ears peeled wide for sounds of curtains withdrawing into the world, like peeking into a gorgeous room and squirming on the floor, too, until finally you push the dogs away.

You cannot stop yourself because in the end you are only human. Your mother didn't touch you, your hero humps you, your brother tickles you and you reduce what it is to live to the body's capacity for awareness, out of necessity, because you will die if you even think there is more beyond. There is something like a faint mist that makes Cummings' proposal different than these teenage encounters. Both are about the body, but the former was a seeking for affection, for comfort, for recognition that you existed at all. Cummings' offer bifurcates who you are, what you think is right, the esteem to which you are entitled. The curtain is coming down.

And what becomes known is this: a human must be seen, must be touched and must matter, or she ceases. And every cell in the body will be in cahoots to prevent her from shutting out existence in the world, for if not in this world then not of this world, and then no longer human. And so to be touched, to be seen, to be recognized, becomes the one way to be human, to breathe, to exist at all. Blistering love, the very fat lining your cell walls, keeps the shit, the putrescence, that is *you* from *I*. And you are expected to identify it as *I* but it is no more *I* than that cock you pray to displace. Bifurcation. Cummings will weld you and your body together. The cutting, the splitting apart you from the body, will wed the body to *I*. And someday, when it is time, *I* may rise, unfurling herself and displaying her magnificent wings. Nothing but being seen and known pumps blood to the heart. Nothing.

You have only imagined *I*. Without *I*, *you* cannot exist. *You*, an imposter, has cast *I* aside. *I* is over there now. What *I* sees from a yard or two off, just out of reach, is an extra body that was produced the day you were born while *I* was shelved. Your body is searching for *I*. So far, there is only perpetual distance, perpetual longing, perpetual *you*.

Now, all you amount to matters. In order to matter, to become matter, in order for *I* to exist at all in the world, *you* must lose its foothold in the world and disappear. The cut means she will become matter and he will – Step away. Fold him back into the idea from which he thrust himself. He never was. He thrust himself into *you* so that *I* could not breathe, so that *I* could not be seen, so that *I* would never be recognized. He will die in that operating theatre. He will lie there unable to rise, unable to see, unable to punch, unable to be. My hands won't grip, my muscles won't serve, my heart won't betray. Decay will begin. But there it is. There it is.

The supplanting of *I* so that *you* can die. For *I* to be *her*, *you* must be *him*. This is what Cummings wants. You must get on your knees and surrender to that other god that shaft that is nothing but muscle and sinew and bloody viaducts for splitting open the world. This is the state of things. You may not inhabit yourself, you may not breathe, you may not live peacefully. You will bend over.

The senator will finger you with Astroglide or Wet or his spit. The senator will get himself hard watching your round posterior in the air. When he is ready, he will take his hand, letting the cum ease back enough to stay erect, and he will place the head of his swollen cock at your door and he will push enough to get past the muscle and you will gasp and take him in and your fingers will extend before curling as the body makes room and then the muscles will unlock and you will breathe and take your mind off before reaching around behind you with Madame Wong's American flag. *I* will need to take it up the rump and forget. To exist at all.

Hoo-da-la, what matters always sickens one at first glance. And so what was revolting becomes acceptable. In order for *I* to be born, *you* can't matter. You have to take it. If Cummings is going to do it then you must. Ah, hoh, but, but you don't need him. You don't. *You* know, now, what it is to matter.

On the top shelf is the house booze. And you know what you have to do. You don't know if you can. Oh God. Okay okay okay. You can do this. If you do it. It will be done. You are not inhuman. You are not a dog. You are a human being. They will have to fix it. But it will be too late to sew you back together. You will be unusable to Cummings. You will send him off and, and, and *I* will matter, *I* will exist, *I* will be recognized.

If you fail then there'll be that low-slung brick funeral home where everyone ends up and the room where they'd keep your body is all enamel cinderblock casting a urined pall over your skin. You will have died eyes open so Peach Michael will have to sew the lids down to the bottom row of eyelashes, it's what he's gotten good at since most people around Bay pass eyes open, and you'll be the same and he'll dust you good, there'll be no need for cutting further and the organs'll be intact since you don't see a reason to donate God's gift to scientists, so you'll be there in a coffin and your kids'll be able to look at you, at it, and Pity is old enough to be cursed right away as to why she couldn't help never understanding until much later, if ever, but Squirrel'll have to wait for his suffering, he'll just wonder where you got off to.

The door bells tinkle, the jukebox thumps. The light from out in the bar leaks under the door. The daddy-long-legs in the corner freezes, suspicious. The cobwebs hung ragged. The floor is scuffed, the boxes sag. You sit. The metal casing cool to the touch. Feel the X-acto and the crate of Tia Maria. Pity probably slumped in the front seat out there, Squirrel in back. Their skin lit in the yellow dome glow of the car. Their sweet breath vapourizing in streams. Gnats and flies a couple feet from you piled up where the walls meet, good and dried dead.

Your blood, roiling now, lurches upward. Your aorta pumps it through, fear hurtles quicker. Thumb out the grey blade, free your waistband. You breathe. The skirt slips to your ankles, the panties below the knees. If the thing is hard, then the blade has something to grab on to.

Light change. Under the door. You don't want to look. You do. Two boots breaking the light. The boots are affixed to breath. Quiet your breast. Under the door, the boots shuffle. The glow blinks Morse code at you.

A knuckle rap. The door frame creaks.

'You know I'm here, I know I'm here. Now –'

Wilson.

'Don't listen if you don't want to. Dol, I got something for you here. I got a little something.'

You lean back and the boxes cut into your spine, you fold your ankles and you rest the X-acto knife on your stomach rising and falling like the top of Rose Lake. The thing between your legs withdraws from the chill.

'You know I think the world of you. More than the world. And I know you got stuff you got to do. This fancypants out here looks like he's getting antsy. Let me in, Dol. I got something to ask you which I don't want to do out here.'

You hold your stomach tight, your breathing strict.

'I got a little something for you, Dol. I have a big thing to ask you. Charlie helped me with it. I can't say it 'cause I don't know what you're going to say about it.'

You listen. You do. Your stomach is moving to sick. You hold yourself tight.

'We've known each other forever. And are going to forever. You look out for me like I'm special so it got me thinking I could help you. But don't think it's charity. It ain't. I really want it. I mean, it'd be charity if I's talking about insurance. Well, I am talking about insurance and I'm not talking about it. If we were to do it, I could put you on my coverage and Vincent says my insurance'll cover your change. So, look, I'm getting ahead of myself but see I got this thing I want to ask and I ain't going to say it while there's a door between us 'cause it ain't right but I'm going to ask you soon as you walk through it and show me your beautiful eyes. Dol. Dol, I never knew that you was so, so, so deep – You're the best thing, Dol. It was like for the first time, there you were. You know I didn't think it was true. You know how you lie to yourself. But I did. I woke up like I never seen you. You could say it's like a healing but it ain't, I ain't sick. I couldn't see. It ain't like I ain't seen my whole life. You're just the the the the person I never seen. And I ain't just saying that 'cause I don't know what you're planning with this bozo out here. He don't look good to me, you got to be careful. People like Burns. They can try and put two and two together. You maybe can't trust him as far as you can throw him.'

Wilson's voice wobbled.

'I don't know why you won't come out and talk to me. I sure feel like a piece of work. I don't not think some little nothing of you. Pity and Squirrel're like my own. They could be. You know. I know it now. Tanya and Michelle're running around like wild animals and if I didn't take care of them who was going to. You remember when you taught them how to put on their Maybelline eye pencil? You can't say we don't go together. And if you did I'd shout you down. I would. Charlie's gone on home. He's probably there right now with his little lady finding out how hard it is to get Pity and Squirrel to sleep. It's hard, ain't it? Julie wasn't so bad, was she? She's a piece of work but once you get past her heart shrivelled like a prune she's nothing but a teeny calf herself.

'I just think you ought to come out here like I asked you to so I can give you something. I ask you something, you say yes or no, and then we'll be on our way. You can go right back to your Atlanta knight or back here – in the liquor closet.

'I ain't in general going to pin you down. I ain't saying there isn't nothing in it for me. There is. I get to be queer. How about that? Ain't that a lifetime aspiration? That is something I did not see coming. Well, how about that. Can we live in Bay together? I don't know. I don't. But they know us here and ain't nobody here's got anything against us. If they loved somebody, Dol, every one of 'em'd go queer too if they had to. Maybe they wouldn't. Maybe they'd kill themselves. I ain't going to. I'm proud of you. It's like love picked me. I was going about my business. Like everybody else.

They will hold us in high esteem. And treat us kindly. And if they don't, well, who wants to be at a party where you ain't invited?'

And so it is that again you remember something of your father. Oh, God help us all. Fifteen. At your dresser. Standing mirror. Your eyeliner isn't straight. Dad opens the door. By accident. He shuts the door. The eye pencil is stuck mid-stroke. He comes back in. He questions you. You tell him. Nothing. You ain't doin' nothin'. He snatches your hair and drags you out of the house. It hurts. Your blouse falls open, the wind bites. Your heel catches on the stair, comes off. You have his arms tight. You will not yell between the one heel you have yet and no traction over the driveway, through the ditch and into the woods. A ways in deep, he stands you just to the other side of a couple of maples.

'Look at you.'

You can't take your eyes off him. He lunges at you, you cover yourself. He gets your shirt at the seams and tears it. He gets the scarf off your head and it catches on his boot tie. Your lousy stinking dress skirt, your stockings the shade of shit and goddamn it to hell your panties come off and are cast onto twigs twisted together.

'Now, look at you. Ain't a game, is it?'

He teeters back away a couple of steps, his chest heaving hard, unable to catch his breath. Ever so slowly, so you wouldn't catch it if you weren't looking, his finger rises till it is aimed up. His eyes get yours as he tells you up there is the sky and this here's down here and you are what you are, son. He pivots and limps off with that finger dropping slower than slow.

You stand there watching him disappear in the trees till it gets too cold and you run back to your room under the blankets till your bones let go of chill – not long before Wilson comes and gets you for work.

And when the X-acto blade slid through the skin, the building shivered in the smacking wind. The muscle separated easier than you thought and it was only a sting, not the cut you thought, but it never is what you think at all. No. That comes in a moment. That came. When you heard Wilson knocking, asking for your hand.

'Hon?'

{ *Charlie* }
8:43 p.m.

Now hes goin to have to order brand new tires goddammit. Even in a podunk town in the armpit of Arkansas in the suck middle of a snowstorm you got hooligans and nincompoops runnin around like wild animals pickin his Luv Most specially in the armpit of Arkansas

Peach Michael the funeral director was on his way to pick up a body from the county morgue Charlie flagged him down on the road outside Averys It wasnt anyone from Bay but Peach had to get over there before the night shift went off When they pulled up to the house he saw the Cutlass still sittin there But the snow was meltin on the hood The lights were on She might have went out huntin him As Peachs rear lights faded Charlie hustled through snow hills made his way to the shed A long way off a rooster was howlin

Was that his boots scuffin or his girl snortin Hed go check on his little lady and screw himself up to go face the big one In the shed Charlie got down on his knees in the grit hay The cement boned into him

Oh it felt so good to take a load off *Come here girl Jesus Christ*

The cold raw cement floor come through his coat pushin his eyes into that architecture of frost layerin at the wall and then to that two by four where hed tied his ol girl Snug bull knot is what to use He blew on his fingers thawin them out so he could get them into the knot

Poor girl all lonesome in here aint you

He puckered his lips at his teeny lady buttin her nose and chirped at her as he picked at the knot

Cause she was a good girl she was bein a real good girl stayin all by herself out here and listen to it out there

The wind hotfootin in from over the back forty was whackin a chain like poundin a steel spike He got a hold of the unyielding piece of rope and rubbed it back and forth burnin the sides of his finger to loosen it up

Julied never gone after him till the girls left He never knew she wasnt right with things till that day the girls drove off He didnt know How was he was supposed to know

How was I supposed to know If you dont say nothin what do you expect Boy that was a rude awakenin

But then they had been blessed

Aint they When Julie come home pregnant and she was hidin that paper Burns give her like it was a secret prize She wanted to keep it from him There werent nothin to talk about was there What the hell has gone on in this world that killin a baby is a choice

Back when Tammy was goin to have that kid and they told her there was plenty of folks whod jest die to have a little baby for their own

You have the baby and then make sure it gets a good home

It isnt a stray dog

Aint a stray dog Whatre you talkin about

It will be a B A B Y Charleeeeeeeuh She insisted with a shake to her voice like he was a couple bricks short of a wall Spellin it at him like he was some kind of bullfrog

A baby Charlie Her whine pierced his hearin

It aint goin to be the first and it aint goin to be the last one

Since when do you care so much about babies Charlie huh Since when How much time you put into them girls Zero Z E R O Charlie

That damned knot wouldnt give He scratched right in that tender valley behind the calfs ear Folks jest had no idea what they were doin They jest dont know Ever since it didnt matter no more if you got kids at home or not or if you had a husband to care for or if you had home responsibilities and they put the Integration in and we had all them negro kids in school ever since then and when you had them National Guards gunnin down them kids and ever since you got the queers you got the Mexicans and you got the Womens Libbers and everybodys got somethin that keeps them separate from the otherns so now we dont have nothin together do we Babies now theyre the ones dont have nothing

The knot could use some more length He breathed on it to warm it

We dont have nothin huh We dont have nothin You goin to be okay girl Dont you know your daddy is with you

But the calf kept on listenin followin the pitched squeeze of the wind that squealed out and then stole further beyond earshot cuttin through Wilsons whippin barbed wire and the little sweet animal twitchin now and relaxin a little and then twitchin again when that chain rattled the steel wall Floatin hay slivers twisted and washed in the rays of lamplight

Stuff jest gets kicked up ol girl It all falls away You goin to be okay little girl

He could follow the slammin weather right into the wall where it shook the steel and attacked them rivets It just might bring it down if it kept up

Then what we goin to do huh girl then what we goin to do We goin to sit here aint we We goin to sit here and make us feel better and ifn it all comes down Well we will jest be sittin here when they come find us

He got a bit of rope from around the two by four

That aint as tight no more is it How much time do I put into you huh sister How much

He pulled the calf towards him The animal took a few clodhops

Thas a good girl Ill help you

He pushed on the small space between the shoulder blades

Come on

Her kneesd bend some but she wasnt givin

Youre a strong one aint you

He pushed harder

Come on

The girl wasnt havin none of it

Jesus Christ look at you Who do you think feeds you Where do you think that water comes from You think the old ladys goin to come out here and put feed out for you

The calf stepped back and regarded him cockeyed

What you lookin at me like that for I aint the animal

The calf stood off from Charlie watchin him She stuck her neck out and down so the scratchin would get deeper then she twisted her neck too long for her trunk lookin away from Charlie then when the sheet walls rattled she flinched and pulled away

Charlie pushed into the neck but it didnt do no good

The calf resisted so he let up and then the calf listened and swung its head towards the door its ears lifted up like them big dinosaur leaves in *National Geographic*

Charlie shoved down again *The wind is jest the weather*

But the animal snatched herself out from under his hand and he shot his head back She peeled back her lips to show her teeth then droppin them just as fast

Jest lay down in my lap for cryin out loud

The baby girl shunted the trunk of her neck right and left and stepped up to Charlies outstretched legs and waited

Thats a girl

He got his arms as far around her as he could and drew her towards him and she let herself go slack and he eased her into his lap When she come down on him with her full weight she mightve broke his femur

What you doin

He could barely breathe

Jesus youre gettin big

It hurt

Christ

Usin his hand as leverage he pushed her up enough by the shoulders to get his legs out from under

Holy Jesus

Her cheek cranked out the BTUs He stroked it The fur there the same as the fuzz comin up on the side of Julies face seein as her hormones were changin again Her right eye black as Vernita Lee wheeled back in its socket keepin an eye on him

That rooster called out again and the caterwaulin slipped in under the door

Hoo boy baby I will tell you You know whats goin to happen You know dont you You know cause youre an animal of the earth Youd know when somethin bads goin to happen Right

Hed read an article in the paper that said all the cattle around a volcano knew it was goin to go They all wandered off Wasnt no way they was goin to stay and get burnt up

The calfs eye didnt move and Charlie couldnt even tell if she was lookin at him anymore But her chest chest was risin and fallin

Youre the future aint you Youre whats goin to happen to me He had got to prepare hisself She might have already done it

Later on hed get up from under her and leave on the night light after all she was a baby and hed go inside and tell Julie he was so sorry for not talkin but he didnt see any point in goin on Hed go in and shed be watchin the TV No she wouldnt shed have her feet up on the couch and the livin roomd be dark and hed go in and the only light shinin where she was lyin would be the spill from the kitchen bulb and shed be layin there her skin the tint of an old blackboard there in the shadow and hed sit down and tell her theyd had some good years and how come she wouldnt jest wait for him to get ready to come talk to her cause he would have removed the burden from her and jest allowed himself He wouldve taken on the baby himself but she wasnt havin none of that was she and so there they were now at this crossroads and he supposed it was time she go his way and hed go his own

What So Wilson can park her fat tuckus on my couch

Julie cant I be civil

Civil

Aint I tryin Why you got to make it so hard

You wanna see hard fella You think youre bringin all your chickypoos into my house eatin my food and sleepin in my bed

Julie

You want me to cut the throats of you your chickees your moocow Every last one of you Charlie

Jesus

You want me to

But then it could go another way

Charlie saw them all a happy family in the summer livin room like there wasnt no disagreement never Naw like it had been okay all along And it had been okay since Julie unfolded her arms and boy he could jest see her all propped up and swollen her belly biggern a watermelon biggern a bale of hay with the biggest baby theyd had yet and he could jest see her in the chair with a grin a mile wide on her face lovin that she was about to give birth cause she patted his arm and told him thats what a womans for

Naw you do a lot hed say

But shed correct and say of course she knows better *Its just that a womans built to bear her man children Thats jest the way it is Charlie I cant escape it You cant escape it No one can*

And hed pull out a jar of cocoa butter and pull off the lid and theyd both sniff it and conjecture on the poolside vacation they were takin once the baby could travel and theyd go to Puerto Vallarta and relax there by the beach and theyd sniff the cocoa butter in the air there and it was his pleasure to rub it gently into her stomach and all around her stretched middle and then as a treat hed gotten her pink mint foot lotion jest as a present cause thats the kind of husband he was and all her friends were always teasin they were jealous but hed stay there on his hands and knees and rub her feet

And jest then the doorbelld ring and itd be Wilson comin in to pay her respects with flowers and a video tellin them how to keep the baby happy and even though they already had two kids itd been a long long time and she didnt think theyd be insulted if she brought this along which shed seen on TV and thought you never know maybe theres new information they could use and bein information gatherers you and Julie are always hungry to learn more to understand more to expand your horizons and youd take it

And nod to Wilson with the weight such a gift deserves and then youd all laugh cause Julies in the chair swollen biggern a Cadillac Wilsons next to her bearin gifts and flowers and who wouldve ever thought that wouldve happened and there you are rubbin the pink lotion into her feet and then here comes the calf comin right in stickin her head in through the kitchen and oh look at her shes chewin a bunch of flowers Julie shes brought you a bouquet of yellow daisies how she got up those creakin back stairs thinner than the hair on his mamas head nobody knows but the calf did and she should cause shes a part of the family shes no different than you even Julie and all of you hold each other laughin and cherishin the moment cause thats the kind of folks you are One big happy family the way you always saw it

But then there were other things thatd come from Julie havin the baby too First hed be there unpinnin the sides of diapers makin sure it all stays in you got to do that and whew this kids been eatin somethin and Julied tease him sayin *Its about time You*

The next that came to mind was how hed always thought Julied make a good Barbara Walters bein a curious girl and he meant that mainly why couldnt she go back to school hed be all for that once their baby was a teenager and this time around he was goin to pull his weight sure why not Julied go to school and become a reporter on TV hell he didnt see a reason why she couldnt work at that station in Jonesboro Theyd be lucky to have her and with all her life experience shed ask the right questions and have the wisdom that raising three kidsll give

Yes

And Charlie didnt see why she wouldnt probably become famous interviewin world leaders and celebrities The president would be their friend hed have to be seein what real people they were Probably shed become a confidante to people like the president and the governor and Oprah and especially cause well Julies got a more rock solid home life than that one on the *Today Show* or the one on *Primetime Live* Not a one of them got a rock of a marriage or kids even is what it says in those movie magazines Julies got stuck all over the living room or the insight really or the vision that you cant help but take from it You got to admit that Julied have insight the others wouldnt have And that was somethin that would affect their lives

And he was ready And he sure hoped she would Oh hell of course shed be ready especially once the little one was grown up practically to a teenager And he wouldnt mind takin the majority of the load Hed be retired then And he could even help her out

The door shook hard as the storm slugged away at it It jest might take this thing down Charlie thought You cant never tell The whole way the weathers goin When he was a kid nobody wouldve dreamed of seein snow in Arkansas but it aint that way no more And Dol wearin a miniskirt Everythin gets to be regular after a while Folks get used to anythin Get used to gruntin at Tanya and Michelle Get used to Julie sourin his stomach Get used to his disappearin

Oh jeez he thought way back when maybe his daddy told him the story he couldnt remember exactly but there was the Choctaw that lived all in through this part of Arkansas which was a miracle by itself with the history shovin them around Wasnt named the Razorbacks back then His daddyd told him it wasnt nothin to see Choctaw or Quapaw men dressed up like women Said one time his granddaddy had been sittin on the sidewalk waitin for his daddy across the way There was planks of wood back then this musta been way way back maybe in the teens or twenties And he was sittin there and one of them Injuns come and sit next to him wearin a dress and beads and carryin a sack of cornmeal You never saw Injuns in town They didnt need no town back then So granddaddyd never seen a real one before This one come to town to get some supplies on account of there warnt no rain so the corn wouldnt come and he come into town to barter for cornmeal Well and now this Injun never seen all these folks neither Lots of men had a lot of time on their hands what with their crops dried up and nowhere to go so theyd come into town and stand around to see whats what and if there was any prospects So a lot of men was standin around lookin at the Injun Gatherin and lookin and spittin their chew and so on Course the Injun was lookin at everyone lookin at him too And so there was his granddaddy sittin on the sidewalk planked out of two by fours and of all the places to set down the Injun sat down next to his granddaddy They said some words back and forth the way folks do to little boys *It ought to rain* They all lookin at you They never seen an Indian and so forth Then the Injun asked him if he was a Believer or what

I aint a what Whered you get your English

Im same as you almost

How come youre dressed like that

I aint dressed like nothin

Like a woman

Aint a woman

You dressin like it

Dressin like me

Huh

You heard of Two Spirit people

Nope

Now you have

The two of them sat there a few minutes one listenin to the breath of the other Each decidin if they were goin to make a friend or somethin else Great granddaddy started crossin the street comin at them after his shoppin The Injun got to his feet went to the water tub and got himself a dipperful of water When he drunk it he smacked his lips aahin like a pet shop bird and wiped his face with the back of his arm Before he walked off he said he was near to an owl only wiser Like a horse only faster Like a man only braver *Like a woman only sweeter* Then he took off

His granddaddys daddy yelled out to him to kindly move off from the Injun what aint goin to do him no good Granddaddy said he never come across him again Once the Indians became Baptist two spirits disappeared A whole gaggle of Baptists flooded in then and the whole way Injuns lived turned upside down God dont like two spirits men in skirts

Guess thats just the way it is Charlie thought *People come and go Whats right and wrong comes and goes* Oh he ought to go in the house and talk to her

$$\left\{ \begin{array}{c} \textit{Wilson} \\ \textit{8:43 p.m.} \end{array} \right\}$$

Maybe Dol wasn't in the storeroom at all. Wilson pressed her forehead into the door. For crying out loud, he couldn't've gone far. This Atlanta fella was still waiting. Huh. She'd bet the best side of a slice of bacon that Dol was in the parking lot or out back. He got right by Wilson without her even seeing – oh, that sneaker.

But Dol couldn't've got past her. Wilson jammed her hands into her back pockets. She wasn't worried – she wasn't. She hadn't been nowhere 'cept here and out there on the front porch. Ain't no way no one could've got past her. My God, she ain't blind. She stood right there, didn't she? Didn't she stand right there jabberin to Charlie? Well, where is he then? Wilson herself sat just right there at that four-top, right there, looking at the ring Charlie brung. She retraced her steps, every one of them. But maybe Dol did get past her, maybe he did. Wilson put her lips, and then her ear, up against the pressboard door. 'Dol? Hon?' I'm going to go around and see if you're out back. You out back? Say something, you in there? If you're in there, say something. Don't be foolin', say something if you're in there.'

Wilson squeezed between Dol's chair and Vernita Lee at the next table. Vernita caught Wilson's sleeve. She didn't take her eyes off Keith Emory across from her.

'Where you wanting to go?'

'None of your business.'

Vernita turned her eyes on Wilson. 'Since when's something of yours nothing of mine?'

'Since my whole life.'

'Go on then if you want to be that way.'

"Kay.' Wilson squeezed on through.

'Hey!'

Wilson rolled her eyes. She ought to be polite. But when she turned around, Vernita Lee was half up out of her chair, leaning on the sides of her feet. Wilson's ring box was moving through her fingers. Wilson heaved into flight.

Even with her awful arches, Vernita was faster. She slid behind Cummings, dangling the ring box along his shoulder. 'Know what this is?'

Wilson swiped at it.

Vernita was faster.

Cummings leaned back in his chair, digging his chin in the crook of his shoulder.

Wilson tripped and thudded to the ground. Keith Emory held his beer up and Pitch Slocum shouted for Wilson to watch what she was doing.

Vernita leaned between two stools at the bar. 'Come here, Francine!'

Climbing back up, Wilson yanked Dol's chair out of the way.

By the time she got to the bar, Vernita was already further along the wall closest to the front door and next to the fireplace. Wilson huffed and puffed past Keith Emory's bald spot bigger than a baby's bare bottom. Pitch and him slumped in their chairs. They pawed their moustaches.

'Hey, cutie. What's this?' Vernita twirled the ring box.

'Give me that.'

'What is it?'

'Gimme it.'

'*Gimme it*. That ain't no way to talk to a lady who's got what I got.'

'Vernita Lee, give me my box.'

'That is exactly what I want to talk to you about.' Vernita swung it over the fireplace.

'Get it away from there.'

'What's in it?'

'Vernita.'

'Francine.'

'What do you want?'

'Tell me what is in it.'

'What do you think is in it? Let it go.'

'Okay.' The box fell.

Wilson lunged but Vernita was faster. Wilson went to the floor.

Every single person in Avery's that night got to get a good gawk in on Wilson's account and that got her gut tight.

'What's inside?'

'None of your business.'

'Why you want to be like that?'

'I'll be any way I want to. Now give it here.'

'No.'

Wilson got to her feet. 'What you want?'

'I saw you looking at this.'

'With Charlie?'

'Uh-huh.'

'Then you know what it is.' Wilson swiped for the box.

Vernita hid it under her arm.

'What're you going to do with it?'

'None of your business.'

'Now why do you say that?'

''Cause it ain't.'

''Cause you want to ask Dol something.'

'I don't want to ask Dol nothing.'

'Yes, you do. You're madder'n a witch at Christmas. Can't be Charlie, can't be Dr. Burns, I know it isn't Pitch or Keith – the one person that that leaves is Dol, you don't like nobody else.'

'See, you don't know nothing.'

'I do.'

'You don't.'

'I know love.'

'Give me my box.'

'I know love.'

'I got to go.'

'Where you going?' Vernita lashed out, hooked Wilson's collar in her grip and pulled her close face to face.

'What's in the box?'

'You already know.'

Vernita got in close, her breath tickled Wilson's ear. 'You're going to be lesbians. Have you thought about that?'

Wilson squirmed.

'I did.'

'Oh.'

'Yes.'

'Oh.'

'About you.'

'About me?'

'Yes. You.'

'Let go.'

'I want a girl like that.'

'Like what?'

'That can, you know, toss me around.'

'Let –'

'You can.'

'Toss you?'

'Yeah.'

'Even with your arches?'

'Yeah.'

Vernita had been drinking beer. Wilson bit her lip. 'I'm going to get Dol now.'

'Are you?'

'Out back.'

'Go on, then. L-E-S-B –'

' – I-A-N. I am now.'

Vernitas lips brushed Wilson's earlobe and she veered some. 'Ain't you going to do nothing about it?'

Wilson flinched. 'That tickles.'

'Vernita, hey! We need beers!' Pitch and Keith tapped their beer glasses on the tabletop.

'You're so lucky, Wilson.'

'That they're calling you? You giving up on me?'

'Yeah, that too.' Vernita tucked the ring box into Wilson's back pocket.

Wilson backed away. 'You're all right, Vernita.'

'Don't tell nobody.'

Vernita flew back to Pitch and Keith. 'If'n I see him, I'll tell him you got a bead on him.'

Wilson moved the box to her front pocket. Her throat got tight. Something wasn't right. She ought to break that storeroom door down. No, she oughn't to. Okay, then. Okay. And how was she going to know until she found Dol? Okay, then. Okay. Head out the door first. Dol could be in the parking lot. Wilson didn't know, she didn't. She had no way of know-ing, she was all tied up with Charlie and getting the ring. Dol probably went to clear the snow off the dumpster, that's what he done, probably. Head out there to clear the snow. He's out there.

Cummings latched a hold of Wilson's sleeve. 'Excuse me?'

'Take back your hand before it don't come back to you.'

Cummings crinkled his brow. 'Where's the young lady I was speaking to? You know her, don't you?'

'You tell me.' Then she bent over so close to Cummings she could smell his rank breath. 'I am not the kind of woman you want to get take a hold of without asking first. I'm different.' She poked him on the tip of his nose in a not-nice way, turned her back and made her way to the screen door. She shoved it open.

Outside, flurries hurtled across. The cold chomped into her scalp through her hair. She should've wore a hat. Look at that. Dol's Dart was still idling there. Those kids'd better not be in that car.

Two long steps and she was on the stairs. Two more and she had taken the stairs and with another three was at the Dart. Large funnels of exhaust rose out of the tailpipe. Those kids'd better not be in that car. A Kleenex layer of snow lay on and then skittered off the windshield blowing a straight line bare.

Squirrel's rose cheeks rounded out what was left for Wilson in this world. His eyes closed. As hushed as dipping a toe into warm water.

For chrissakes, Charlie Ceame. What did you do? Take off and not even think of these kids? Oh, for cryin' out loud. And where is Pity? Wilson wrenched herself around. Charlie's Luv was still there – but with a flat tire.

'Pity? Pity? Jesus H. Christ. Now isn't that just the goddamned cat's meow.'

One at a time. First, she'd get Squirrel inside in a chair or somewhere, and then find Pity and then that goddamned father of theirs. Ol' Dol must've made a deal with God for a kid what sleeps as hard as Squirrel. The little guy grumbled but she dragged him out of the car, up the slippery stairs and inside where it was warm, laying his sleepy face in Vernita Lee's lap, and was back out the side door in no time.

The weather had picked up. As soon as she stepped on the stair to the side yard, driving snow bit into Wilson's face. Blinking into the onslaught let her see some now in spite of the weather on account of the slushed and grumbling sky absorbing the lamp light and casting it off. Flickering yard lights stretched and glowed up through the knee-high drifts collecting in the side yard. Not far off, at the elementary school, the steel-link halyard rang against the flagpole.

'Dol?'

Boot tracks came towards her from around the building from out back. They were a lady's, Wilson was sure. Too small to be a man's and the steps too close together, they passed the stairs where she stood and curled around the front porch.

Wilson stepped into 'em. Tight fit. Tracked in the wrong direction. Water'd come off the roof and frozen before this latest dump, and her toes had to grip it to stay steady. She put her fingers straight through the snow clinging to the siding and gripped the edge. Much as she could, she dug her weight into the building so she wouldn't slip.

The bootprints'd get her back there. Whose was they? Too big for Pity. Maybe they was Dol's.

Bet he's sitting out here now, right around the corner of the building up ahead and shivering like a witch's you-know-what. Propped up on the trash cans out back like they was some kind of La-Z-Boy. Sitting there, stuck, smoking, griping and shivering. That joker from Atlanta said something to Dol, Wilson bet. He didn't like it, stalked off, Wilson knew, and he'd yell at her too, call her all nosy.

Better nosy than up to your neck. Then she'd do it, on her knee, you betcha.

'Get up. I got something to ask you.'

Dol's eyes'd widen and land bowled over on the back forty. He'd lower his cigarette. 'I'll put this out on you.'

'Get up. Now.' And then Wilson'd go to one knee and ask it.

And the universe, like an excited aunt, would draw Dol's smoke away as Wilson raised the wedding band. Dol's lips'd part. Wilson'd see the tips of his teeth like a fork in the road.

'You what?' he'd say. 'You want to what? You crazy stinking thing! You didn't say nothing. You didn't let on.' He'd jump off the trash cans. 'And here I am, sitting on the garbage! Are you crazy?' His voice would catch. 'Yes. You are. You are crazy. You're crazy and I love ya for it. You can't marry me. You can't. Wilson.' And then he'd jump in her arms. 'Hold me. Oh, Wilson. Yes. The answer is yes, yes, yes.' And they would kiss because he'd maybe accepted it in the flash of proposing. His lips would be pillows.

They would gather Pity and Squirrel and everyone in the bar and Vernita Lee would buy 'em a beer and her speech would say how she knew it ever since the very first day she came in dancing on the sides of her feet trailing behind Pat Boone's fur coat, and no one had an idea except her, and she'd shake her straightened hair and then comb it down over her forehead with her fingers, and blabber on that Wilson had told her just a few minutes before but don't worry she told her without telling her so no one should feel left out and boy, then, first thing tomorrow, Wilson'd take Dol and the kids to Lake City where the kids could stay with Reading is Saturday Fun run by the Jaycees, and then she could take Dol to Freebird's to choose a new pickup so he could get back and forth to Avery's in one piece.

Wilson got to the rear of the building. Nothing. The trash cans were empty. It all was. The snow on the rusted aluminum lids hadn't been touched, ain't even been leaned on. The start of 'em tracks crawled around. The old woodpile Avery had cut when he thought he'd get a Franklin stove lay under two inches of snowfall. No one'd leaned on that darned thing neither. She clapped her hands to keep the blood flowing, she slapped her cheeks. The scrub maple and pine twisted up through the fence put up back when they was in junior high. Past that, moonlight made the field heading to Scott's Woods the flush of Rose Lake at dusk.

Out there, in the back-forty field between Wilson and the dull line of the woods, a greyish thing skittered. Scuttled some and slowed, run off and jerked north like a lost coon. The snow barrelled in in a last-ditch effort to make a difference. A person – there was a person walking out there. 'Dol?' The figure stopped, and then went on. 'Hey?' He oughtn't to be out there.

Wilson heaved a leg and got blown over. She hauled herself up and deep into the drifts. No tracks, she made it to the fence and got her breath. 'Hey?'

Whoever it was stopped again, and then kept on.

'Dol?'

Whoever it was couldn't make her out. Probably couldn't tell her from a red maple, couldn't recognize her from that far off – they'd stop moving if they knew who she was but they couldn't hear her and probably wouldn't over the fierce wind stomping on her yell. There was just no way she'd get seen or heard on this side of the fence. The snow'd piled up soft on her side same as in the side yard so she got a grip of a pine branch, hoisted herself up over the fence then down into a drift that got a hold of her thighs and hauled her down so far she was up to her waist.

Wilson waved her arms – for crying out loud, she still couldn't make out who it was. Whoever it was was walking on top of the snow. Well, that'd make it faster to get to 'em. She flayed her arms out away from the fence. The drift's surface was hard enough almost maybe to carry her – she could walk on it too probably. Once she got up, she sank a couple of times but after a few steps got her tank legs ginger enough so she flew, she kept herself up as she went on like a drifting feather, never dropping her full weight.

The person began moving towards her – now they seen her. 'Hey, Dol?' Whoever it was squawked back at her, barely breaking the din.

It was not Dol – as the person got closer, that was plain. No, it was not. Pity. It was Pity. That kid could die out here – oh, for Holy Toledos crying out loud, that little know-it-all shit-sinker. Oh, she was going to get it for running around out here in a storm, don't even have the sense of a wild animal to stay out of it. She oughtn't to be wandering around out in the middle of nowhere – this damned blizzard'd cover her up and they'd never see her again until she thawed out in spring. Didn't she know? What kind of idiot kid would put herself out here? She was a crazy crazy kid, like her dad.

'Goddammit, Holy Jesus H. Christ, get over here!' Wilson hammered one boot down and the whole of her sank goddamned through. Then, on top of that, she tipped backwards. She turned on her side and pressed down to push up. She broke through again. Oh, crikey. She sank on her belly.

Pity, however, didn't sink. 'Is that you, Wilson?'

'Get over here.'

'I ain't in trouble, am I?'

'Oh, you don't think you oughta be? You better bet your sweet patootie y'are.'

Pity tugged her hat down and folded her arms.

'Give me a pull.' Wilson heaved herself to the right and then the left.

Pity planted herself. 'What?'

Wilson reached out her arm towards the nine-year-old. 'Get over here. Where's your father?'

'I don't know, he ain't nowhere, he don't care a hill of beans for me.'

'That is not true.'

'Where is he then, you seen him?'

'You watch your mouth, little lady. No, I ain't seen him. But that don't mean nothing. You can't be always thinking of yourself, Pity. You got to think. Your daddy has got to work. You like to eat, don't you?'

'No.'

'Oh, you don't?'

'No.'

'You are some kid.'

'So?'

'So. Don't talk to me that way. Jesus Christ.'

'You can't say that.'

Wilson gave up. She sat back in the snow. All the fears she was fearing and all the worry she was worrying and all the hopes she was hoping came up through her esophagus and out her eyes. She ate a handful of snow. And noticed the stillness return, the wind'd died.

Pity unfolded her arms.

Wilson shook her head. 'Go on then. Keep going. All of you just keep going. Leave me alone.' She studied the sky finally letting up some.

Pity looked past Wilson, then back behind her. She drew hair through her mouth. She folded her arms.

'I come out here,' explained Pity.

'I told you go on.'

'I heard you. You feeling sorry for yourself.'

'I am not.' Wilson dragged herself up out of the snow.

'You are. My daddy's going to say yes. He is. You just got to ask him.'

Wilson froze. 'How do you know? Say yes to what?'

Pity already had her mind somewhere. 'There a lady out here?'

'Say yes to what?'

As she spoke, Pity moved closer to Wilson. 'I come out here when there was a lady in the parking lot when she was hunting for something, 'cause she lost me, and she wouldn't come, then she went off out over there 'cause she took off'n didn't come when I called her and – '

'A lady?' Wilson got to her feet. 'What lady? Not your daddy?'

'No. Out in the parking lot! It was another lady, and when she was hunting around, she couldn't find nothing, and I was going to help her but she didn't want me to when she was looking, but she wouldn't come out no more and – '

Wilson got hold of Pity's coat and held her close.

'And I got mad, and when I couldn't find her, Wilson, since when she went off then there was all these rabbits, and they was a rabbit family, and I know I ain't supposed to leave Squirrel but when he was sleeping, and he always just goes on, he don't ever wake up, so when I come to see the rabbits then they took off and they gotta be off over there – '

Wilson drew her closer, she was betting that the tighter she held her Pity, this little thing, this little sweet thing who was going to be her Pity, the more strength it'd give her. And when she could face it no more, her face got prickly, starting first back by her jaw hinge and working its way electrically through the nerves of her neck which clamped her throat shut.

'There was little ones and big ones and they didn't act scared of me at all.'

After she could swallow again and when Pity was ready, Wilson slung her over her shoulder like the bag of rocks she was and carried her back across the field to Avery's while they saw how sparkling the lights were from out there but they couldn't reach and Pity sussed she liked the dark better. The peculiar sky had absorbed a charred red as if a cut had been cast behind the stars and the wound left to age in the oxygen; still, it was clearing up. Pity wondered if didn't Wilson ever want to be somewhere where lights couldn't reach and as she bore on, Wilson's stomach bunched up until her throat cinched again, and a new awful coalesced sharply before her eyes, stinging with the wind pricking into 'em, until her panic increased because of what she saw so clearly now and where Dol was, to where she wrung Pity out of the snow, gathering her under her arm, stumbling back to her love lighter than a jackrabbit, only to stick and fall and have to snatch this baby back up like she was a bloodless rag doll.

After she flung open the front door, oh God, she knew it she knew it she knew it. She rushed towards the back, past where Cummings' table was, where the salt and pepper were upturned and the doctor wasn't there but his coat was. She jerked her head around: no Burns neither. Dol's purse sat open as open can be on the counter. Wilson pounded on the storeroom door. No sound.

{ *Charlie* }
8:53 p.m.

He used the biting cold cement to push himself up and thats when it was he heard it first That steady and repeatin crunch like Saran Wrap bein torn far off Steps

Listen

Charlie pushed at his girl She swung her head up and bucked to get her weight around to help her Once she got far enough off he pulled his leg out She was gettin big He got to his knees Between the wind whackin and the calf kickin on the floor he couldnt make it out

Shhh

The calf gave up its kickin and laid back on the floor The one eye facin him had him locked in it The animal didnt hear nothin But Charlie did Footsteps in snow near to frozen like two sheets of paper rubbin together

Charlie cringed on his knees real low and then lower still till he was on his belly usin his shoulder muscles to pull back the bent corner of the door That crunchin wasnt so far off

Jesus Christ

Julie was stompin at him like a fuse sizzlin

Oh jest look at her Jesus Christ

His big huntin coat engulfed her Her arms stuck out from her sides Her knees didnt bend She was on fire Comin at him relentless What she want to come out here for She aint got no business here What the hell was she goin to do out here She ought to be inside out of the cold She ought to have her feet up

Goddammit

Oh he shouldve showed himself He shouldve gone straight in the house Whats the matter with you Charlie you know bettern Well here goes He got to his feet and was just about to open the door when he had an idea

Hed face her all right Yeah Come on Come on in here Come on in here Miss High n Mighty I aint scared of you Ill face you When she got here hed give her a good silent look in the eyes No wordsre needed His eyes would say it all He wouldnt say nothin What was there to say Hed show her Hed hurry right on out the door and leave her here Hed leave her here and take the Cutlass and go He didnt have to talk to her if he didnt want to Who was she that he had to answer to her There wasnt no reason he had to She couldnt make him do it He was a grown man This is too much Her harassin him every which way and that Who did she think she was When she reached out for the door and pulled the rope for the bar to lift hed yank it open

He got another peek at Julie comin at him She was trampin Her eyes were shadowed by the cast of the lamp Wilson shouldve got that 240 watt halogen Them lips like jar cherries were gone Her mouth was cut like a harvest tool curvin down to the ends the way they do when she aims to teach somebody a lesson Oh she had it in for somethin He backed away from the door

He kissed the calf on the cheek pet its head His girl could always tell or so it was to him when he was leavin

Hay dust glittered down

You

There was room for him up there He could go up and lay real flat behind them shingles what Wilson never finished and whats left of them

bales what the calf aint eat Them two by foursd hold him if he spread out
See what shes up to

What you got to say

Her snout hooked up taggin behind the waterin eyes Them eyes
turnin over like rivers takin storm runoff He flipped the light switch off

Tell me after

He withdrew his hand from the Coleman switch stood up in the
darkness and reached his fingers into the black He stepped in the direction of the loft ladder behind him and on the other side of the shed
wigglin his fingertips so that they might catch what he might bump into
before he did His girl was as quiet as an accomplice ought to be He was
sure her head cocked a little the way animals do when they watch humans
fumble Cats can see in the dark but he did not know if cows could Once
he caught hold of the sides of the ladder he nervously but quickly stepped
up the rungs climbed into the loft and pulled the ladder up behind him
God he hated heights

Seein him there would only get her mad and also scare her half to
death He wanted that child but no wordsd come to get her to see things
his way He lifted the ladder so that it wouldnt scrape the edge of the loft
and laid it on its side directly in front of him If he set her off in the wrong
way if she got mad enough the next thing shed make an appointment
with that vacuum cleaner That aint right We signed the contract we pay
the piper

And he took a deep breath

{ *Julie* }
8:55 p.m.

When I come around the corner of the house, a blast of wind burned into my eyes and when I got them back open, I saw how the snow had drifted into dunes. The very tip-top of the drifts shifted alive and seeking, first this way and then that, glittering in Wilson's halogen. I was going to claw my way back to Charlie's heart if it killt me.

Between where I was and the kitchen behind me, all that snow was lit up – grey on white, on silver, on blue, on gold. It never took on that brilliance to my eye before. I never seen it come up and cast through the storm like that until all that anger and lonesomeness and being trapped like an animal was there, in me. The night was so pure in feeling, so clean, so atomic, that the light spread farther as I went on – the path was icy and the night took me.

A bowl hollow caving in was up ahead, it yawned, yearning out from where we took dirt fill for them flowerbeds we put in, I put in, a couple years back. Puffing down into it, holding my breath, I had to grip the ice tight – if I was sliding down the side of a greased-up mixing bowl that would be what it was, and my toes went right up the other side, landing me right up so close to the shed door I had to throw up my hands and press myself away from it. But then I saw.

Somebody else'd come there already. I was standing in indentations that could be the remainders of someone else's tracks. Behind me, and coming up to me, deep small hollowed boot steps snaked all the way around that pocket I just come through to where the snow fence comes to the corner of the house right there where I was just standing. There weren't no lights on in that shed. Did that worm beat me to it, pussy shithead goddammit. He got home and then scooted right back to that bar before I even got this far, jerk. How'd he do that? I seen everything, how'd he get past me? Sonuvabitch.

Headlights crossed behind me, I got down to my haunches. They lit up the shed playing the shadow of me bigger'n King Kong on the door. For chrissakes, it was probably Charlie or it was Tibs, I had to hide myself. If Charlie saw me, I could just call it a night. He would see that porch, unshovelled, and then step up to the front door, and then see the living room lamps lit up, see the busted glass like his heart was gonna be and that'd get him thinking – he'd see me stirrupped at Burns'. And then he'd have to come on out to this shed to see if his baby baby baby was all right – that made my heart jump. It made my heart jump so far because I could almost tell how it would play out. I'd've loved to see the look on his face. To walk in there and see his itsy-bitsy beast child flayed out like strips of raw jerky – that picture got me going and I stole up to the shed door.

Girls like me can't bitch about synchronicity. Cut and climb was what I was thinking. I would hide up there in the loft, don't that beat all, and watch that calf's blood pool in the straw. I'd watch it catch sticks of hay flowing on down to the drainage. When they laid the cement floor, Charlie and Wilson gently sloped it, and that did beat all, 'cause little did they know. After this, I could call myself a psycho killer and it wouldn't be too far-fetched. Little Miss Me was at the only end of a knife you want to be at. Negotiations have been called off – I have walked away from the table. I'd lie up there on my belly after soaking up all that blood, I'd listen and watch and smile as wide as my pearly whites could stretch, feeling feeling feeling what it feels like to be me almost for the first time, and it'd go like this.

First, I'd hear Charlie crunching and moping up towards the door. Then he'd yank the door too hard 'cause he's got no measure. He'd step in – I'd watch his face fall. His girl lying there, throat cut, kicking. Help me, help me – oh Lord. And his grief – he might even howl. All that feeling in him would throw in like the Red Sea crushing Pharaoh, it'd just drown him. That got me lost for a second. The idea, the idea that Charlie's anger might, please-dear-God-kick-me-in-the-pants, show itself. Oh God, I wished for it. Hell, I'd quit smoking if he showed just a little real feeling to me. There wasn't no way he could avoid it – he'd have to say something, he'd have to act, he'd have to get raged, he'd have to talk. From then on, our together'd be changed: every night we'd probably sit on the porch watching the sun set. After a time, Wilson could come over 'cause Charlie'd know what I was capable of and that'd take care of that. Tibs would be there too – if Charlie could have a buddy, I could too. Them two'd never know where these new touches, these sweetsies, all them nice coos'd come from – me and Charlie would, though. Charlie didn't know of what I was capable, but he would.

A great iron chain cranked in me and caught on a lung – I couldn't breathe. The wind'd horned up good. I gathered my coat around me and the knife in my right hand, my good hand. I dug in my heels. I could leave, I ought to, I ought to turn around, I ought to pack a bag, I could get the hell away before he ever knew. He wouldn't come for me – I could save my soul. I never killed a living thing in my life but murder is in me. I'd sell my skin to have Charlie for mine, to own him. And I couldn't see no other way around it and I didn't want to. I couldn't tell you the rot bubbling in me. But, boy, I ached for him, real, beyond compare. I couldn't never explain it if I wanted to, so I got that knife in tighter. Them headlights shining on me went on past and the wind shoved me on.

The shed door popped open. He don't see fit to lock it up. The air in there heated my cheek – it could've come out of a register, that's how warm it come.

A glow was coming into the place and that animal was all in shadow, its eyes were watering though. Them, I could make out – they inched at me as soon as I got the door open.

A shadow was pressing to me, crawling over the cement, first covering the toes of my boots, and then clear on out the door till it had me covered and come to a point out on a drift blown up behind me. Light was on me, Wilson's halogen. Slivers of hay flit crazy in the light and wind wailing in. Kerosene from the Coleman stung my nose. Charlie, out here pressing his heart and God knows what else. My tummy strung itself up – stay on your toes.

Someone'd be here soon, this had to be quick and neat. I shut the shed door, cutting the wind and shadow. Furious, the wind tore at that sheet metal. Oh, it was a wrawling sound, prying at the rivets while while while the two-by-fours wheezed. Them walls didn't seem like much more than Reynolds Wrap. Under all that, though, that calf was breathing low, down low and way inside – we both was.

I closed my eyes – instinct, I guess. I couldn't see nothing but that calf inching at me. I backed up against the wall, the studs digging in my back, and I felt out to my right, along the horizontal stud, until I got hold of the vertical one, and when I got that far I got down on my haunches 'cause that's where the Coleman'd be sitting, had me whether it was a switch-on or a screw-on, so I got it and stood up and didn't move for fear of how close that animal was or where that porcelain heating coil hung 'cause who knows if Charlie'd moved it. And I could feel the top of it was a dome so I went to twist it to get it on but nothing turned there and I turned it over feeling along the bottom and there was the switch.

The black beat back. The animal stood right there looking pitiful. Crying – swear to God, crying. Fur all knotted up, goddamned Charlie. Ahead of its hind legs, the muscles tightened and, eyeing me, let go. Thinking. That's when that beast who wasn't too far south of a hamburger squeezed out a pile of crap.

'Oh, for Christ's sake.' I buried my nose in my sleeve.

With some light, I got a good look around. If I was going to do it right, I was going to have to untie the thing and bring it close to the drainage hole, I might as well save some mess. I got a gulp of fresh air coming in near the door and set the lamp by the drain slope – I could taste that goddamned steaming pile of shit inside my mouth, so I spit when I undid my coat, and I wasn't going to get it all over me, and to do anything I had to have my breath and my arms free, and I let some air out, and I was cussing, and running back out towards the door, past the light, and getting some more air until it wasn't no use, and maybe the storm'd rip the sheeting off outside, and we'd get some real fresh air, and that's when I found where Charlie'd square-knotted the animal's rope to an iron eyebolt he screwed into the wall, which is the closest he's come to doing something technical, something useful, something that'd do somebody some good, then down on my haunches I worked that knot till it loosened up and I still had to run more out of the light, and get some more air, and then run back to the knot, and God knows how long it'd been, damn, there had to be a shovel in here somewhere, and I couldn't find one so I kicked some hay over the pile of shit, and I had to stop some of the stink to breathe, I don't know why it was so closed up in there, and even without air it was just then, when I stood up, getting that rope in my hand, that the siding out there let loose, shrieking, tearing off, letting gusts in from that mean sky strewn purple, and that hay I covered up the shit with got blown right back off and at me, and sonuvabitch I couldn't breathe, and whoever heard of weather like this down here, unnatural and backass backwards.

'Jesus H. Christ. Come on, thing.'

That rope was around its neck, I pulled it.

The calf half-cocked its head, screwed up its snout at me, not budging.

'Come on, you you. Make nice.' I used my muscle this time, it didn't budge.

'Oh, for heaven's sake.' I got over next to it, squatting and petting it until I wrapped my arms around it like it was a little baby to see if maybe I could lift it. Nope. I got on my knees and when I did, the thing turned full to face me and leaned into me.

'I can't lift you.' I got around and stomped my feet to scare it. 'Move.'

And then what was going to be come into my head.

{ *Wilson* }
8:58 p.m.

Wilson saw keys on the counter. When they wouldn't fit the lock she threw 'em to the floor. Behind the bar, her fingers upended a shot glass, swiped unused order chits to the floor, scattered paper clips, rubber bands and pens. Dol had the keys.

Wilson found a screwdriver in the drawer underneath the register and stuck it in the doorknob lock. She wiggled the knob first – maybe the latch'd get triggered. Then she did it harder, sweating and stabbing at the door.

'Wilson?' Pity leaned on the stool seat. Strands of her hair quivered with static. Her eyes were on the door. 'Where's Daddy?' Her stocking cap hung limp and twisted in her fingers.

Wilson hid the screwdriver. 'He might've run home for –'

'Nuh-uh. Our car's here. He's in there, ain't he?' She pointed to the storeroom.

'I don't – No. I don't think so. Somebody gave him a ride.'

'Where to? How come he don't come get us?'

Wilson had no answer for that so she grimaced. Pity climbed onto the bar stool and watched the storeroom door.

'Uh. You want a Coca-Cola?'

'Yes'm.'

Wilson squirt the Coke out, setting it on a napkin on the bar. 'How's that, uh, well, now you got to go over there and take care of your brother.'

'He's sleeping and he don't – '

'You're the big girl.'

'That ain't my fault.'

'No, it ain't. But you are. And I got to find your daddy, so dry up and get over there and take care of your brother before I swat you one!' She'd never stung Pity with her tongue before.

Scared bad, Pity screwed her brow. 'My daddy has the key to that door!'

'Yes.'

'Wilson?'

'What?'

'Is that rabbit you shot, is that still in the freezer?'

'No.'

'I want to look at that bloody rabbit, I got to see the rabbit.'

Wilson hurried over to the deep-freeze, all the time her aim on that storeroom and what was being dealt with behind it, turned over the frozen fries, the jalapeno poppers and chicken fingers before snatching that old flattened rabbit in the Ziploc, handing it to Pity and even leaning on the counter for a split second, so fast no one would ever know something horrible was dawning, drawing her finger over the freezer-burnt animal so as to leave off the frost gathered there but not to worry her little sweet thing who sure enough wouldn't have a fine day tomorrow. Wilson pressed her fingers so hard into the Formica she could've broke the tips off – oh, she had to move, she had to go. Like she was playing piano, Pity placed her fingertips on Wilson's.

'Whyn't you go show Pitch Slocum that rabbit?'

'He don't want to see it.'

'Doesn't. Pitch doesn't want to. Show Vernita then.'

Pity picked at the shut eyes, the matted fur and the darkened claws. 'Vernita don't like nothing good like this.'

Then it all happened faster than Wilson could ever describe it later. Behind her, a bottle crashed. Liquor leaked out from under the storeroom door. Another bottle broke. Alcohol smell struck her nose. Wilson shook the doorknob with every muscle she had, Pity beat that rabbit carcass into the door. 'Daddy?'

Gin leaked first under the door, pooling around their boots and then thick ribbons of blood followed. Blood and liquor spread wide around 'em, and then into the treads of their boots, and then past 'em behind the bar, soaking into the unused chits still laying there and disappearing into the bar mats already stained worse than blood could ever do.

Pity's lips flattened.

Wilson ran to the register, then turned back, with the screwdriver. She stuck the point into the lock and slammed the heel of her hand into the handle. The screwdriver jammed into the lock but didn't turn. A mess of folks piled behind Pity and when she peeked back at 'em, she moved closer to Wilson. Vernita weaved through the gawkers and hooked her arms under Pity's to lift her up. 'Come 'ere, hon. Wilson'll get in there.'

Pity lunged at Wilson and held tight. 'Wilson?'

'Get out of here, Pity.'

Pity fought free and rushed the door, banging on it. 'Daddy, Daddy, Daddy!'

Wilson swung Pity up, her mouth slightly ajar, now silent as that snowfield they'd just come through, back over to Vernita's arms, who passed her to Pitch Slocum who shook as he set Pity farther back, steadying himself as much as quieting the child. Cummings appeared, clasping his hands and peeking through the gawkers.

Wilson kicked the door. The pressboard caved through to its hollow inside but didn't bust completely so the door itself remained shut. 'Goddammit. Come 'ere, you guys.'

Keith and a couple of 'em that couldn't do nothing but stare stepped forward and Wilson showed 'em how she wanted 'em to hit the door with their shoulders all together. All of 'em moved four feet back, knockin' the microwave and hunched together same as squirrels over a handful of peanuts, and then, so far back their rear ends were pressed against the deep-freeze. There being no room to stand shoulder to shoulder, Keith and Wilson got in front to lead and with the other three following charged the door, the three behind pushing their force into the two in front, their shoulders all of five, their weight of one.

The door burst open and slammed into the boxes behind it before swinging back and cutting off the sight, and when they saw him, Keith couldn't move his eyes off, Pitch's hand pulled his cheek and Wilson reached out for Dol. Then the door swung shut on 'em, and with all her force, Wilson growled and shoved the door open so fast that if a person were timing it it would've taken no more longer than a finger snap. And she got inside and went to her knees for what must've been an eternity shorter than a heartbeat, not knowing where to start. There Dol was, strewn and propped on a stack of boxes, his bare midsection soaked red. Wilson steadied herself on the floor but when she brought her blood-soaked hands to him, Dol moved.

One of the guys propped the door open while Wilson gathered Dol's panties snagged to pumps she hadn't seen before. The raw mangle of Dol's penis, hunched, mound-like as a parasite.

'Girl.'

Barely conscious, Dol lifted his leg a little, hissing some as if he'd been burned.

The lump rose from the landscape of his groin as one of them Indian burial mounds do, and to Wilson didn't even look as real as one of 'em plastic wounds Pity put on for Halloween.

Wilson carefully got around to the right of Dol and, leaning him forward so so so gently, got her arm in to hold him good and then the other behind Dol's knees and pulled him to her breast, standing.

Cummings, being a doctor, was at the door now, since Keith and Pitch had backed off at the grim sight. He clamped his teeth and kept his eyes on the floor as Wilson brought him out.

Pity squealed that she wanted her daddy. Vernita covered the little girl's eyes but Pity fought her. Wilson thrust her chin at the bar behind the onlookers. If she could get Dol out of here fast enough, he might not lose all his blood, he might not die right there in her arms – he'd cut himself good. Squirrel's eyes got big as coin dollars, and the guys were cater-wauling at Wilson to come on, do this and do that, what was she waiting for, and Jesus Christ look at that, he cut it off, holy shit. She told Vernita, whose tears were coming as fast as she could wipe them off, to watch over Pity and Squirrel.

And then the strangest feeling that wasn't ever hers before floated itself up to balloon inside Wilson as the blood from Dol's wound seeped in through her flannel shirt, soaking in so that the skin covering her own stomach grew viscous and firm.

Planted long before, the feeling and an arranging of ideas flowered up, taking root deep down: all of them gawking men and women looking upon the pitiable figure Dol made in Wilson's arms thought that they were separate, that somehow they were not complicit, that Dol could cut himself or that he could break 'em bottles alone. What she would tell 'em someday if she could was that suffering happens in plain air, in weather, amongst the living, it happens where breath is, under noses and when we look away from that torture, we are all a part of it, maybe it would happen no matter what, maybe no natural thing could stop that inner tide 'cept casting a gaze on that creature and maybe seein' 'em, seein' 'em for what they are, mappin' the terrain of their insides, the breadth of their thoughts and the majesty of feeling, this is what thins pain, getting sounded out and being heard and seen, and then, then, then it ain't too much to live with for most days. She would do that for Dol, his blood gaining oxygen in the wound and sticking Wilson's soles to the floor so she mostly had to peel them up with each step and dilly-dallying there a few feet shy of the front door. With all of 'em oglers ogling and the kids screaming, them's the thoughts that came to Wilson.

And that she'd save Dol.

Wilson's arms strained under Dol's increasing dead weight. She hurried to the front door propped open for her, and after the door bells tinkled the sounds of Pity and Squirrel shriekin' wore down as she stepped so she wouldn't fall down the stairs while those behind her crouching and reaching and afraid to get in the way were praying to the sky and to Jesus and Wilson was asking herself how come Dol was to do this because she hadn't known Dol thought all was lost or come to not knowing what to do next. Them experts would've done it right if he waited and where was Burns?

When Wilson laid Dol in the front seat she didn't know where she would take him. His skirt'd become like a second raw skin and his whole nice top Wilson hated to see him in was soaked. Burns' clinic.

"S Burns' place open?' Wilson shouted at the surging crowd who'd followed her out and got the truck door open for her and then stepped back, afraid some of what Dol done might rub off on them, afraid that being driven so far is contagious, and afraid each of them could be driven into such a storm so far they could cut themselves too, but understanding that the first step in fallin' is gettin' mixed up in the distance between the cliff and where you stand. Their palms were wet, their throats sucked dry. A chopped-off, sharp shout came back: 'He said he was going home –'

By then, though, Wilson had the wheel in hand, was spinning out of the lot and into the loosened night.

{ *Julie* }
8:58 p.m.

I flaunted my knife and the animal shifted.

'Know what this is?' I dangled the blade.

Head now low, it graciously backed right up to the drain.

'Well, I'll be.' That warmed me some to it. I had to feel for such a generous living thing.

I was going to cut for Charlie and me. New life don't just appear, you got to carve it out. Let's get to it. That Coleman sat to the left. Over here by me. But, but, but. A queer light flowed from the far side of the calf – that was the first time I took note of it. My feet, right next to the Coleman, were in shadow, that animal's shadow. Now, that was queer. I shifted my feet, still shadow.

Maybe it had another shit coming. It come towards me, nudging its snout on my calves. Time to stop pussyfooting.

I sized up my options: I could stick the blade to the jugular, or straddle it and cut a necklace ear to ear, or just stab at it until it was dead. It shouldn't suffer, I ain't soulless. A necklace, then.

I got alongside the animal, on my haunches, and reached around it end to end. I was going to lift the thing closer to my breast if it didn't want to budge. I pressed my chest into it to hold it still and got my left hand around its front. The crook of my arm was right under its neck, right where, that day I walked in on Charlie out here, the palm of his hand lay too. In the powdery fur. I gripped the thing, it went stiff. I was passing the knife from my left hand to my right when it saw the blade and swung its head back at me. It bucked its head back and peeled its lips.

We eyed each other.

The handle was warm in my right palm.

That thing jerked, lunging at me, baring its teeth, biting into my shoulder and I fell back on the floor. It backed itself over the drain, sniffing down in it, eyes cocked on me. My mouth wouldn't work and I was afraid to see if it got a chunk of meat off me. When the pain went back a bit, I cussed, holding my shoulder – my pulse come through my shoulder is how hard it bit me.

Sonuvacottonpickin SOB shit. I peeked at the skin and there was stinging teeth marks. I had my coat on, you piece of turd pie.

It turned and squared off in front of me.

'All right, come on, you little SOB steak. Charlie is going to eat you. You, you, you chuck roast.'

I got to my feet before it done anything else. I was going to just stab the thing to death now, and I raised up the knife to show it. 'You ought to run, thing.'

It eyed me.

My shoulder hurt, I rolled it the bit I could to soothe it and lunged back. Them little fine gold hairs along its head and out across its back were lit up by the Coleman. The calf reared up to its hind legs and come at me. She threw her whole self up into me, jabbing her hooves. She got me in my belly, pulling me in and pulling me up. Under the ribs, she got me closer. Back down in the gut and, pistons punching, she just kept coming, driving her legs and pinning me. I froze, the wind lulled.

And I heard the ladder crash to the floor and saw Charlie's fingers draw back out of sight. He'd been up there the whole time. She give me a final kick. My back recoiled hard into them studs where I first come in and knocked the wind from me. I dropped the knife next to me on the floor, losing my air.

That lady dropped back to all fours, taking note.

And, oh God, I thought I was going to pass just then. Pain and a hundred cannons to the gut yanked me up. My lips would not move, hay dust flit in the Coleman. And then I got one. A breath. Clenched. When I couldn't exhale no more, my womb seized. The fetus come where no air would. Maybe Charlie'd come down, maybe he'd open the door. I wouldn't be scared if he'd hold me now. Each seize rounded up through my womb, buckling and stabbing. If I could get to a squat, if I could let my breath out. The calf spied up at the loft where Charlie was peeking at me.

Charlie would climb down soon then, before the weather took me up and passed on.

{ *One Last Part* }
9:25 p.m.

A s she climbed the slope, past a mob of wheelchairs, towards the entrance, digging her toes into her boots for traction, the doors opened and a red alert light began turning on its axis and blinking. Some dog barked off somewhere. Wilson stepped carefully under Dol's weight as the beating snow drove into her face. She blinked, the flakes collected on her eyelashes. She took in details and reminded herself to remember them as she might want to recall them later.

There was the blinking light, a row of wheelchairs against the wall, the snail crawl of the automatic doors, and then, after stepping through, the booth marked TRIAGE and a nurse whispering into a telephone. Carrying Dol in her arms like King Kong or the Creature from the Black Lagoon carried their ladies, she unstuck her fingers from Dol's skirt now soaked through and coagulated.

As soon as they saw her standing there with bleeding Dol, emergency personnel in green scrubs rushed to her. One came to hold her arm while the other hurried away for a gurney down a long hallway. As he went, he snatched a phone from its cradle, snapped an order into it but with a face appearing extremely calm, given the circumstances, and a dial tone followed by the sound of punching number buttons come on over the loudspeaker, while the other man put his arm on her bicep as if to steady her. The woman from the triage booth came out and asked Dol's name and did he have insurance? They all had badges saying NURSE'S AIDE.

Wilson hadn't noticed her own shaking till then. Her knees were givin' out, she thought she would fall and sure wished they'd come and take Dol in for chrissakes what was takin' 'em so long he was gonna die didn't they know, should she tell 'em, she didn't want to be a pest but Dol was bleeding to death here, his face now drained to grey and purple pale. That other nurse aide ran the gurney to Wilson and the two of 'em took Dol from her arms and laid him on the gurney. Wilson steadied herself on the metal frame.

'Oh, take him in, please?' Wilson's voice now carried in it a tinned and exasperated wail. The aides wheeled the gurney around from her hands towards two large orange doors marked RESTRICTED ACCESS. One punched a flat, circular switch as if to hurry it up.

Wilson hurried after the gurney, hoping to keep up. Her boots shed dirty ice. When the doors yawned open, the other aide whipped firmly around to Wilson and told her to stay there.

Another flashing light, beyond the doors, signalled their entrance. A ponytailed nurse hurried to 'em from somewhere out of view. Them doors looked like Singer's loading dock. Her heart was palpitatin' and she couldn't catch her breath. She wanted to explain, 'He cut himself on account of, he cut himself on account of, he cut himself on account of –' But she couldn't get no volume. Dol and his gurney disappeared around a corner.

The automated doors behind her, and through which she'd brought Dol, began their quick, tart opening. Julie in a wheelchair. A blanket over her, full with blood and a heavy dusting of storm. Then Charlie, pushing. Julie's head'd slumped to the right as she muttered something through her clenched teeth. The snow that'd collected on Charlie's hair and eyebrows now began to fade to water in the warmth of the foyer. He stood there lookin' for a place to go or a face to recognize.

The nurse, now returned to her booth, was back on the phone. She put her call on hold, dialled a number and shouted, 'Triage, Triage, Triage,' into her handset. She rushed out of her booth and told Charlie, who had not yet seen Wilson standing there, herself a bit dumbfounded by chance, not ten paces in front of him, 'Sir, they'll be here in a minute. Bloody night.'

'She's bleeding real bad,' said Charlie. 'She won't stop bleeding, I put towels and a blanket but she won't stop, she lost the baby, I think.'

'She's pregnant, sir?'

Charlie nodded. 'Can't they take her in?' His voice now tremored with incredulity.

'They're coming, sir.'

The orange doors peeled open and the same aides that took Dol in came for Julie. When they took the chair from Charlie, the blanket snagged in the wheels and exposed a ferocious map of blue, green and red welts, pulsing, on her belly. Her head lifted and her eyes popped open as if she were seeing something but she could not be because, though her eyes opened, she was unconscious. It was some nerve ending or some native instinct come to help her through.

The aides worked the blanket from the wheels and hurried Julie through the orange doors. Charlie slowly followed, not wanting to interfere. The aides turned to him and told him to stay there, that they'd come and get him.

Charlie turned around. To Wilson, it was if he were recording every detail of the lobby. The black scuffs on the walls. The green specks in the linoleum. The gummy residue dripping down the side of the garbage can. The nurse now back on her phone. He was stunned.

Wilson approached him. 'Charlie? What happened?' She took his upper arm to support him the way the nurse's aide had taken hers and guided him gently to a plastic chair rooted to the floor. She sat next to him.

After a while, not very long, the orange doors unloosed again and the nurse with the ponytail announced to the mostly empty waiting room, 'Which one of you is with the drag queen?'

'His name is Dol Heyer.'

'Could you come with me, please?'

She squeezed Charlie's leg and saw how the nurse's eyebrows were set like she had in her mind something particular she didn't want to lose sight of. Wilson pressed her hands together to put a stop to her heart beating so fast.

Inside the orange doors, she saw a glassed-off MRI room and beige rubber bumper strips running the course of a long hallway where Dol and Julie lay on gurneys side by side. Julie's right arm hung limp and motionless. The nurse disappeared back out to the waiting room and in a moment led Charlie into the same area.

'We'll get them in soon, gentlemen,' said the nurse, petting Charlie's arm. 'The doctor was called away to a worse emergency in another wing.'

Wilson turned her back on her and wrapped her arms around Charlie, holding him close and feeling that, of all the possible outcomes for her life, one had already been chosen. She didn't know which. Charlie had begun to weep. No sobbin', just 'em tears spilling out and down his cheeks. His light breath carrying the scent of beer, his tears cool on her cheek. 'She'll make it, Charlie.'

'She don't stop bleeding.' Charlie lifted his head from her breast, staring. Wilson followed his gaze over her shoulder and, if Charlie hadn't seen it she'd've missed it, but Dol, twisting in some muscular agony, reached out and touched Julie's arm.

About the Author

Thom Vernon's roots are in the North American Midwest, South and Far West. Other than geography and writing, his core interests are performance, arts education and the exile experience. He lives in Toronto with his partner, Vajdon.

Acknowledgements

Thanks to Vajdon, Cubby, Alana, Michael B., Dad and my crew.

Typeset in Albertina and Oneleigh
Printed and bound at the Coach House on bpNichol Lane

Edited and designed by Alana Wilcox
Author photo by Samer Muscati

Coach House Books
80 bpNichol Lane
Toronto ON M5S 3J4

416 979 2217
800 367 6360

mail@chbooks.com
www.chbooks.com